PROLOGUE

T he driver flexed his hands on the steering wheel and glanced at the wire cage belted in the passenger seat. The occupant, a handsome black and white rat, stared fixedly at the door handle.

"This is how you want us to take our leave of one another?" the man asked. The words quivered with suppressed emotion. "Years may pass before we see one another again."

The rat's whiskers twitched, but he didn't turn his head.

"Rodney," the man pleaded, "you must understand. Were you to fall into the hands of the Coven, the Order's survival would be in peril."

A tiny paw lifted and came to rest on one of the silver bars.

Wincing, the driver said, "You must endure the indignity of being housed in that cage for the benefit of the humans. We do not wish them to see you as vermin to be exterminated, therefore you must pass as a domestic pet. I don't like it either."

Nothing.

Swallowing against the lump in his throat, the man tried again. "You'll enjoy living with Fiona. I haven't seen her in years, but she resides above the most powerful fairy mound in all the realms. After I put you on the doorstep, I'll watch from the other side of the square until you're inside."

Only the sound of the tires on the pavement answered his assurances.

Tightening his grip on the wheel again, the man sighed. "Very well, but I will reach out to you when action can no longer be avoided. I know you will respond. You are a noble creature, Rodney. You would never fail to come to the aid of your compatriots."

The remainder of the drive passed in silence. The nondescript sedan entered Briar Hollow, North Carolina, gliding unnoticed through the deserted streets and into a parking spot in front of the courthouse. Across the street, a cobbler's shop and general store had not yet opened for the day.

Getting out and going around to the opposite side of the vehicle, the man removed the cage and carried it to the store's doorstep.

"I have to go now," he said, looking down at Rodney who stared up at him accusingly. "Until we meet again, my brother."

At those words, the rat relented slightly. He extended one paw, touching the index finger the man slipped through the bars. They held each other's eyes for a long moment. Then the man turned, trotted briskly across the street, and moved the car to the far side of the square, backing into an alleyway between two buildings.

Fifteen minutes later, a yellow cat exited the cobbler's shop. He yawned and stretched before the cage caught his attention. From his hiding place, the man stiffened, but the cat made no move to menace Rodney. Instead, the creatures appeared to strike up a conversation.

After a moment or two the shop door opened and a gray-haired woman came out. She bent and spoke to the rat, then lifted the cage, glancing up and down the street before carrying it inside.

As the door closed behind them, the yellow cat limped to a nearby bench, hopped onto the seat, and stretched out in the sun.

"Well," the man whispered, starting the car's engine, "that's that — for now."

1

Most people spend months planning home renovations. I walk downstairs to the lair and never know what I'm going to find. On the day this story begins, I discovered a better coffee machine than the one sitting upstairs in the espresso bar. Considering what Tori paid for that thing, I'm not making a small statement here.

Briar Hollow may be a sleepy backwater off the Blue Ridge Parkway, but we live over a sentient fairy mound that tends to take matters into its own hands.

If it has hands.

Which I don't think it does.

Never mind.

Spending too much time attempting to impose logic on the workings of my world leads down a sure path toward insanity.

Here's the important detail: I was about to enjoy coffee. Really good coffee.

No sooner had the dark liquid filled my cup, however, than a burst of static and a flash of light to my right sent me wheeling round with hands extended prepared to do battle.

Thankfully, I hadn't picked up the cup yet, so there was no coffee spill, but my sharp movement attracted Tori's attention. She got up from the FaeNet terminal and walked over to where I was standing.

"Down, girl," she said, laying a hand on my forearm. "And I hope that's decaf in that cup."

Normally I don't keep my magic on a hair trigger, but the last few weeks had left me prepared to expect almost anything.

That "almost" did not, however, include the top half of a Douglas Fir — as in a Christmas tree — sticking through the shimmering opening of the Shevington portal.

A stalwart brownie strained to pop the tree through to our side, his whole body leaning into the effort. If the branch broke, he was in for one heck of a ride.

As we watched, someone in the Valley must have given the trunk a mighty shove. Without warning, the tree catapulted through, sending the brownie sprawling, just as I predicted.

Outclassed, but undaunted, the little guy got up and began dragging the fir toward a line of waiting carts — three of which already held Christmas trees of different types.

With my focus trained on acquiring caffeinated goodness, I hadn't noticed Festus, iPad in paw, supervising the whole operation.

I gave Tori a sheepish grin. "Sorry," I said. "I guess I keep looking for some kind of invading hordes to come through the portals."

That's right. "Portals" — plural.

To facilitate our movements in the Otherworld, the fairy mound has given us direct links to both Londinium and Tír na nÓg in addition to the existing gateway to the Valley.

"Well, I'm glad you didn't let loose with any electrical bolts," Tori said, "or you might have started a forest fire. Let's go talk to Das Furball over there and find out why we're suddenly running a Christmas tree lot."

I started to reach for the waiting coffee and stopped myself. It wasn't decaf. Pouring rocket fuel on my already tense nerves suddenly didn't seem like a great idea.

As Tori and I walked toward the portal, more branches poked through the opening.

"You do know it's not even Thanksgiving, right?" I said to Festus, by way of greeting.

Checking the Douglas Fir off his list with a pat of his paw, Festus replied, "I'm aware."

"Then why exactly do we need *five* Christmas trees down here in the middle of November?" Tori asked.

"Six," Festus corrected her. "Douglas Fir, Balsam Hill Blue Spruce, Norway Spruce, Virginia Pine, Noble Fir, and Fraser Fir."

If asked to come up with an adjective to describe Festus McGregor, "festive" would not make the cut. Whatever the werecat might be doing, he wasn't indulging a spontaneous burst of holiday cheer.

"I'm guessing you didn't choose those six trees for their pretty branches," Tori said. "What gives?"

Making a disdainful hacking sound in the back of his throat, Festus shot her a withering glare.

"*Pretty*?" he demanded. "Would you ask Roger Federer if he bought a tennis racket because it was *pretty*? Did David Beckham pick *pretty* soccer balls? For your information, I am a professional athlete, and these trees are my training equipment."

Ah. So that was it. Festus was getting ready for the annual tree destruction contest at The Dirty Claw, his drinking hole of choice in the Valley.

Neither Tori nor I managed to respond to his announcement before the werecat's ears went flat against his head. Arching his back in the universal sign for feline disapproval, Festus roared, "Hey! *You!*"

The brownie with the Douglas Fir froze.

"Yeah, you," Festus growled. "The Half Pint in the lederhosen. Careful with that tree. I need those branches intact. You hear me? In-*tact!*"

To my surprise, the brownie all but went down on his knees in apology.

"Please forgive me, Mr. McGregor," he said, his eyes shining with admiration. "Can I just say, sir that it's an honor to meet you? The judges robbed you of the championship title last year. There is widespread speculation among your fans that the ribbon that failed to fall from the tree had been rigged."

A beatific expression instantly replaced the scowl on Festus' furry features and his ears perked up at the praise. The quickest way to the crotchety werecat's heart runs straight through his ego.

"Now, now, young man," Festus said. "Grace in defeat is also the hallmark of a champion. A true competitor looks forward, never back."

This time *I* almost tossed a hairball at the werecat's carefully orchestrated humility and Tori hid the words "self-impressed, much?" in a fake cough.

The brownie didn't even know we were there. With his full adoration trained on Festus, he said, "No one will ever touch your shattered ornament record. "Did you really smash 247 glass globes in 4 seconds?"

"Two hundred and forty-*eight*."

Although I've never seen anyone swoon, I think that's what the brownie did in response to the correction.

"You're an artist, sir," he said in a hushed, reverent tone. "I, uh, I hope one day to excel in my own field of athletic competition by aspiring to your level of dedication and discipline."

Fairly radiating feline paternalism, Festus said, "What's your sport, young man?"

The brownie ducked his head shyly. "I'm training for the Domestic Chore Decathlon," he said. "I haven't mastered all the categories yet, but I am ranked in the top five in competitive dusting."

Thankfully, Festus managed not to give voice to the pitying scorn that passed through his eyes. Instead, he opted for a reasonably gracious response.

"Well, that's excellent, Half Pint. Deliver that tree to my training area in good shape, and I'll give you my paw print for inspiration."

"Oh, thank you, sir!" the brownie gushed. "I won't lose a needle, sir, not a single needle."

As he trundled away with the Douglas Fir, Festus shook his head. "How in the name of Bastet can anyone call *dusting* a competitive sport?"

Without giving my words any thought and before Tori could stop me, I said, "Well, he can practice at my place any time he wants."

Beside me, a horrified gasp told me I'd said the wrong thing in front of the wrong brownie.

"You've done it now," Tori muttered under her breath.

Steeling myself, I looked down into Darby's indignant face. As soon as my eyes met his, he said, "There is not a *particle* of dust in your home, Mistress Jinx."

Outrage dripped off every syllable.

That's the problem with the brownie power of invisibility. You never know when they're going to pop in at exactly the wrong moment.

Since I didn't see how I could talk my way out of my predicament, I fell on my sword. "Forgive me, Darby. That was a stupid thing for me to say."

"It was *inaccurate*, Mistress," he huffed.

"You're absolutely right," I agreed with feeling. "In fact, I think that young fellow there would appreciate some advice from you in the dusting department. If you can take the time, of course."

All traces of offense fled from Darby's features, replaced by a happy smile. "Do you really think I could *coach* competitive dusting, Mistress?" he asked breathlessly.

"I can't imagine anyone who could do a better job than you," I assured him, ignoring the snickering from Festus.

As Darby went over to introduce himself, Tori said, "Nice save."

"Something tells me we're going to be breathing a lot of lemon-scented Endust down here," I replied.

Festus shook his head. "That would be against the rules. They're not allowed to use anything but untreated dust cloths."

Talk about leaving yourself wide open.

"I thought you didn't regard competitive dusting as a sport?" Tori said. "So how come you know the rules?"

The werecat suddenly got interested in his iPad again. "I may have seen a round or two out of sheer boredom. Now would you two please quit distracting me? I'm managing a major freight shipment here."

"Fine," I said, "but just keep your insta-forest out of the way."

"*Please*," Festus said. "I'd never be able to focus listening to you people yakking all the time. My training ring will be at least three rows back in the archive — and it's strictly off-limits to spectators, so *you* stay out of *my* way."

Rather than go another round with him, I let Festus have the last word. As Tori and I walked away, I heard Darby introducing himself to "Half Pint," whose real name sounds enough like "Bartholomew" that we've taken to calling him "Bart."

Risking a glance over my shoulder, I saw Darby lending a

hand with the Douglas Fir. Thankfully my *faux pas* led to a beautiful new friendship — one predicated on dust — but more on that later.

FROM THE SHELF over Beau's desk, Rodney watched Festus supervising the delivery of the training trees. His roommate had been talking non-stop about the contest for the last month.

Even during their favorite TV programs, the werecat went on and on about new techniques he intended to try and why his lame hip gave him an *advantage* over the younger competitors. More than once Rodney wanted to point out that Festus was the one being the squeaky wheel now.

Rodney had come down to the lair to see if Glory was around, but as usual, she was busy with Chase. The rat's whiskers twitched, and tears filled his eyes. He missed the days when he and his friend watched Elvis movies and stayed up late talking.

It never occurred to him that when Glory became normal sized, she'd forget about him. Finally one night Rodney confessed the extent of his hurt feelings to Festus. In a surprising show of support, the werecat patted him awkwardly on the head with one of his big yellow paws.

"Most people are oblivious, Rodney," he said. "They only see what's important to them in the moment. Sometimes they forget the friends who helped them get where they are. They hurt you without even realizing what they're doing."

As Rodney watched the werecat ordering around a brownie struggling with a Douglas Fir, he knew in his heart that Festus would *never* do to him what Glory had done. Festus might talk mean, but out of every single person in the lair, he knew the most about loyalty.

Fiona was like that, too. The first Christmas Rodney lived in the store, they had the same kind of tree the brownie was working so hard to load onto the waiting cart.

Sitting on the end table in the apartment upstairs, Rodney had watched while Fiona floated ornaments out of their storage crates and decorated the branches with magic — all the while singing holiday songs at the top of her lungs.

Then, she made a doll's cup of hot chocolate for him, and they'd watched *White Christmas*.

"These are our special holiday traditions now, Rodney," Fiona had told him. "We'll always do these things together."

When Fiona made everyone else think she was dead, Rodney, like Myrtle, knew the truth. That meant in Fiona's eyes, there was no difference between him and the powerful aos si.

Then, when they all went to the Valley for Christmas the first year Jinx lived in the store, Fiona remembered their special traditions. She and Rodney had their hot chocolate as they watched the movie.

She even made some of the ornaments on Barnaby's tree float around the parlor when Rodney asked her to.

Fiona practiced magic the way Rodney remembered it should be used, spontaneously and joyously. He enjoyed making his home in the store, just as a friend had once told him he would, but Rodney missed living in a place where pure magic infused the world — and he missed the days when all his friends weren't so busy.

He watched now as Jinx said goodbye to Tori, went into her alcove, and pulled the curtain shut. Even though Rodney knew she wouldn't mind if he joined her, the best evenings were when everyone sat around the fire talking and laughing. Like when the WAGWAB women were in town for Halloween.

That had been a special night with Knasgowa joining them from the other side. When none of the others were watching, she held out her hand to Rodney. He ran up her arm, riding on her shoulder into the darkened stacks.

In a spot where no one would hear them talking, Knasgowa gently lifted Rodney onto a shelf directly across from her face.

"I have a special job for you, my friend," she said. "Darby tells me that you are brave and resourceful. Will you help me?"

Rodney nodded, listening closely as she held out a wand like the ones she'd given to Jinx and the others earlier in the evening. As he watched, Knasgowa made the wand grow smaller and smaller until it fit in his paw.

"You must find a place to hide this wand where it will not be discovered," she said. "Guard it with your life. The one who will wield it for the good of all has yet to be born, but in time, she will be the closest friend of your heart. When you give it to her, the wand will shape itself to fit her hand, growing as she grows. Do you understand?"

Nodding again, Rodney closed his paw around the wand. The wood hummed, making his eyes go wide.

"You recognize the power, don't you?" Knasgowa asked. "Yggdrasil itself gave the wood to form the wand you now hold. It belonged to the greatest wizard in all of Britain. You will scamper again in the branches of the Great Tree, Sir Rodney. You have my word. Now go. Do as I have asked of you and tell no one."

Later, when all the witches left to send Knasgowa back into the shadowy place between the realms, Rodney carried the wand high into the walls, climbing the staircase carved for him by the fairy mound.

There, halfway between the storeroom and the basement, in a spot where two large beams met, Rodney had made a room to call his own, a place to gather his thoughts and to nap in peace.

Reverently he placed the wand atop the longest beam, which he used as a shelf for his treasures. When he stroked the golden ash, the familiar voice of Yggdrasil rose in Rodney's mind, speaking words from a long-ago night in a place far from Briar Hollow.

"As the last of the Rodere, you must hide in the human realm until the day when your kind fights again in the service of pure magic."

Going down on one knee, Rodney had bowed his head before the World Tree in acquiescence. After all, being a good soldier meant doing the things others could not or would not face.

But that had been long ago. Rodney no longer saw himself as a soldier. He was a rat with a good family he loved, including Glory, even though he was mad at her. Rodney would guard the wand and deliver it as Knasgowa had asked, but he hoped she was wrong.

He didn't want to see Yggdrasil again, for to do that, Rodney would have to leave Briar Hollow — and that he couldn't do. Not even for the Greatest Tree of Them All.

J ust after supper, Beau Longworth stepped onto the sidewalk, buttoning his coat against the cool evening air. He wasn't scheduled to put in an appearance as the Confederate ghost for at least another week, but the colonel enjoyed stretching his legs after supper with a few circuits of the square.

A movement in one of the front courthouse windows caught his eye. Squinting in the dim light, he saw the apparition of former Briar Hollow mayor Howard McAlpin making a rude gesture.

Rather than dignify the insufferable man's jealous display with a response, Beau turned resolutely on his heel and began his walk. The day had been a satisfying one involving close coordination with the head librarian at the University in the Valley.

To fill the position, Barnaby Shevington had sought out the services of the Valley's premier bookseller Horatio Pagecliff. To Beau's surprise and delight, the Lord High Mayor also formalized Beau's own position as the fairy mound archivist.

Now, working together, Beau and Pagecliff were preparing the collection to be used by the school's faculty in instruction and course development. While the colonel had always considered himself to be a gentleman scholar, being afforded the opportunity to take part in a bona fide academic endeavor gave him enormous satisfaction.

Lost in his thoughts and plans for the collection, Beau crossed the street and started down the west side of the square. He didn't hear local historian Linda Albert calling his name until the woman was only a few feet away.

Hastily remembering his manners, Beau quickly removed his hat and bowed.

"Forgive me, Miss Linda," he said. "I fear I was indulging in a state of inner preoccupation rather than attending to my surroundings. Good evening.

Linda smiled at him fondly. "I do love the way you talk, Beau."

Chuckling with self-deprecation, he replied, "I am afraid my manner of address strikes most people as quite antique in nature."

"I'm not one of those people," the librarian said, ducking her head slightly. "I was working late and saw you start your walk. I came out to ask if . . . if . . . would you like to join me for Thanksgiving dinner?"

The embarrassed rush of the invitation caught the colonel completely off guard and left him momentarily speechless.

"Well, I, uh, I will need to consult with Jinx and her mother to determine what celebrations the family has planned," he finally stammered.

Now blushing furiously under the dim glow of the street lamps, Linda said, "Oh, of course. I didn't think about that. You want to be with your family. How are you related to Jinx again?"

"I am her uncle," Beau said, "by marriage."

"On her mother's side or her father's?"

"The connection is matrilineal and somewhat distant," Beau

hedged. Out of the corner of his eye, he spied the light come on in Chase McGregor's cobbler shop.

"If you will excuse me, Miss Linda, I have an appointment with Chase. Thank you for your gracious invitation. I will be in touch as soon as I have ascertained my obligations."

"You don't have to come for dinner," Linda said a little desperately. "You could just have dessert with me. A man always has room for more dessert, right?"

"I have never been known to push away a slice of pie," Beau admitted.

"What's your favorite?" Linda asked eagerly. "I'll bake whatever you like."

"As Miss Tori would say, I am an equal opportunity consumer of pie," the colonel said, adding gallantly, "and I have no doubt any pie you bake would be of a most excellent quality."

Warming under the praise, Linda said, "Well, I don't like to brag, but I have won ribbons at the county fair. You think about it and let me know. I don't want to keep you from your meeting."

Excusing himself with another bow, Beau replaced his hat on his head and hurriedly retraced his steps toward the cobbler shop. He could feel Linda's eyes following him.

When he knocked on the shop door, Chase pulled the shade aside and then opened the door with a puzzled expression.

"Beau?" he said. "What . . . "

Jumping in quickly, Beau said, "Please forgive me if I am late for our meeting. I was speaking with Miss Linda."

Chase's eyes tracked to the corner, then back to Beau's pleading eyes. Dropping his voice, he said, "I don't think she can hear you all the way over here."

Then, in a more normal tone, he added, "You're not late at all, Beau. Come in. I wanted to discuss the historical accuracy of a design I'm working on."

As the door closed behind them, Beau's ramrod-straight posture sagged. "Is she still watching?" he asked.

"Not anymore," Chase said. "She's walking back to the library. Am I seeing things, or has Linda changed her hair? She's had a bun for as long as I can remember and now it's gone."

Hanging his hat on one of the hooks by the front door, Beau shrugged out of his coat. "Is it?" he asked. "I confess I did not notice. I was too taken aback when she extended an invitation for me to join her at Thanksgiving dinner."

"And that's bad?" Chase asked.

"Under normal circumstances, I should be quite pleased to have attracted the attentions of a woman like Miss Linda, but given the state of my existence, I do not think pursuing a relationship is fair to the lady herself."

From the doorway to the office, Glory said brightly, "Because your dead and all?"

In spite of his discomfiture, Beau laughed, "A most succinct way to summarize my condition, Miss Glory. Good evening."

"Hi, Beau," she said brightly. "Come on back here in the office where it's warm. Chase has a fire going in the pot-bellied stove, and we're both doing paperwork."

Following them into the tiny office, the colonel accepted the offer of both the rocking chair and a glass of bourbon.

"Your father would be scandalized," he said, sipping the amber liquid, "but I still regard the fiery nectar of my home state to be the superior spirit."

Sitting down at the desk, Chase said, "Dad's been known to put away his share of Kentucky bourbon when there was no Scotch to be had. You need to let me have those boots for an hour. You're getting down at the heels."

"A product of my gait," Beau said, crossing one long leg over the other to examine his boots. "Do you care to do the work now?"

"As opposed to tackling the monthly accounting?" Chase said. "That's an easy question. Let me get you a boot jack."

After Beau removed the tall cavalry boots, he sat in his stocking feet and watched Glory, who was parked on the floor busily sorting through stacks of papers arranged around her in a semicircle. From time to time, she consulted an iPad in a bright pink case propped on her knee.

"Miss Glory," he asked, "are you laboring to complete your weekly column with the *Banner* or assembling the WAGWAB newsletter?"

Looking over the top of her yellow polka dot framed readers, Glory said, "Oh, this is for a *new* project. I'm comparing letters I got online from the cemetery with questions living people sent in. You know, I don't really think there's that much difference between being alive and dead, except for the breathing part."

"A most droll observation," Beau said with a tolerant smile. "I can vouch for the fact that the afterlife can come with problems quite similar to those experienced by the living. How, pray tell, have you come to commune with the deceased in this manner?"

"Well," Glory said, taking off her glasses and leaning forward as if sharing a confidence, "you know that Mayor McAlpin caused an awful stir when he wrote to me from the courthouse."

"I do," Beau said. "That man specializes in inciting dissension and mayhem."

"You can say that again," Glory agreed. "The ghosts out at the cemetery got all upset after he wrote to me. They want to be able to ask me questions, too, but, well, we just can't have dead people writing to the *Banner*. It's hard to explain."

"How do the spirits in the cemetery contact you then?"

"Oh, it's not just the spirits in the cemetery anymore. I mean really, can you just imagine how many problems the *nonconformi* must be having? Tori and Adeline set up a website for me on the

FaeNet for readers who are *special*. I don't mean *special* special, but you know, *special*."

From the other room, Chase translated. "She means unorthodox readers. The ones her human fans don't need to know about."

"Ah," the colonel said, "I see, but how will these special consumers of your advice access the material you create for them?"

"You tell him, Chase," Glory said. "All that techy speak doesn't mean a thing to me."

Chase appeared in the doorway. "Tori and Adeline thought ole Howie's original point about the dead being technologically deprived was valid. Adeline came up with the idea of creating afterlife cyber cafes. They're recruiting the more recently deceased to act as teachers and monitors for the equipment."

Beau's eyebrows shot up. "Equipment? They are installing computer equipment in the cemetery? Will that not attract undue human attention?"

"Tombstone mounted micro-terminals powered by fairy dust," Chase replied. "They're as small as the GNATS drones, but equipped with holographic displays. Tori has already set up the first units at the graveyard to work the kinks out before they go wide with the system."

"While that is a most ingenious solution," Beau said, "are you not concerned that the spirits will make an effort to contact their living loved ones via electronic means?"

"Tori thought of that," Glory said. "The ghosts can do a lot of watching and reading, but they can only talk on approved channels. Seems like boredom is also a major problem for the dead."

The colonel nodded. "Another aspect of the afterlife experience whose veracity I can affirm," he said. "During my long sojourn in the cemetery, a means to continue to learn about and to observe the world of the living would have been a welcome respite."

"Beau," Glory said, "I hope you don't think I'm getting too personal, but, well, I understand that you wouldn't move on because of what happened to your soldiers back during the war, but do all ghosts stick around because they're guilty about something or because they have unfinished business? It would help me to know how to talk to them."

"Personal motivations vary," Beau said. "I do not think there is a single answer to your question. I have known spirits who walked the earth for decades before deciding to investigate alternate levels of existence. Others never seem to comprehend that such options even exist."

Glory chewed on the inside of her lip. "But you don't stop being who you are just because you're dead, right?"

"Indeed not," Beau said. "My sense of self has remained intact since the moment I awakened on the battlefield and realized I no longer dwelt among the living."

"Then don't you think that's why you don't want to go on a date with Linda?"

The abrupt change in the direction of the conversation startled the normally unflappable old soldier. "I am afraid I do not follow your meaning," he replied stiffly.

"She means you still see yourself as a married man," Chase said quietly. "You can't bring yourself to go out with Linda because it would feel like cheating on your wife."

All the color drained from Beau's face. He started to speak, but the words refused to break free until he cleared his throat.

"My wife has long since gone to her own rest," he managed finally.

"But you weren't there when she died," Glory said, "so in your mind, she's still at home waiting for you to get back from the war, right?"

Overcome by his emotions, Beau looked down at the floor.

"Miss Glory," he said softly, "I do not think you require any insights from me regarding the conundrums of the departed. You are quite correct. I do still think of Almira as last I saw her, standing on the porch of our home dressed in a lovely green velvet frock, her hand raised in a gesture of farewell, but that is hardly a memory I can share with Miss Linda."

"No," Glory said, "but you can tell her you're not over losing your wife, which is true. You're a nice man, Beau. It would hurt you to hurt Linda. If you don't tell her something real, she's going to think you're just brushing her off, and that wouldn't be nice at all."

Beau raised his head. "Chase," he said, "are you aware that you have the privilege of keeping company with a most remarkable woman?"

"I am," Chase answered, regarding Glory with a warm gaze. "Aware and grateful."

3

Howard McAlpin floated from window to window in the courthouse watching Beau Longworth taking his evening constitutional. It irked the former Briar Hollow mayor no end that the colonel had found a way to have a solid body — to have a *life* — a case of amulet envy Howard would rather die all over again than admit.

The deceased politician spent hours of his endless ectoplasmic existence plotting ways to get that blasted magical bling away from the dead soldier. The sticking point was Howard's manifestation anxiety. In the presence of observers, he could manage, at best, a half materialization — generally his lower half.

Unless he could learn to snatch the amulet with his feet, thievery didn't seem to be the answer to Howard's after death dilemma.

As these thoughts were going through his mind, he spied Linda Albert rush out of the library and launch into a *gushing* conversation with Beau. McAlpin's irritation surged to a new level.

"Would you just look at that idiotic woman," he muttered.

"She's let her hair down and *colored* it — all to chase a dead man. I wonder how moonstruck she'd be if she knew the truth about Beauregard T. Longworth."

He spoke the colonel's name like a teenage boy mocking his rival, drawing out the syllables in a sullen, singsong rhythm. That's exactly how Beau made Howard feel — like the awkward, unpopular adolescent he'd been at Briar Hollow High.

But where were they now? The good-looking jocks who had mocked him?

Where were they?

Alive, that's where they were, in a cosmically unfair turn of events that drove Howard nearly mad endless day after endless day.

All this because he'd altered the math in a swordfishing tournament and greased a few palms to guard against potential weight recalculations. How was he supposed to know that winning meant so much to Abe Abernathy the man would drive all the way from Wilmington to Briar Hollow to get even?

But the worst part was when Abe stabbed him with the very trophy they were arguing about, no one believed Howard had been murdered! When, exactly, had he, the Honorable Howard McAlpin, *ever* been so inept he'd manage to stab himself with a brass swordfish? Didn't anyone in this miserable town care about *justice*?

The lack of interest in his untimely demise showed the people of Briar Hollow as the pack of ungrateful rubes and hicks he'd always known them to be. After all the years he'd spent trying to drag this backwater nowhere kicking and screaming into the 20th century . . . or was it the 21s century? *Whatever*!

And all Dead Colonel Beau had to do to be beloved was pass himself off as the living descendant of the Confederate ghost when he *was* the Confederate ghost. The whole situation was *intolerable*!

Well, death wasn't going to be enough to derail Howard's life plans, and now he had a friend, one who knew those people in Fiona Ryan's old store, were up to something. Glancing at the clock hanging from the ceiling in the hallway, Howard floated away from the window and toward his old office.

Grudgingly he conceded that Tori had kept her word about giving him a "secure" way to get online so he could at least enjoy some interaction with others of his kind — like FBI-JEdH who could talk conspiracy theories — and shoes — for hours on end.

Oh, yes. Tori thought she had Howard contained and entertained, like throwing a penned dog a bone. With a few cyber conversations to gnaw on during long nights in the courthouse, Howard wouldn't be any trouble at all. But for all her cleverness, Tori hadn't counted on SpookDude96.

Luckily, the first email message came in before Jinx and the others caught Howard on camera using the computer in the mayor's office. That gave SpookDude enough time to teach him how to hide their correspondence before they could get caught.

Howard appreciated that act of collusion, but it wasn't enough to get him to lay all his cards on the table. Instinct told him that if he ever needed the people in Fiona Ryan's old store again, revealing the existence of the FaeNet was not in his best interests.

The important thing, for now, was that SpookDude believed Howard McAlpin died at the hands of a murderer and was prepared to help the late mayor prove it.

MINDY CROSSED her arms and scowled at Kyle across the living room of the rented HBH headquarters in Fish Pike's old house. "You *seriously* want us to believe that you are *emailing* with Howard McAlpin's ghost?"

"GhostFish knows every detail of McAlpin's life," Kyle insisted. "No matter what I ask him, I can't trip him up. He knows things that go on in the courthouse that he couldn't know if he wasn't in the building *all* the time. I've tested him. I hid stuff, like when you geocache, you know? GhostFish told me exactly where everything was *and* what was going on when I put it there."

Nick, who had been pacing back in forth, stopped in front of Kyle's chair.

"Okay, genius," he said. "Let's say you *are* talking to McAlpin's ghost. What good is that going to do us? You can't even prove those emails are coming from inside the courthouse."

"Thanks for pointing out the obvious, Fearless Leader," Kyle said sarcastically. "I'm working on it, but that Tori dame is good. She's monitoring all the computer traffic in and out of that place. I had to drop GhostFish to the dark web through a VPN."

Mindy threw her hands up in frustration.

"Kyle, get *real*," she said. "Tori Andrews is a former *waitress* turned shop girl. She's not some mega tech genius operating a secret computer network out of a general store in Briar Hollow, North Carolina. That's a crazy story even for you, and you're like the king of crazy stories."

"Oh, right," Kyle jeered, "Blame the whole 'we got vampires' thing on me — *again*. You were there, too."

Refusing to back down, Mindy said, "While we're flipping through your greatest hits, *Kyle*, let's not forget the Glory Goes Green fiasco that almost got us sued."

"You can't be stupid enough to buy that online copper cosmetics story," Kyle snorted. "I saw that woman turn green and start shrinking, *and* I got it on camera."

Mindy looked like she wanted to lunge over the coffee table

and throttle him. "She *tripped* on her pants legs because they needed to be hemmed."

"Right," Kyle said, "the old 'I can't sew' alibi.'"

That did it. Mindy hurled a magazine at her fellow ghosthunter. "Oh. My. *God*. That's not even a *thing*!"

"Fine," he huffed, "but you can't dispute the evidence about the *War and Peace* cam."

"Watch me," Mindy said. "You bought that thing on sale at SpiesRUs.com. Are you really surprised it turned out to be a piece of junk? Malfunctioning bargain basement electronics do not a conspiracy make."

"There is nothing wrong with the *War and Peace* cam. How many times do I have to tell you that *Tori Andrews* made the video *loop*? Mindy, you are such a . . ."

Nick stepped between them. "Knock it off! Both of you!" he ordered. "Kyle start at the beginning and tell me everything about GhostFish again. And go slow."

"You're not going to encourage him, are you?" Mindy demanded, her eyes going wide. "Please tell me you are *not* going to encourage him."

Pulling one of the armchairs closer and sitting down, Nick said, "I'm not encouraging him, but I am going to listen to him. *Somebody* is sending those GhostFish emails and I want to know why."

AS WE WALKED BACK into the lair, Tori said, "You want that coffee now?"

I would have cheerfully committed a capital crime for a cup of real coffee, but heeding her earlier advice, I asked for decaf.

The complicated series of commands she punched into the

machine touched off an even more heavenly aroma than the one I'd created on my first attempt.

"What are you brewing for me?" I asked, peering curiously at the coffee maker's LED screen.

"If you have to drink decaf the only way to go is bold," Tori said. "It's a proprietary drip sequence . . . "

My upraised hand cut off the stream of barista-ese. "Will it be good?"

"Will it be *good*?" she scoffed. "You may never drink regular coffee again."

That I doubted seriously, but she was right about the "proprietary" decaf. The coffee hit my taste buds in a smokey, complex cloud of wonderful that made my eyes close as I sighed in appreciation.

"That'll cure what ails you," Tori said, watching my reaction, "without making you jumpy enough to fire off lightning bolts. What was that 'shoot first ask questions later' business about anyway?"

If she'd had my week, she would have understood.

"Hey," I said, "give a gal a break. We've had two special ops missions in five days and I still have reports to file. That's where I was headed when the portals started sprouting trees."

By this point in the conversation, we'd wandered over to her work table. Shoving bubbling beakers and a stack of iPads to one side, she began stuffing select items into her messenger bag.

"Headed to the Valley?" I asked, sipping and savoring my coffee.

"Yeah," she said. "Adeline and I have a meeting with the alchemy faculty at the university. Then I've got a dinner date with Connor. Adeline's waiting for me, so I have to get a move on."

Glancing around the cluttered corner of the lair, I saw

Adeline's darkened telepresence robot parked under the stairs. "She didn't take her wheels with her?" I asked.

Adeline's new existence as an AI still confuses me. She can pop into every tablet and phone we own at will, but she likes trundling around in an iPad mounted on a powered stand, which Brenna enchanted to be perpetually charged.

"She has a second telepresence bot at the school," Tori said, closing the straps on her bag. "Don't stay up all night working. I think you need some sleep."

"No argument there," I agreed. "Give everyone my love."

4

A fter Tori left, I went into my alcove and pulled the curtain closed. Blissful silence surrounded me. A newly requisitioned FaeNet terminal waited for me on the desk. Every member of the team has one, even Rube.

Protocol demands we record our individual observations for the team's logs as soon as possible after a mission. Like I told Tori, I was behind by two reports.

That's why I remember the date — Sunday, November 20, 2016. We'd been back from our first visit to Tír na nÓg for less than five days.

Hold that thought about Tír na nÓg. I'll get back to it shortly. First, let me tell you about my "work" problems.

The first rogue *nonconformi* incident happened early in the week on Attu Island.

Don't worry. I'd never heard of the place either. When I asked exactly where we were headed, Lucas had swiped a glowing globe off the screen of the main FaeNet terminal in the lair and highlighted Alaska.

Imagine those scattered islands that make the state look like it has a tail — the Aleutians. Attu is the last one to the west before you hit open water.

There's a myth in those parts involving a white-faced bear with white feet. It's a cautionary tale about what happens to hunters who get overzealous killing animals — or at least that's the human telling of the legend.

The real white-faced bear, who is also the *nonconformi* behind the sightings of a giant polar bear on Kodiak Island, claims distant relation to both the Yeti and the Sasquatch. Like many creatures the humans call "cryptids," he only wants to protect the natural world from the incursion of so-called "civilization" by using a time-tested equation: scare the crap out of people, and they tend to run fast in the opposite direction.

While it's hard to believe droves of people head out to the westernmost tip of the Aleutians, birdwatchers are a hardier bunch than I realized — thus setting the stage for a confrontation.

When we found the white-faced bear none of us — not even my Welsh-speaking water elf boyfriend — could pronounce his name, so Rube christened the *nonconformi* "Eugene."

The story Eugene shared with us came with a familiar ring. We'd heard variations on the same theme since the Conference of the Realms lifted the Agreement.

Eugene hadn't been out of the In Between since World War II. For two weeks in 1943, he witnessed the only battle of the war to take place on American soil.

U.S. ground troops supported by the Canadian Air Force fended off the Japanese in bloody hand-to-hand combat. The memories of the fighting left Eugene scarred and determined.

When he came out of the portal after the Agreement was lifted and spotted a group of those intrepid birdwatchers, Eugene charged on impulse no questions asked.

Thankfully the eco-tourists were too panicked to get clear images for social media, but the story of a "monster" loose on Attu still cropped up on the paranormal discussion boards online.

We had to get the whole thing sorted out before some Bigfoot hunter in search of a winter project decided to book a flight north. Thankfully, Eugene proved to be reasonable and sweet.

After we brought him up to speed on the current state of global politics, he realized his mistake, apologized, and agreed to enroll in Intro to Human Society 101 at Shevington University.

Which brings us to the next source of confusion and chaos in our world: the fast-track construction of the campus in the Valley.

Over the summer, the dwarven engineers in the Valley managed to erect the administration building and the main academic halls in time to welcome the inaugural class for the fall term.

While the residence halls are still under construction, students are bunking all over the city, with some of the aquatic species taking rooms with the merfolk in Qynn.

As you can well imagine, the *nonconformi* are changing the face of the Shevington — dramatically.

Walking the High Street has always been an experience, but as the city is transitioning to its new life as a college town, Tori has declared it "wilder than Mos Eisley."

I have a layman's appreciation of *Star Wars.* Tori operates at a Jedi level. I had to ask for a translation.

She's referring to the crazy cantina scene in the original movie, which apparently you can't call the "first" movie, a complicated bit of chronological confusion I cannot begin to fathom. Anyway, the scene with the funky alien band.

Find a clip on YouTube and watch it again. Throw in a couple of unicorns, the stray dragonlet, and a few fairies in combat fatigues, and you'll have a decent approximation of what Shevington looks like these days.

The *nonconformi*, still exhilarated by their newfound freedom to travel the realms, have touched off a few ... rowdy ... but good-natured incidents, including an all-out bar fight with the werecats at The Dirty Claw.

My brother, Connor, currently serving as acting mayor, has decided to call on the services of Major Aspid "Ironweed" Istra and the Brown Mountain Guard to maintain order.

Even though Connor has the authority to make that call, the new assignment doesn't sit well with Ironweed. He's told Connor in no uncertain terms that his elite fairy troops are not a bunch of campus cops. They'll only help out until the university gets an in-house security detail.

Frankly, my grandad, Barnaby, the president of the university, shares Ironweed's frustration over the sudden population influx. Even though enrollment is technically closed through the spring term, overly enthusiastic *nonconformi* continue to come through the portals daily.

Barnaby and Moira have their hands full trying to organize workshops and symposiums to keep everyone occupied regardless of their place in the degree track.

Just between us, I'm not as sympathetic about all that as I should be. The situation may have caused chaos in Shevington, but every *nonconformi* that turns up in the Valley counts as one less the special ops team has to run halfway around the world to manage.

Eugene was one of our successes. They're not all in a listening mood. Two days after Attu, we hauled ourselves to Russia to deal with the Brosno Dragon only to find out the real problem was the volcano at the bottom of the lake ... but that's a story for another day.

I started telling you all this to illustrate how busy we've been since Halloween. Running around with the special ops team putting out cryptid brush fires hasn't been the most complicated thing on my plate. That would be Tír na nÓg.

Just to refresh your memory, on Samhain, the Celtic holiday that extends through November 1, my ancestor Knasgowa gave seven wands to the Chosen Ones: Tori, Mom, Gemma, Amity, Greer, Brenna, and me.

Using the wands, we opened the locked door to the land of Tír na nÓg and discovered not just the fate of the lost Rowan witches, but also the existence of a sanctuary for pure magic — run by Brenna's mother, Bronwyn Sinclair.

I'm going to tell you the story of how that place changed our lives and how it changed me. You see, until I went to Tír na nÓg, I was one self-satisfied witch. I would have sworn my powers had grown at a steady pace, and in a way, I guess they had.

I'd gone from being a dimwit novice who used an Internet spell to accidentally raise a whole cemetery full of ghosts, to a witch competent with telekinesis, psychometry, everyday spells, and the hurling of the stray energy bolt.

Bouncing around the realms no longer bothered me. Truthfully, for as exhausting as I'd found those last few days, I already loved my work with the Special Ops team.

What I didn't realize is that I'd also gotten very comfortable at letting other people fight my battles. Whether it was Myrtle, my mother, Greer, or Brenna, I always had an older, bigger, badder magical practitioner watching my back.

If faced with a life or death choice, would I make the wrong decision? And if I did, who would pay the price?

Nobody suggested that I was in any way "less" than I should or could have been. I hadn't even had the thought myself that night in the alcove, but looking back, after what we've now survived, I see that I was only half living my purpose.

To be blunt, I wasn't all in.

You can't get away with that kind of thing forever.

Destiny has a way of slapping half-awake people into full consciousness.

Yes, I'd done some brave things, and I'd become a pretty good leader in the sense of "managing" things. But my first exposure to Tír na nÓg — to the vibrant force of spontaneous magic infusing the very air around me — began a transformation whose ramifications I had not yet begun to feel.

Although, when you see what my pen had to say to me that night, you'll get a sense of how quickly that was about to change.

"Graduation" day loomed, a transition I would face armed with a weapon crafted by one of the greatest wizards in the history of the Fae world. From where I stand today, I look back at the convoluted series of events and revelations that constituted my journey up to that moment with a new understanding.

What started with my inheritance of Aunt Fiona's store and her magic would come full circle under the boughs of an apple tree. To find out what that means, you'll just have to keep reading.

For now, know this. Life presents each of us with a path.

Sometimes the road goes straight forward. Sometimes it winds back on itself.

There are detours that take you into mud bogs, while others dump you into such a comfortable place you never want to move again.

I had reached a dangerously attractive pit called "complacency."

Here's the problem with being complacent.

In settling for the present, you sacrifice the potential of the future.

Since my magic awakened, my friends and I have vanquished two foes and uncovered an older, larger threat that won't be so easy to contain.

But the foe I needed most to vanquish was myself. That's what Tír na nÓg made possible.

In this story, we're going to meet some bad witches, and learn the true history of one of my dearest friends. Prepare yourself. It's not going to be a smooth passage.

Think about Bette Davis coming down that staircase in *All About Eve*. (If you haven't seen it, you need to.)

Downing her martini in one gulp, with smoking cigarette in hand, Bette delivers one of the greatest classic movie lines of all time:

"Fasten your seatbelts. It's going to be a bumpy night."

5

After I dictated my reports, I spent reflective time with my grimoire. All witches share a personal relationship with their spell books and journals. Committing our magic to writing seals the bond forged with an incantation or methodology, but I have an added advantage. I write with an enchanted pen.

Under its watchful nib, thoughts and ideas flow effortlessly onto the page springing from wells of creativity and insight I could not reach alone. Most of the time I don't even hold the pen, much less direct its movements.

As my mind wanders down winding corridors of contemplation, the instrument takes flight, landing, and dancing on the surface of a book that will never reach its final page. Lost in that magical communion, time means nothing to me.

That evening, I didn't notice when Darby slipped a supper plate onto the corner of my desk. At some point, my nose detected a buttered biscuit, which lifted into my hand when I absently gestured toward the scent.

Darby rolls his biscuit dough in sugar. That's what I do

remember. The warm, sweet taste on my tongue as I re-experienced our first visit to Tír na nÓg — the crashing of the waves on its rocky coast and the twinkling of the lights in the castle city high above the cliffs.

I finished half my plate before I even realized what I was doing, but by then the flavor of Darby's hearty winter stew had morphed in my imagination into the thick peasant bread and pungent cheese we'd eaten around the open fire pit in Bronwyn Sinclair's great room.

The sight of Brenna's mother on that night will never leave me — her porcelain face flushed with the pleasure of reunion with her daughter, the verdant green of her eyes dark with passionate outrage as she revealed Reynold Isherwood's crimes against Fae children.

Later, before we all retired to our rooms, I saw Brenna and Bronwyn standing together in the courtyard under the beams of the moon in perigee. Bronwyn lifted her hand and gently brushed the hair away from Brenna's face, showing me the tears that flowed down my friend's cheeks.

Before I turned away and gave them their privacy, I saw Brenna Sinclair, once a sorceress who terrorized the courts of Europe, lay her head on her mother's shoulder. As Bronwyn's arms came round her, Brenna's body shook with the force of her sobs.

She'd walked a long and lonely road to that embrace, one pitted with traps and snares engineered by men like Irenaeus Chesterfield and Reynold Isherwood. Brenna killed the former, and we were about to take down the latter together.

They say revenge tastes best when it's served cold, but the blood of the women who sat around the fire that night ran hot with a different animus. We wanted justice.

Pulling my focus away from the memory of Tír na nÓg, my

eyes settled on the page before me. Ruby ink flowed from the nib. Drawing in a deep breath, I willed my thoughts to calm, but the force of my psychometry rose unbidden, merging with the pen's enchantment.

As I watched, a drawing took form on the page. First, the pen drew a ruby the size of a hen's egg, the stone of kings, more prized by the ancients than its cold cousin the diamond.

Switching to gold ink, the nib sketched a nest of intertwined Celtic knots cradling the gem. The design elongated, forming the pommel, grip, and crossguard of a sword as silver ink flowed down the page to make a blade.

Before the pen came to rest, it engraved two words in the steel. "*Accipe me.*"

"Take me up."

That was enough to break my trance.

Take up the sword?

That was not what I wanted to come of the re-opening of Tír na nÓg.

"Enough," I commanded the pen. "We're done for tonight."

Obediently the ebony cap placed itself over the nib, but as it twisted closed, I saw the eyes of the crimson phoenix on the barrel looking at me. The bird blinked slowly and shook its head.

"That'll be enough out of you," I said. "Go on, put yourself to bed."

The pen did as it was told, sliding silently into the butter-soft leather of its loop. The grimoire closed itself, the brass clasp latching with an authoritative click that sent the wings of the dragonlets on the embossed cover fluttering.

Even they seemed disturbed by the impromptu vision. I needed company — and conversation that didn't involve what had just sounded like a magical call to war.

Standing and stretching, I pulled back the curtain only to find the lair mostly deserted, with the one usual exception. Greer sat in her habitual place by the fire with my cat, Winston, snoozing in her lap.

Without looking up, her sharp vampire senses immediately honed in on me. "Good evening, Jinx," she said. "You wrote for a long while. Has something happened to disturb you?"

"No," I lied, crossing the room to join her. "Why would you ask that?"

Word to the wise. Lying to a baobhan sith doesn't work. Greer let me get away with it, but she knew. She totally knew.

"At the edge of my consciousness, I maintained an awareness of the scratching of the nib on the paper," she replied. "The noise ceased somewhat abruptly."

So much for soundproofing.

"You heard all that through the privacy incantation?" I asked as I sat down on the hearth.

"When the lair falls quiet," she smiled, "and when I am on watch, the magic does not present a barrier to my perceptions."

The warmth of the fire felt good on my back and began to calm my nerves. I didn't want to admit it, but the experience with the sword drawing rattled me.

"On watch for what?" I asked.

"Whatever might come along in the dark of the night," she replied, closing her book and setting it aside.

I saw the flames reflected in the emerald depths of her eyes, but the borrowed embers paled next to the real fire dwelling within the baobhan sith. There was a time, early in our friendship, when I found Greer's power disconcerting. Now it warms me to my core.

But that still didn't mean I was ready to talk about my vision — if that's what I'd just experienced. The pen had drawn my dreams before that night, but it had never joined its enchantment with my psychometry.

"What time is it anyway?" I asked, changing the subject.

"A quarter of one in the morning," she replied. "Lucas sent word awhile ago that he has been detained at the British Museum."

Lucas could have contacted me himself over the FaeNet. The fact that he didn't, raised my suspicions about what he'd called a "business as usual" run to Londinium that morning.

Doing my best to keep my voice light, I said, "Anything serious?"

"Nothing the laddie can't handle. His Uncle Morris continues to protest the interagency nature of the special ops squad. Otto Volker asked Lucas to stay for dinner so they might discuss the matter."

Morris Grayson. I should have known. The director of the DGI had no use for me.

The feeling was mutual.

"Shouldn't we all have been part of that conversation?" I asked.

Greer shook her head. "Otto hopes to use his position at IBIS to foster a rapprochement between uncle and nephew. Our presence in Londinium would not be helpful toward that end."

Pursing my lips, I said, "Don't you mean *my* presence?"

That acerbic question brought a sparkle of humor into the redhead's eyes. "Come now, Jinx. You rather put Morris in his place on your first meeting. You don't really expect his fragile ego to have recovered from that encounter so soon, do you?"

Still annoyed, I said, "Did Lucas take Rube with him?"

"No," she said, "Reuben and his associates on the wrecking crew are in the treehouse playing poker with Festus."

Glancing toward the tree that towers beyond the back wall of the lair, I saw the canopy of leaves in full bloom.

After the fairy mound created the arboreal hangout for Rube and his fellow raccoons, we all complained about the noise generated by their frequent all-night card games. In response, the fairy mound added a lever on one wall of the tree house and a second one at floor level we can reach.

When either lever is pulled, a noise-canceling canopy of thick leaves pops out from the tree's uppermost branches, effectively cutting off the poker buddies raucous antics.

"Well," I said, "if everyone else is settled for the night, I guess I should go to bed. Is Winston staying with you?"

Resting one elegant hand on the cat's head, Greer softly stroked his fur. "Winston may stay as long as he likes," she replied fondly. "The other three went upstairs hours ago, but he chose to remain with me. I take his presence as a compliment. Do you mind?"

"Not at all. He's just never been much of a people cat."

Winston opened one eye enough to regard me with a thin sliver of amber.

"Shh," Greer crooned. "Go back to sleep. There is no need to editorialize."

As the cat's eyes drifted shut again, she said, "I've always had something of a way with animals. My powers allow me to attune myself closely to their thoughts. He objects to your description of his nature. It's not that he doesn't like people, he prefers to characterize his loyalties as 'selective.'"

I couldn't keep from smiling. "No wonder the two of you get along," I said. "That could be a description of you."

Greer rewarded the observation with a warm chuckle. "I learned to keep myself removed from a parent well versed in the art."

Hesitating slightly, I said, "How is your mother?"

"As she has always been," Greer said, with a touch of something I took to be wistfulness in her voice. "Impossible and utterly magnificent."

The idea that a being as powerful as Greer MacVicar might get lonely for her mother gave me comfort, and it caught me off guard. That's what happens in the small hours of the night. The things you refuse to think about by the full light of day come calling and won't be ignored.

When we returned from Tír na nÓg, my mother stayed behind in the Neverlands. Even though that was only a few days before, I missed her with the kind of longing panic I remembered from my first day of school.

Back then, when I was six-years-old, I knew I had to stay where I was, in Miss Austin Duncan's first-grade class, but it still took all my willpower not to bolt for the door and run home to my mother as fast as my legs could carry me.

Under the force of that memory, I looked anxiously toward the dark portals off to my right. Even with a direct gateway to reach Tír na nÓg just yards away, the distance between my mother and me seemed immense.

Greer cocked her head and studied me with probing eyes. The frankness of her gaze sent the first wave of a blush spreading across my cheeks.

"Does Kelly's ascension to the role of Roanoke Witch trouble you?" she asked.

Turning my eyes back to the fire rather than face Greer's scrutiny, I said what I was supposed to say. "Mom's destiny lies on Tír na nÓg."

The words lacked conviction even to my ears.

"A mother's destiny can never be truly severed from that of her child."

Hot tears filled my eyes, and my throat closed. If a floating teapot hadn't intervened, I honestly don't know how I would have answered the baobhan sith's kindness.

Yes, you read that right. A floating teapot.

While I struggled to regain my composure, Greer said wryly. "I believe someone wishes to speak with you."

Wiping my eyes as surreptitiously as I could manage, I sat up straighter and found myself face to spout with the levitating china.

"Something I can do for you?" I croaked.

The pot's lid lifted in what I took to be a smile, while the spout gestured in the direction of Myrtle's quarters.

An invitation. Of the kind Myrtle hadn't issued to me in a long while.

"Most people would just come to the door and ask me in," I pointed out, "but you do love your theatrics, don't you?"

The lid clattered up and down in an approximation of both laughter and agreement.

"Alright, fine," I said. "At least you're not going totally over the top and winging arrows past my head to get my attention like you did back in the old days."

The words were hardly out of my mouth before Greer's hand shot out and caught an arrow with bright purple fletching.

"Really, Myrtle," she scolded. "Now you're just showing off."

The shaft pulled impatiently against Greer's hand. When she released it, the arrow turned over in mid-air, pointed toward Myrtle's door, and quivered as if straining against an invisible bowstring.

"She's never liked being made to wait," I said, standing up and starting to walk away. Then my responsible cat mother side kicked in, and I added, "Don't let Winston miss breakfast."

The cat's eye slit open again and fixed me with a look that plainly said, "Seriously?"

"Do I need to translate that for you?" Greer asked with fake solemnity.

"Nope," I laughed. "That one I understood. Fat chance he's going to pass up a full food bowl. I'll see the two of you later."

With that, I followed the teapot and the arrow to the door of Myrtle's quarters, which swung open at my approach. I might not be able to have a conversation with my mother, but there were a few things I wanted to talk to my mentor about as well. Thanks to her impromptu invitation, there appeared to be no time like the present.

houldering through the foot traffic on the High Street, Tori stumbled and careened into a Japanese Satori. With her free hand, she caught the monkey-like creature as it tumbled toward the gutter.

Before she could apologize, the clairvoyant Satori read her mind, thanked her, and hollered, "Duck!"

Only quick reflexes saved Tori from being thwacked by a thick, serpentine tail lashing through the air over her head.

"*Hey!*" she yelled. "Dragon Snake Guy! You do know you have a tail, right?"

The two-legged *nonconformi* stopped and looked down at her. "I am a Lindwyrm," he replied in a thick, growling voice, "not a 'Dragon Snake Guy.' These streets were not constructed with one such as myself in mind. Apologies, Mistress."

All around them, pedestrians got up and dusted off, hurriedly scrambling past the Lindwrym before it started to move again.

"I'll mention the narrow streets to the mayor," Tori said, standing and checking herself for damage. "He's a friend of mine. I assume you're a new student?"

The Lindwrym dropped its head in a sort of bow, "I am, Mistress. Birger Henrikkson, at your service."

"Tori Andrews. I'm with the alchemy department."

"It is an honor to meet you, Professor."

"You can drop the whole 'professor' thing, Birger," she said. "Call me Tori. Are you headed to campus?"

"I am."

"Okay, good. I'm going to stop at Madam Kaveh's for coffee and then I have a meeting at the university. Why don't we walk together and see if we can keep that tail of yours under control?"

"As you wish, Professor Tori," Birger replied, "but I will not be able to walk quickly unless I use my tail for balance."

"I think we're good with slower and safer," she assured him. "Madam Kaveh's is just down this way. Follow me."

While the Lindwyrm waited in the street, Tori went into the coffee shop and ordered a cup to go from the proprietress herself.

Glancing out the window while she worked, Madam Kaveh said, in her heavily accented English, "You walk with big snake?"

"Yeah," Tori said. "He's a Lindwyrm studying at the University. I'm trying to get him off the High Street before he knocks a wall down with that tail of his."

Madam Kaveh snorted. "Agreement was bad, but this mess worse." She gestured with the spoon in her hand toward the congested street. "*Big* mess."

"Come on now," Tori said. "The crowds have to be good for your business."

Settling her round, black spectacles more firmly on her hawkish nose, Madam Kaveh sighed. "I make coffee. Customer buy coffee. Is what I do. But still, *big* mess."

Even though she didn't say it aloud, Tori had to agree. Shevington was caught in the throes of rapid growing pains, and currently, it *was* a big mess.

Connor admitted as much to her the night before, during their mirror call. "The changes are exciting, honey, but the logistics are a nightmare."

He wasn't going to be thrilled to hear about a Lindwyrm almost taking her head off on the High Street, but if she didn't tell him about the incident, someone else would.

Now that Tori was dating the Lord High Mayor Elect, she had renewed admiration for how low key Moira had managed to keep her relationship with Barnaby for hundreds of years.

Thanking Madam Kaveh, Tori collected the waiting Lindwyrm and pointed him toward the outskirts of town. As they walked, she studied the knot of newly constructed buildings occupying the lower end of the big meadow.

With the fairy barracks on the west and the stables to the east, the upper field now lay at the center of an immense quadrangle. In deference to the long-standing tradition of kite flying in that grassy expanse, Barnaby had insisted the university be placed farther from the city.

Tori suspected the layout was also intended to create a greater buffer zone between the peaceful citizens of Shevington and the swelling student population.

Until the residence halls were finished, however, the road from town to campus bustled with traffic all day and well into the night.

At the front gate of the school, Tori parted company with the Lindwyrm, holding her breath as he slowly and carefully threaded his way toward the political science building. During their walk, he'd explained that he had aspirations to serve in the Assembly of the Realms.

"I would be the first of my kind to hold such an office," Birger told her. "As an elected representative, I can speak for all the *nonconformi*. Differences should be celebrated, Professor Tori, not condemned."

Spying Moira waiting on the top step of the alchemy building, Tori pushed through the knots of students in the yard as politely as possible.

"Wow," she said, winded by the exertion. "Is enrollment slowing at all?"

"Alas, no," Moira said. "When we developed the educational plan in Londinium we hoped the *nonconformi* would be receptive to the idea. We certainly did not anticipate this level of success, however. Adeline and Gareth are waiting for us in his laboratory. Shall we join them?"

Tori looked confused. "I thought we were meeting with the full alchemy faculty."

"My dear," Moira laughed, "the four of us and your dear mother *are* the alchemy faculty. As you know, she could not be with us today because she is with Kelly in Tír na nÓg."

"Tell me about it," Tori said. "I've been running back and forth between our shop and the apothecary helping Brenna run the place. Jinx's dad shows up every night in the lair for supper with all his dogs and chaos ensues. If staying in Tír na nÓg was a plan to make us appreciate them, the moms have proven their point."

Chuckling, Moira said, "While I am sure they will be glad to hear they are missed, Kelly and Gemma are needed in the Neverlands."

Together the two alchemists entered the cool, dark hallway with its vaulted ceilings and high stained glass windows.

"This place reminds me of a church," Tori said in a hushed voice. "I feel like I have to whisper."

"You do not," Moira assured her in a normal voice. "Would that novice alchemists practiced their trade with the reverence of clerics at the altar. I do need to warn you . . ."

Her words came too late. A wave of noxious fumes hit Tori full force, touching off a furious fit of coughing and gagging.

As her eyes began to stream from the acrid stench, Tori hastily covered her nose with her hand. "What on earth is that smell?" she croaked.

Unperturbed, Moira replied, "I'm afraid my *Introduction to Elements* class had an unfortunate incident involving sulfur. Dewy is endeavoring to eliminate the odor."

Prolific swearing emanating from a room on the right gave Tori a point of focus.

"From the sound of things," she said, "being put on Stink Eradication Detail is not making Dewey any happier about being your teaching assistant."

Peeking cautiously through the door, she saw a short man shaped like a barrel pumping furiously at an old-fashioned insecticide canister. The nozzle in his hand spewed clouds of purple smoke toward the rafters.

"It does not seem to be," Moira admitted. "Nor is he happy that I have asked him to use lavender to counter the smell of rotting eggs."

"What's not to like about lavender?" Tori asked.

"The herb imparts a sense of calm and tranquility," Moria replied. "Two states of being Dewey utterly detests."

When Tori snickered, the corners of the alchemist's mouth twitched. She tried to suppress both her smile and the giggle that accompanied it, failing on both counts.

"Under that rough exterior, Dewey is a dear," she said. "He would do anything for me, and he has cared faithfully if gruffly, for Barnaby during his convalescence. Frankly, I did not know how Dewey would react when Barnaby left the Lord High Mayor's house and moved temporarily into my workshop."

"You're married," Tori said. "Did Dewey think you'd continue to live in different houses?"

"No, of course not," she said. "Even Dewey is not that unreasonable, but he has become quite set in his ways through the centuries. Once the issue of the toast was resolved, however, we have all gotten on quite well."

Renewed banging from inside the classroom made them both jump back.

"Perhaps we should continue to our destination as we talk," Moira suggested. "We would not want to distract Dewey from his task."

It was Tori's turn to grin. "Don't you mean you want to get out of here before he sees us and pitches one of his fits?"

"That, too."

A few paces farther down the hall, Tori said, "Okay, now, tell me about the toast."

"Ah," Moira replied, "well, you see, Barnaby prefers to butter his own toast."

"Uh, don't most people?" Tori asked.

Moira seemed to consider the question. "I rather imagine they do," she said, "but Dewey insists the butter be applied with surgical precision symmetrically reaching the crust on all sides. My dear husband tends to, well, smear."

"Remind me never to eat toast around Dewey," Tori said.

"I would not recommend it," Moira agreed, "the initial impression you make with a butter knife can be quite difficult to pry from his mind. Here we are."

She opened the door to a room flooded with light pouring through floor-to-ceiling windows that overlooked the mountains in the upper valley. From behind a complex mass of glass tubing and beakers, Gareth greeted them happily as Adeline rolled into view beside him.

"There you are!" Adeline said. "Thank you for handling the matter of the Lindwyrm."

The comment surprised Tori. "How did you know that?" she asked. Then the answer came to her, and she snapped her fingers. "Wait. You're using GNATS drones over the city, aren't you?"

"A necessary tactic," Adeline said, splitting her screen into two windows with her face on one side and a live feed from the High Street on the other.

"Given Major Istra's aversion to his elite troops serving as what he insists on calling 'truant officers,'" she explained, "Festus consented to my commandeering one of the drones assigned to Briar Hollow to help keep an eye on the students."

Tori met the explanation with skepticism. "Festus *agreed*? What did you have to do for him in exchange?"

The image of Adeline's face flickered slightly. "It is possible," she said, "that I may have electronically assisted him with the placement of wagers on a series of sporting contests."

"Don't tell me," Tori said, holding up her hand. "I want to maintain plausible deniability."

"A prudent choice," Adeline agreed.

Squinting at the screen, Tori said, "So how are you handling incidents like my Lindwyrm wreck?"

"For minor infractions of decorum and etiquette, I record the transgression and send the footage directly to Barnaby's office. For more serious matters, we dispatch the fairy guard. Major Istra seems more willing for his troops to participate in scenarios requiring physical action."

"I'll bet he does," Tori said. "Ironweed has the worst case of short guy syndrome I've ever seen."

"In all fairness," Moira demurred, "he is quite tall for a fairy. He stands at least six and a half inches."

"Tall being a relative term," Tori said, turning her attention to their spacious surroundings. "Gareth, I think you snagged the best lab in the building."

"Hardly," he said. "Moira's workshop occupies the whole

second floor." Then, remembering himself, he added hastily, "As it should be."

"I will be teaching the advanced students there," Moira said. "We will require the room for our more ambitious projects. My lab in our home will be considerably more modest."

"How close are the builders to finishing the house?" Tori asked.

"Come and see," Moira replied. "They are putting the roof on today."

The two women moved to one of the tall windows and Moira pointed to a building site at the base of the foothills. Sitting behind a mostly decorative rock wall, the house had the look of an English country manor. Crews of dwarves swarmed over the rafters, hammers in hand, laying down shingles.

"They're working fast," Tori said. "When do you and Barnaby hope to move in?"

"The foreman assures us we will be in residence within a fortnight. A deadline that is also having a deleterious effect on Dewey's disposition."

"Gareth," Tori asked, "do you plan to stay in Moira's old workshop?"

"For the time being," he said, "but it's too much space for me. I plan to take rooms here at the university when the construction is finished. I think we'll be quite happy with something smaller."

Tori frowned. "We? Are you seeing someone?"

The question made Gareth blush bright red. "Oh, no," he said. "Not at all. I was referring to the Liszt set. It's become the primary focus of my alchemical research. We're working together on a treatise examining the sentience of enchanted objects."

"Well," Tori said, "I guess the two of you were more or less roommates when you were trapped inside the board."

"My imprisonment was Chesterfield's doing," Gareth said defensively. "The set itself is blameless. The board has cooperated fully in Isherwood's prosecution."

Holding up a hand in apology, Tori said, "I know, my bad."

Mollified, Gareth said, "Come and say hello. The board remembers you from the time it spent in The Witch's Brew."

The Liszt set occupied a place of honor in a cozy sitting area arranged before the window with the most commanding view of the mountains.

"The board likes this vista," Gareth explained, drawing back one of the chairs. "Please, sit down."

Tori sank onto the cushion, and eyed the board hesitantly, not quite sure how to address a chess set. "Uh, hi," she said awkwardly. "Come up with any good moves lately?"

In response, several pieces slid around the board in rapid succession.

Tori looked at Gareth blankly. "Is that supposed to mean something to me?"

Studying the arrangement, Gareth said, "A variation on the Sokolsky opening. In its spare time, the set is working out a new theory of tactics. It was never free to think for itself when it was under Chesterfield's control. Now it's like a sponge. By demonstrating this opening, the set was attempting to give you a literal answer — that it has come up with new moves."

"Does 'it' have a name?" she asked, bending closer to study the intricate pieces.

"Not the board itself, but the spirit within is known as Memoriae."

"That's Latin for memory," Tori said.

"Yes," Gareth said, running a hand along the edge of the polished playing field. "Memoriae has proven to be an excellent witness against Chesterfield and Isherwood. It watched for years, forced to do their bidding, but forgetting nothing of their crimes."

"How do you talk to it?" Tori asked curiously.

Still looking lovingly at the board, Gareth said, "Why, I go home, of course."

Tori's jaw dropped. "You go back inside the set?"

"Oh, yes," Gareth said cheerfully. "I can now come and go as I please. Memoriae felt bad about my imprisonment, but there was nothing it could do to set me free. We've become wonderful friends and colleagues. Moira, I do wish you'd re-consider putting Memoriae on the faculty."

"Now, Gareth," Moira said placatingly, "we have discussed this. Until you and Memoriae develop a more standard means by which it can communicate, such an appointment is out of the question. Surely you understand that I cannot sanction sending students inside a chess set to attend class."

Gareth set his mouth in a firm line. "Respectfully, Alchemist, that is ossified thinking. If the *nonconformi* have been liberated from their segregation, why do we continue to treat sentient artifacts as *things*?"

"Let us handle one societal upheaval at a time, Gareth," Moira said. The inflection in the statement indicated the conversation was over. "Shall we begin our curriculum review?"

Tori could tell Gareth wasn't happy with the response, but he bustled toward his desk to retrieve his notes.

"Do I sense an activist in the making?" Tori asked under her breath.

Sighing, Moira said, "Gareth is himself rather a project in the making. He has not yet learned that while a man's reach should exceed his grasp, being armed with both passion and a *plan* tends to garner the greatest success."

"He may have a point about the sentient objects, you know," Tori said.

"I do know," Moira replied, "but would you add a chorus of clattering grails and talking walking sticks to the current level of chaos in Shevington? The mission of this university is to broaden the minds of all the species in all the realms. Our work at the present is with the *nonconformi*. The sentient objects are not the ones spilling into the world of the humans and causing cryptid sightings."

Tori refrained from saying the one word that instantly popped into her head.

Yet.

7

As I stepped across the threshold, Myrtle called out, "Come in, Jinx. Share a cup of chamomile with me before you turn in for the night."

I found her sitting by a smaller version of the lair fireplace. A cup and saucer waited for me on a low table next to the empty chair. Myrtle's place always reminds me of a hobbit hole, right down to the irregular lines and round doors. If she'd told me we needed to talk about a gold ring and Mount Doom, I wouldn't have been surprised in the least.

"You haven't sent me an animated invitation like that in forever," I said, claiming the chair and reaching for my tea. "You're like a kid in a candy store now that Tír na nÓg has fully restored your magic."

Her laughter filled the room with the sound of tinkling bells. "I stand guilty as accused," she admitted. "How I missed playing with the fairy mound as we just did! The arrow was her idea, by the way, not mine."

The pronoun choice surprised me. "The fairy mound is female?" I asked.

"Yes," Myrtle replied. "She has been my companion since childhood."

Having the aos si to myself and in a talkative mood boded well for my plan to go after answers to some of my more nagging questions.

"Can you explain a few things to me?" I asked, taking a sip of the warm, fragrant tea.

"Of course," she said. "What do you wish to know?"

Even though I had expected Myrtle would say yes, I found myself briefly stymied about where to begin. I could have taken a deep dive into Fae politics, but as I looked at the lovely, golden woman sitting across from me, I realized that wasn't the most vital important information.

To understand Tír na nÓg and its significance in our shared journey, I needed to know more about Myrtle herself.

"I'm confused," I said. "You've always said that you were born in the roots of the Mother Tree, but you've also said that Tír na nÓg is your ancestral home. Now you tell me that you grew up with the fairy mound. How does that all fit together?"

"Each of those statements is true," Myrtle replied. "I was born in the roots of the Great Oak when the Mother Trees dwelled in the land of Tír na nÓg before the Great Dispersal. The magic of the trees springs, in part, from the fairy mounds in which they were first planted. This mound began as my nurse-maid, and over the centuries evolved into my friend and confidant. One with a rather wicked sense of humor, in case you hadn't noticed."

I'd noticed all right. Since I informed Morris Grayson the special ops team would be based in Briar Hollow, the fairy mound had busily expanded — and decorated — to meet our every need. The process was not, however, without a goodly number of whimsical touches — like the leaf lever in Rube's treehouse.

"You lost me at Great Dispersal," I admitted.

Holding out her hand, Myrtle drew her cup closer on a current of shimmering light. "In the time before there was time," she began, "the Tuatha Dé Danann dwelled in the Neverlands . . ."

Listening to the rise and fall of her voice, I allowed myself to be drawn completely into the tale, seeing the images Myrtle painted with her words like living pictures before my eyes.

She spoke of the days when all the Great Trees grew together in a single grove at the roots of the World Tree, Yggdrasil. In time, however, the Tuath Dé, which is Gaelic for "tribe of the gods," grew curious about the human realm.

"We are not, of course, gods," Myrtle said, "but in those days when we exhibited our magic freely in the company of humans we seemed as such to them. When we crossed the In Between and entered their realm for the first time, we found peoples already struggling with questions of belief and bloody territorial disputes. Even in their infancy as a culture, humans suffered from bouts of contentiousness and division. Still, at their best we found them to be delightful and sought, as we could, to guide and mentor them."

An act of Fae generosity to be filed under "no good deed ever goes unpunished."

"To serve as a stabilizing influence," Myrtle continued, "Yggdrasil bade the Great Trees to leave Tír na nÓg and to position themselves at points of power around the globe. The fairy mounds went with the trees. The Great Dispersal created the structure that ensures the coherence of the realms, and it spread the magic of Tír na nÓg far into the world. There it remained and thrived until the days of the Fae Retreat."

She was referring to the time when the Fae largely removed themselves from the affairs of humankind ahead of a growing wave of persecutions that mainly took the form of witch hunting. Those events roughly coincided with the Fae Reformation and my grandfather's exodus to the New World in 1584.

Now, with Isherwood unmasked, those atrocities had been revealed as part of his master plan to dispense with his rivals and to pervert natural magic for his own greedy ends. He'd done far more than just strong-arm The Agreement through the Ruling Elders and cast the *nonconformi* races into exile in the Middle Realm. Isherwood built the Creavit heresy on the stolen magic of Fae children.

"So the Mother Oak left Tír na nÓg during the Great Dispersal and settled in Kent," I said, "with you and the fairy mound."

"Yes," Myrtle said, "and when the Oak fled to the New World, the fairy mound and I came with her. Our magicks are intertwined. Together we form a triumvirate of sorts, one that was weakened when the Orb of Thoth poisoned me."

Even though I knew there was likely a reasonable magical answer, I couldn't stop myself from asking the next question. The instant the words passed my lips, I knew I sounded like a petulant child.

"Why didn't you just go to Tír na nÓg then and heal yourself?" I asked. "Wouldn't that have been better than going into the Mother Tree and leaving us here all alone?"

I'm honest enough to admit I wasn't thinking about "us" at all. I was only thinking about myself.

During the long months when Myrtle was gone, I struggled to find my way without her wise counsel. Whether I had a right to be or not, I was still hurt and a little resentful.

Myrtle had been back for eleven months. Even though I realized she cut short her recovery from the Orb's poison to return — a sacrifice I appreciated — our relationship still hadn't found a new "normal."

Or course, the aos si heard the wounded undercurrent in my

words. Myrtle isn't one to just leave elephants sitting in the middle of the room.

"I could not risk exposing the existence of the sanctuary. I am among the last of the Tuatha Dé Danann. Had I crossed the barrier to Tír na nÓg, ripples would have been felt throughout the Otherworld."

There it was. The perfectly reasonable answer, but I wasn't ready to give in yet.

"But you were in Tír na nÓg waiting for us when we unlocked the passage with the Wands of the Chosen," I said stubbornly. "How did you get there undetected then?"

"On the flight of the baobhan sith," Myrtle replied. "I rode the wind with Katherine MacVicar. Her magic cloaked my presence. We knew the Chosen Ones would open the gateway within hours. With the ascension of the Roanoke Witch and the Power of the Seven in place, we could well afford the risk at that moment."

Something about the phrase "Power of the Seven" nagged at me, but the soothing effect of the chamomile was starting to slow down my thought processes. I let it go. Instead, I blurted out, "Why have you been avoiding me since you got back?"

Myrtle leaned forward and rested her hand on my knee. The warmth I felt in the gesture didn't come from her powers. "Dear child," she said, "I have not been avoiding you. Matters of great import have demanded our attention — yours and mine. Jinx, every moment I dwelt within the Mother Tree I missed you."

A sob caught in my throat. "I guess I thought you'd come back and everything would be the way it was before."

The answer of a child. Which Myrtle gently forgave.

"I was not the only person to change in those months," she said. "In my absence, you became a leader. Things will never be as they were before, nor should they. Beyond that, when I returned, I had another to prepare."

She could only mean one person.

"My mother?" I asked.

"Yes," Myrtle said. "Before the truth of Tír na nÓg could be revealed, I had to help Kelly rediscover her confidence so that she could serve as the Roanoke Witch."

"But didn't the Amulet of Caorunn restore her confidence?"

"An amulet can be taken from the neck of its wearer as easily as it can be placed there," Myrtle said. "What the trinket began, Kelly has finished on her own. In the absence of her mother, it fell to me to help her complete that task."

Did you have to take her from me while you were doing it?

I don't think I spoke those words aloud, but Myrtle heard them anyway.

"Sometimes to find the mother within yourself, Jinx, you must feel, even if briefly, the pain of the motherless."

Myrtle watched as Jinx's eyes grew heavier and her head lolled to the side. When the teacup slid from her limp grasp, the aos si caught it and the remaining liquid with her magic, returning both to the safety of the table.

The clinking of the china against the wood surface roused Jinx. "Sorry," she mumbled. "Past my bedtime."

"You are welcome to sleep here," Myrtle said.

Blinking blearily, Jinx stood up on wobbly legs. "Thanks," she said, shuffling toward the door. "I'll just go to my alcove. Soundproof."

Smiling indulgently, Myrtle gestured again, opening the door before Jinx walked straight into it. Then, thinking of all the objects in Jinx's path, the aos si rose and followed her friend.

As they passed Greer by the fire, the baobhan sith looked up and smothered a laugh at the sight of the half-conscious witch and the protective Myrtle trailing behind.

At the door of the alcove, Myrtle watched as Jinx climbed into her daybed and pulled the quilt up around her ears. Satisfied that her charge was well tucked in, Myrtle turned to leave. A motion on the desk stopped her.

The Phoenix pen slipped from its leather loop at the side of the grimoire, slid to the edge of the desk, and floated serenely down to the rug. When it landed, the pen rolled across the short distance to Myrtle and stopped at the toe of her shoe.

The aos si bent and retrieved the writing instrument. Balancing it across the palm of her hand, she asked quietly, "Do you wish to speak with me?"

The pen levitated to stand on its base and nodded first toward Jinx and then at the door.

"No," Myrtle whispered, "I do not wish to awaken her either. Let us return to my quarters. May I place you in my pocket for the journey?"

When the pen nodded, Myrtle tucked it into her robe, stepped into the lair, and drew the curtain closed over the alcove.

Greer looked up again. "You must make a remarkable cup of chamomile," she said. "Did you enchant it?"

"No," Myrtle replied, "I believe the special ops team's hectic schedule of late has proved too much even for Jinx's indefatigable spirit."

The baobhan sith nodded. "Two missions in five days is unusual, but there are many changes afoot in the realms."

"Indeed there are," Myrtle agreed. "Goodnight to thee, baobhan sith."

"And to thee, aos si."

Behind the closed door of her quarters, Myrtle took the pen

from her pocket and laid it beside a fresh stack of paper on her desk.

"How may I help you?" she asked.

The cap rotated free and stood to the side while the barrel assumed a writing position and moved over the first page.

"Forgive me, aos si, but the grimoire and I share a concern. Something happened tonight we take as cause for alarm."

Myrtle rested her hands on the desk and studied the words.

"The magic which gifted you with sentience forbids that you break the confidence of the Witch of the Oak," she said. "You cannot speak with me of what Jinx may have asked you to write."

The nib traced out a new series of words.

"What we were asked to render did not come from the Witch of the Oak. Something has changed in her magic."

After considering that statement, Myrtle said carefully, "Do you know the source of the content you were asked to render?"

"We are not certain, but it came from within the fairy mound and carried with it the essence of the World Tree."

The aos si sat back in her chair. "The eighth wand," she muttered.

Then, turning her attention back to the waiting pen, she said, "You have given me sufficient information by speaking those words alone. You cannot share more. If you break the terms of your enchantment, you will destroy yourself."

The pen hovered over the paper as if thinking and then wrote. *"Our charge is to keep the secrets of the Witch of the Oak, but also to protect her."*

"A fair point," Myrtle agreed. "Do you and the grimoire judge this information of such importance that you would risk your existence?"

In flowing script, the pen wrote, *"Yes. We love her, too."*

"Then pause and think with care, my brother," Myrtle

cautioned. "Show me only enough to make me understand your concern. Nothing more."

The ink rose from the page and flowed back into the pen leaving the paper clean and smooth. Then, with infinite precision, the nib began to draw a sword.

odney finished his nightly 30-mile wheel run and
looked at the clock in the storeroom. Festus had been
downstairs for hours playing poker with Rube and
the other raccoons. Wide-awake, and curious as always, the rat
decided to find out how the game was going.

Scampering down his personal staircase, Rodney paused on
the tiny landing above Beau's desk and surveyed the scene in the
room. Greer MacVicar and Jinx's cat Winston sat by the fire,
while Jinx herself was just stepping through the door into
Myrtle's quarters.

No one else was around, and the privacy leaves were in place
over Rube's treehouse. The game must have gotten rowdy. Festus
was probably drunk, which meant he'd be overly enthusiastic
with his paws and garrulous in his greetings. A "pat" on
Rodney's back could easily send the rat sailing over the table
and possibly straight out of the tree.

Not anxious to have that experience, and disappointed that
Glory was still off somewhere with Chase, Rodney decided to
slip into Jinx's alcove and look for something to read. There, he

could access a shelf of pocket-sized classics that fit his paws perfectly.

Maybe *A Tale of Two Cities* would put him to sleep. The first lines of that book explained more and more how Rodney was feeling.

It was the best of times; it was the worst of times.

Running along the top of the newly erected back wall, the rat jumped onto the curtain rod over the alcove door and slid halfway down the fabric before springing onto the nearest easy chair. From there it was a single leap to the desk.

Jinx's grimoire lay in the middle of the blotter. As he started to cross the green felt toward the bookcase, Rodney stopped with a gasp of surprise when the brass clasp on the book clicked. The grimoire's front cover rose followed by a rippling fan of sheets until the volume lay open in front of him.

Whiskers twitching, Rodney stood on his hind legs and peered at the page. There on the thick paper lay a perfect sketch of a sword, so detailed that the weapon might have been lifted from the page and wielded in battle.

But it wasn't the detail of the sketch that caused him to grow still, his snowy chest rising and falling with heavy breaths. He knew that sword, from the glowing ruby set in the handle to the words ornately etched into the silver blade.

Accipe me.

Take me up.

Between his guardianship of the Eighth Wand and now the appearance of the Sword of Merlin, Rodney knew what would happen next.

Lucien St. Leger would find him again.

Innis served dessert to Connor and Tori in the parlor of the

Lord High Mayor's house. She'd thoughtfully arranged a table near the hearth to create a cozier atmosphere.

As the brownie housekeeper poured their coffee, she asked, "Will you be needing anything else, young sir? The dishes will carry themselves to the kitchen when you're done."

"No thank you, Innis," Connor said. "Dinner was wonderful."

"You're welcome," she replied. "Shall I put the Lady Ailish to bed?"

Connor looked down fondly at the Elven Gray Loris curled in the crook of his arm. "No," he said. "She can stay here. If she wakes up alone, she might be afraid."

After Innis left, Connor shifted his beloved pet onto a cushion, tucking a lap robe around her sleeping form. When he returned his attention to Tori, he found her grinning at him with laughter-filled eyes.

"What?" he asked. "Did I do something funny?"

"'Young sir?'" Tori asked in a teasing imitation of the housekeeper's voice. "'Lady' Ailish?"

Connor blushed. "I wish she wouldn't do that," he said, "but honestly, Innis likes Ailish a whole lot more than she likes me. As long as she's around, Ailish is set for 'sticky sweet honey' for life."

"I don't think there's any danger that either one of you will go without anything," Tori said. "How are you adjusting to all this?"

Her upraised hand circled the room to elucidate the question.

"It's an adjustment," Connor admitted. "I liked living over the stables, but Grandad did something really sweet to give me the best of both worlds. Want to see?"

"Sure."

He got up, making sure not to disturb Ailish. "Over here," he said, leading Tori to the door that used to open into Barnaby's study. This time, however, it revealed the interior of Connor's old loft.

"Barnaby did this?" Tori gasped. "Is it a copy or the real thing?"

"The real thing," Connor said. "Grandad doesn't use his personal power of transmogrification anymore, but he has some way to extend the ability beyond his body. He moved his study to their new house and brought my loft from the stables here. I don't understand all the magical details. You'll have to ask him about that."

"I will," Tori assured him. "I'm used to the fairy mound remaking itself at will, but this is a really impressive piece of personal magic."

As they returned to the parlor and their dessert, Connor said, "Grandad has been using his power much more freely since he and Moira got back from Londinium. I don't know if it's being married or because he doesn't have to worry about his brother now, but I've never seen him happier. Did you see him today on campus?"

"No," Tori said, reaching for her fork and slicing off a thick bite of Innis' spice cake. "I met with Moira, Adeline, Gareth, and the chess set."

Pausing with his own fork halfway to his mouth, Connor said, "The chess set?"

"Gareth has gotten passionate about the rights of sentient objects," Tori said, chewing thoughtfully, "and I'm not sure I disagree with him. If the *nonconformi* can move openly between the realms and aspire to get elected to the Assembly, those freedoms should be universal."

"You met someone who wants to run for the Assembly of the Realms?"

Connor listened as Tori described her encounter with Birger, frowning when she recounted their collision.

"I'd like to close the High Street to the larger *nonconformi*," he said crossly, "but that would go against the new climate of acceptance."

Meeting his eyes over the rim of her coffee cup, Tori said pointedly, "Yes, it would."

"He knocked you down," Connor insisted stubbornly.

"Okay, " Tori said, putting down her cup. "Part of me wants to tell you that's sweet and the other part wants to chew you out for saying it."

An uncertain look came into his eyes. "Uh-oh. What did I do?"

"Nothing yet," Tori said, "but don't treat me like I'm made of glass. That kind of thing got Chase and Jinx in trouble. Let's not go there."

Connor sighed. "Understood," he said, "but that won't stop me from worrying."

"That's okay," she said, reaching over and squeezing his hand. "You want to protect the people of Shevington, and you want to protect me. Those aren't bad impulses if you channel them the right way."

"Finding the right way is the difficult part," he said, "especially when you're not always getting the level of cooperation you need."

Frowning, Tori said, "That doesn't sound like we're talking about me and the Lindwyrm anymore. Did something happen today?"

"The chief engineer of the dwarf crew *refuses* to move at any speed other than his own," he blurted out in a rush of frustration. "We needed those residence halls finished last week. That alone will cut the foot traffic on the High Street. Sometimes I think the more I urge him to work faster the slower he gets . . . "

The stream of words stuttered to a stop when he realized Tori was staring fixedly into the space between them with glassy eyes.

"Honey, are you listening to me?"

"Hmm?" she said, blinking back to reality. "Oh, yeah. Sorry. I just had the strangest feeling."

"About what?"

"I know this sounds nuts, but I think Jinksy just had a vision."

"Do you need to get back to Briar Hollow?"

She shook her head. "No, I don't think she's in any danger. It was just a quick flash."

"What did you see?" he asked curiously.

"I'm not really sure," Tori admitted. "I think it might have been a sword. It's probably nothing. Go on, tell me about the chief engineer."

9

R eynold Isherwood paced the length of his cell in the Tower of Londinium. Twenty steps from the west wall to the east and twenty back again. Compared to human jails and discounting the cold seeping through the ancient stones, the disgraced Ruling Elder knew his situation could be far worse.

For one hour each afternoon, the gargoyle guards allowed him to walk in the interior courtyard under the gaze of the Tower ravens. The birds watched him exercise with their bright eyes, silent but judgmental.

During his weeks in prison, and deprived of his magic by the enchanted restraints cast into the walls, Isherwood learned to keep time in the fortress by surprisingly human means. He watched the sunbeams slanting through the windows and listened for the scrape of his captors' claws on the flagstones as they made their rounds.

Using both, he calculated that his single hour of relative freedom was about to begin. At the far end of the hall, the wizard heard a gargoyle approaching. A ring of keys rattled in the lock, and the door swung open on well-oiled hinges.

"Time for your walk, Isherwood," the creature snapped, his beak clacking sharply. "Put your coat on. It's cold out there."

Shrugging into the heavy garment, Isherwood followed dutifully through the labyrinthine prison. At the door leading outside, the guard stopped him.

"You're going to have company," the gargoyle rasped. "If you tell anyone she was here, I'll call you a liar. This wouldn't be happening, but she scares me more than you do."

Nodding curtly, Isherwood stepped out into the pale, winter light. He half-expected, half-hoped, that he would find his wife, Thomasine, waiting for him — except the gentle woman he had married and wronged for centuries lacked the capacity to inspire fear in anyone.

A figure in a long, hooded cloak stood with her back to him.

"Who are you?" Isherwood said. "What do you want of me?"

With a swirl of black fabric, the woman turned. At the sight of her face, the wizard's veins filled with ice. "Morgan," he gasped.

"Hello, Reynold," the woman said, her crimson lips curving into a seductive, dangerous smile. "You're thin, old friend. Are they not feeding you?"

A bitter draft passed between them. Shivering, Isherwood drew his coat tighter. "They feed me," he said, the words clipped and nervous.

"Now, now," the woman said, a dangerous imitation of sympathy filling her azure eyes. "Why so apprehensive? We've known one another since the days when my insufferable brother ruled this wretched island."

"England has never been wretched nor was Arthur insufferable," Isherwood said. "You created your own difficulties, Morgan le Fay."

The words hardened her eyes. "Careful, Reynold," she said.

"I have never been known for my patience. Let us walk. I should think you would be loathe to waste this hour."

In a mocking tone, he replied, "I am also loathe to trust you."

"Walk," Morgan commanded.

The wizard took a hesitating step, flinching slightly as the woman moved alongside him.

"As you know," she said, "I have not set foot on these shores in many centuries. You have, however, created something of a dilemma for my sisters and me. Shall we say the Coven is not pleased?"

Stealing a sidelong glance at her profile, Isherwood said, "You mean *you* are not pleased. The Coven does nothing save by your command."

Morgan laughed, a sound both musical and cruel. "My sisters are loyal, a quality you would do well to emulate."

"I have said nothing," the wizard protested. "The fools they send to question me believe that I am the architect of all that has occurred."

"You are the architect of many transgressions, Reynold, beginning with the Creavit heresy."

"A dark deal crafted with magic *you* provided," he countered.

Overhead, a single bolt of lightning crackled across the sky. The ravens shifted on their perches, but still uttered no sound.

"You have not begun to see the darkness of my magic," Morgan said. "The pathetic restraints woven into the walls of this prison will not hold me as they hold you. Mind your tongue. I am here because the Vessel of Pure Magic lies once again within my grasp. My plans depend on your silence."

"I told you. I have said nothing."

The woman stopped and faced him. As the hood of her cloak fell away, the rising wind caught her ebony hair, coiling the tendrils in dark waves around her pale face.

"I do not trust you," she said. "You have become accustomed

to your creature comforts. Wine and meat. Your quaint collections and pastimes. If I have learned one thing since the days of Camelot, it is that no woman can leave her fortunes to the mercurial nature of a man."

Isherwood took a step back, raising his hands to defend himself, but unable to produce more than faint static at his fingertips.

Morgan lifted one hand, curving the fingers into a bowl as a pinpoint of light appeared over her palm. As the ball of energy expanded, the glowing light illuminated Isherwood's pale, terrified features.

"You can't do this, Morgan," he said. "You can't murder me in the Tower of Londinium and just walk out of here as if nothing happened."

"Reynold," she purred, "I don't walk anywhere. The guard who brought you here will remember only that he performed his regular duty. Anyone looking out onto this courtyard will see only you, pacing your weary route around the walls. And the birds on the parapets know better than to cross the Goddess of the Crows. I am hardly an amateur at matters of subterfuge, and what you call murder, I call tying up a loose end I can no longer allow to dangle."

Before Isherwood could say more, the magic flew from the sorceress' hand, engulfing him in an envelope of flame. His mouth opened in a scream, but before the sound left his burning throat, his body exploded into a cloud of fine dust. The wind caught the particles and lifted them over the walls leaving the courtyard pristine and empty, for with the same burst of magic, Morgan le Fay was gone.

As silence fell over the scene, a single raven danced nervously on his perch before spreading his wings and flying away over the rooftops of Londinium.

"Pour the metal slowly," Seneca commanded, tilting his head as he surveyed the work of the Key Man. "The finished product must have no seams."

The workman's thick mutton chop sideburns twitched with irritation. "Patience thy name is not raven," he grumbled, annoyance filling the rheumy blue eyes behind the gold spectacles. "You act as if I've never cast an article for enchantment. May I remind you that I learned this process from you, brother?"

"In a time when I possessed hands, not wings, and could ply my trade alone," the raven replied.

The Key Man shook his head. "Centuries have passed, Seneca. We have both gotten by as we are."

A sharp rapping at the back window of the shop interrupted their conversation. Without looking away, the Key Man called out, "Yes, yes. In a moment. I cannot stop what I am doing."

As the last drop of molten silver fell, Seneca chanted an incantation in Latin. The surface of the cooling metal roiled in response and instantly hardened. Carefully removing the article from its mold, the Key Man held it up to the light.

"Perfect," he said, "like every key we've ever made."

The sound from the window came again, sharper this time.

"I'm coming. I'm coming," the Key Man said impatiently as he placed the newly enchanted item in the velvet interior of an ornate mahogany box and closed the lid.

Shuffling through the detritus that littered the shop, he turned the latch on the grimy window and opened the hinged pane. A second raven stepped through.

"It's about time," the bird said, ruffling his feathers. "A body could catch his death of cold out there."

"Theatrical as always, Munin," the Key Man said. "What brings you from the Tower to our humble shop?"

The raven fluttered across the cramped area and came to rest on the worktable. The newcomer, although a robust and healthy bird, seemed to shrink next to Seneca's muscular form and broad chest.

"My Lord," Munin said, dropping his beak to touch the scarred wood.

"Munin, my loyal friend," Seneca said. "What news do you bring us on this cold, wet day?"

Raising his head, Munin said, "I bring you news of the Morgaine, returned this day to Britannia."

Behind them, the Key Man wiped his hands nervously on the stained fabric of his blue work shirt.

"You must be mistaken," he rasped. "The enchantress Morgana quit these shores for the hidden forest of Brocéliande in France in the days after the death of Arthur Pendragon at the Battle of Camlann."

Seneca clacked his beak impatiently. "You read too many human books," he said. "The Morgaine did not go to France. She went to the icy lands of the Vikings. You are sure you saw her, Munin?"

"Yes, my Lord," the raven said. "The Goddess of the Crows came to the Tower to see the wizard, Isherwood. She told him the Vessel of Pure Magic once again lies within her reach."

Nodding, Seneca said, "The Chosen Ones have opened the doors of Tír na nÓg. The Rowan Witches have returned, under the leadership of She Who Serves the Two Trees. What did Isherwood say to this news?"

"He said nothing, my Lord. The Morgaine rendered him to dust in a storm of fire."

The Key Man rammed his hands into the pockets of his cardigan. "This is none of our business, Seneca."

"Perhaps not," the raven said, his obsidian eyes glittering in the dim light, "but it has come to our doorstep all the same."

10

The smell of fresh coffee brought me blinking awake, momentarily disoriented by my surroundings. When my eyes focused, I realized I'd slept in the daybed in my alcove with no memory of stumbling there from Myrtle's quarters. Whatever she stirred into that chamomile tea put me out like a light.

Darby stood just inside the curtain holding a silver tray in his hands laden with a steaming pot of coffee and a good-sized mug.

It took me awhile to convince the faithful brownie that tiny porcelain cups don't work for me even if he does consider them "ladylike." Now he finds the most ginormous mugs I've ever seen, yet another reason I love him. This one was emblazoned with a smiley face rising sun and the words, "Seize the day!"

"Good morning, Mistress," Darby said. "When you went to bed last night, you asked that I awaken you at 8 a.m."

"I did?" I asked my voice sounding thick and bleary.

Wow. I *had* been down for the count. My memory of that conversation amounted to exactly zero.

"Yes, Mistress, you did," he assured me. "You also . . ."

Before he could finish whatever he was going to say and remind me of whatever *I* had said, the lair reverberated with the sound of an outraged werecat.

"Now see here you cranky old hag, I am an athlete in training."

"*Hag?*" came Amity's shrill response. "Festus McGregor, did you just *dare* to call me a *hag*? Coming from an alcoholic wastrel, that takes some *nerve!*"

Sliding out of bed, I hastily grabbed the coffee cup and took a quick gulp. You never have to worry about burning your tongue when Darby makes the coffee. He always gives it to you with the temperature perfectly set for instant consumption.

"What am I getting ready to walk into out there?" I asked, now fully awake.

The brownie filled me in quickly. The poker game from the night before broke up sometime around 4 a.m. Festus, thoroughly sauced, decided to make a few tree destruction training runs, egged on by Rube.

Little did Festus know the whole thing was a set up for one of the raccoon's infamous practical jokes. Rube had managed to fill the ornaments on one of the trees with explosive powder and glitter.

Yes, I even managed to sleep through *that*.

When the decorations blew, the foundations of the fairy mound shook, and a torrent of red and green glitter doused the werecat. Festus was still trying to lick the metallic flecks out of his fur *and* argue with Amity at the same time.

The concussive wave from the blast shattered several pieces of expensive pottery in her gallery. Amity expected Festus to pay for the breakage, which he stoutly refused to do.

From Darby's description of the fight, Festus was alternately flinging invective at Amity and spitting out glitter while Rube and the Wrecking Crew enjoyed the show.

"Where is the baobhan sith?" I asked, shrugging into the baggy old sweater I kept in my alcove against the lair's perpetual chill.

"Mistress Greer received a mirror call from Londinium a few minutes ago and is in her apartment," Darby said. "Master Beau attempted to intervene, but retreated when Mistress Amity turned on him."

"Can't blame him for that," I muttered, taking another slug of coffee for courage. "Okay, time for me to wade in."

As I came out of the alcove, Festus, who was sitting on his desk, arched his back sending a shower of glitter rocketing out of his fur.

"Bastet's *whiskers!*" he roared. "Rube, you stinking gutter *rat!* How the hell much glitter did you put in those things?"

Rube, who was reclining in one of the chairs by the fire, dissolved into a fit of helpless laughter. I willed myself *not* to join the raccoon in his fit of hysterics, but it wasn't easy when I caught Beau's eye, and the colonel grinned in spite of himself.

When he caught enough breath to answer Festus, Rube said, "I used enough to make you look like a unicorn with a bad case of Rainbow Mange. Somebody take a picture. This is just too freaking suh-*wheet!*"

"I'll make you think, *suh-wheet!*" Festus said. The force of the words brought on a hacking cough that sent even more glitter spewing out of his mouth.

I had to look down to keep a straight face. When I thought I could maintain a neutral expression *and* speak at the same time, I put as much authority as I could muster into the words. "Okay. Everybody just settle down."

"Jinx!" Amity said. "I'm glad you are *finally* awake. This *scrofulous* tomcat is responsible for damaging almost a *dozen* vases crafted by regional artisans, and I *demand* that he be made to stand good for them."

Furiously wiping spitty glitter out of his whiskers, Festus said, "Who are you calling *scrofulous*, you sorry excuse . . . "

"*STOP!*" I commanded. "Both of you just *stop.*"

Unwilling not to have the final word, Amity grumbled sullenly, "*He* started it with his drunken carousing."

Summoning all my patience, I pointed out the obvious. "Amity, you're a witch. Just use a reintegration spell and put the vases back together."

In a fair imitation of a fish out of water, Amity opened her mouth, shut it again, and then regarded me with bulging, indignant eyes.

"Yeah," Festus sneered, "didn't think of that one, did you?"

Festus can never be bothered to leave well enough alone.

"Can it, Glitter Puss," I said. "This whole thing serves you right for getting drunk and smashing Christmas ornaments at 4 in the morning. And as for you, Rube . . ."

Greer's voice cut me off. "I am afraid your admonishment of Reuben will have to wait. There has been a development in Londinium."

This morning was just getting better by the minute.

"What's happened now?" I asked, already dreading the answer.

"Reynold Isherwood has escaped."

Whatever I expected to hear, that wasn't it. Greer's announcement instantly put everyone's mind back in the game. Beau went next door to tell Chase the news, while Amity disappeared into the stacks. I didn't find out until later that she'd gone to the apothecary to get Brenna.

Greer sat down at the FaeNet terminal and accessed the IBIS network, calling up the first reports on the early stages of the investigation, with Rube perched on the back of the couch reading over her shoulder.

"Who called?" I asked, leaning against the couch myself.

"Jorge," she replied, swiping windows off the screen and arranging them in the air around the terminal. "Lucas and Otto are in a meeting with Morris at DGI headquarters."

"What do we know so far?"

"Precious little. The gargoyle guards escorted Isherwood to the inner courtyard for his daily recreation period. When they returned at the end of the hour, he was gone."

I couldn't believe what I was hearing. "You mean no one was watching him during that time?"

"Apparently not," Greer said, still studying the screen. "No one has ever escaped the Tower. The Captain of the Guard says sentries were posted inside the doors leading to the yard, but Isherwood was alone outside."

Out of the corner of my eye, I saw Glory come out of the passageway to the cobbler shop with a brush in her hand. Following her movements, I watched as she began to de-glitter Festus. Normally the werecat would have protested the grooming, but he was too busy deploying the GNATS drones to argue.

"I don't know why I let Adeline talk me into sending a drone to the Valley," he groused, studying his bank of iPads. "Pickle, do my ears first. I need to put my headset on."

"Be still, Dad," Glory fussed. "You're wiggling too much."

At the word, "dad" everyone in the lair froze. Even in the opening stages of an international manhunt, we all tensed to dive to Glory's defense when Festus lit into her.

Except that's not what happened.

With a completely unreadable expression on his furry face, Festus said, "What did you just call me?"

Blushing furiously and taking a step back to put some distance between herself and the yellow cat, Glory said, "Oh, Festus. I'm so sorry. It just slipped."

I can't tell you what combination of miracles conspired at that moment. It could have been that Festus simply wanted the detested glitter out of his fur, or maybe his hangover slowed his reflexes.

Or maybe, just maybe, Festus picked up on the hopeful pleading in Glory's eyes.

Regardless, he did an astonishing and immensely kind thing.

"No fur off my back," the werecat said gruffly. "Call me whatever you like, Pickle, just finish my damned ears."

Pure, radiant joy infused Glory's face. She immediately set about eradicating every lingering trace of Rube's prank before helping Festus on with his communication gear.

Without missing a beat, Festus got to work positioning his drones on the square, but not before he muttered, "Thanks, Pickle. Appreciate it."

The whole exchange made Glory so happy, I would have stopped and hugged them both if I hadn't been in such a hurry to get upstairs and dress.

Thankfully Tori and I had agreed the day before that she'd open the shop that morning. She looked surprised when I emerged from the basement in my pajamas, but I managed to slip behind the espresso counter without attracting the attention of the early morning patrons.

Flipping on the coffee grinder to mask our conversation, she said, "Good morning. Just a heads up. The Monday morning crowd can't stop talking about last night's earthquake."

I covered my eyes with my hand. "How many people felt the explosion?"

"Everyone in a one-block radius of the square," she replied. "It cracked the front window down at George and Irma's. How's the glitter situation downstairs?"

"Festus let Glory groom him."

Tori almost dropped the coffee pot in her hands. "He did *what?*"

"Yeah," I said, "I know, but trust me, that's far from the biggest news of the morning."

Sharing what little I knew about the developments in Londinium, I said, "Greer, Rube, and I need to get over there to help Lucas. I'm going upstairs to change. Can you hold down the fort and make do with the JinxBot for now?"

"Sure, go," she said, "just remember to send the bot up from the lair wearing the same outfit you come down in. If you don't, someone will notice, and the natives are restless enough already. The dominant theory is secret government weapons testing up in the mountains."

"Good," I said, "encourage the conspiracy theories. It keeps the attention off us."

I turned to leave but stopped when Tori put a hand on my elbow. "Did something happen last night?" she asked.

"Other than the glitter bombs?" I said. "I don't think so."

"You didn't have a vision?" she pressed.

My hesitation gave Tori all the answer she needed. "It was a sword, wasn't it?" she asked. "With a big ruby at one end?"

Since our first fight with Brenna, Tori and I have shared a mild telepathic connection, but the link had never been strong enough to send an image from one realm to the next.

"You saw that?" I said. "In the Valley?"

"Just for an instant," she answered, "but it didn't feel like you were in any danger. What did you touch to set it off?"

"I didn't touch anything," I admitted. "I was writing in my grimoire. The vision connected with my pen somehow and it drew the sword."

"Well, that's new," she said. "Did you tell Myrtle? This might have something to do with Isherwood."

"No," I replied, "and she's already left for Tír na nÓg. After I get the lay of the land in Londinium, I'll fill her in."

UPSTAIRS IN MY APARTMENT, I hurriedly packed a bag and called Darby's name. The ever-vigilant brownie materialized instantly. "Would you please take this to the lair," I said, "and take care of my cats while I'm in Londinium?"

"Mistress," he said, "I would never forget the cats. They are my *friends.*"

Even the cats looked offended on his behalf.

After my crack about Darby's dusting prowess the night before, you'd think my brownie sensitivity meter might have been working in overdrive, but oh no. Not me. I can *always* manage to put my foot in my mouth.

Still looking miffed, Darby blinked out with my bag. I said goodbye to the cats — who were doubly annoyed due to the appearance of a travel bag — composed myself and went downstairs looking for all the world like I was starting just another day in The Witch's Brew.

To reinforce that image, I puttered around the store for a few minutes before giving Tori the high sign. Right on cue, she asked me to bring up more cup lids from the basement. The JinxBot was waiting for me on the landing.

With a wave of my hand, I duplicated my outfit on her. "You good to go, JB?" I asked.

"I've got your back, sister," she said, holding up her hand to give me a high five.

Tori's lessons in personality and vernacular were paying off, but I secretly nurse the fear she's making my simulacrum *way* cooler than real me.

With the JinxBot deployed, I descended the stairs. Greer and Rube sat waiting by the fire and, thanks to Amity, Brenna was present as well.

"Do you want me to come with you?" the sorceress asked

immediately.

Honestly, the idea hadn't occurred to me, but no one other than Adeline knew the intricacies of the Chesterfield/Isherwood conspiracy better than Brenna — at least until the 1670s when she left London for the Orkneys.

Adeline would be with us via the FaeNet, and with Brenna along in person, we would be well equipped to go after Isherwood.

"That would be great," I said. "Can you be ready in 10 minutes?"

"I will be ready in five," she replied, turning on her heel and heading for her room.

While Brenna packed, I walked over to discuss security with Festus. "We don't have any reason to believe Isherwood will come here," I told him, "but we also have no reason to believe he won't either.

"Don't worry about it," the werecat replied, walking me through the live feeds from the drones. "We have the front and back of the store blanketed with cameras. Rube's leaving Leon, Booger, and Marty here so I have extra operatives. If I need him, I can always call on Chase. We're good. Go get that traitorous bastard back in a jail cell where he belongs."

My sentiments exactly.

Shouldering my backpack, I nodded to Greer and Rube, who moved toward the portal. As Brenna fell in beside us the baobhan sith said, "I spoke briefly with Lucas. He needed information on connections I maintain in Lundenwic. He said to tell you that he will see you at IBIS headquarters when we arrive. He and Morris have declared a temporary truce. The DGI and IBIS are casting a wide search net for Isherwood."

"Good," I said. "The faster we get him back in custody, the better. We'll leave our stuff at Claridge's when we arrive and head straight for the British Museum."

Siegfried managed to contain his pleasure over our return to Claridge's, but just barely. In greeting, he clicked his heels smartly and said, "Madam is looking well."

"Thank you, Siegfried," I said. "How have things been here at the hotel?"

Quirking his mouth in consternation, the brownie said, "I wage a never-ending war against inefficiency, madam, but in the midst of my travails, I strive to maintain a positive attitude."

Nodding sympathetically, I said, "I admire your fortitude."

"Thank you," he said crisply. "I have requested that you be assigned to your previous accommodations. I hope that is acceptable. The remainder of the floor has been reserved for the use of your party. I assumed you would need the additional space to coordinate your efforts to apprehend that swine, Isherwood."

"Thank you, Siegfried. You've thought of everything. We're going immediately to IBIS headquarters. Will you see to our luggage?"

"But of course, madam," he said. "Do not give it another thought."

Jumping into action, Siegfried took charge of a line of lesser brownies in the hotel's pecking order. Shouldering our bags, they headed for the elevators. It wasn't lost on me that Siegfried took personal charge of my backpack, securing it on small cart he pushed with effortless dignity.

As we exited the hotel, my eye fell on a copy of *The Londinium Times* lying on an end table. The banner headline splashed across the top half read: *Isherwood Escapes Tower*.

Hopefully, by the next edition, the news of his capture would dominate the space above the fold.

11

Gemma raised and lowered her index finger smiling with delight as her plate obediently followed the motion. Across the table, Kelly said, "I can't believe I'm saying this to you at your age, but stop playing with your food."

"Aw, come on Kell," Gemma laughed, settling the plate on the white linen cloth. She gestured toward the fork, which instantly came to her hand. "You have to admit this is fun."

"You're not doing anything you can't do back in Briar Hollow," Kelly said. "You could levitate dinner plates when you were six."

Loading her fork with a gooey bite of cheese omelet, Gemma said, "Not like this I couldn't, and you know it. I haven't thought *once* about using my magic here on Tír na nÓg. It just flows right out of me. The power feels completely different here like it's an extension of my mind."

Beyond the open air summer house, the morning sun danced across the waters of the Atlantic. Perched high above the beach and safe within the city walls, the setting might have been brought to life from the pages of a storybook.

As Kelly studied the ocean vista and the verdant garden that surrounded their breakfast table, a bright blue bird fluttered down next to her plate.

"Well, hello there," she said, breaking off a bit of toast and offering it to the newcomer.

The bird accepted the bread with a dainty motion, flying away again with the treasure held tight in its beak.

Still chewing on her omelet, Gemma said, "Okay, confess. What came into your head that led to that visit?"

"How do you know I was thinking anything?" Kelly said, avoiding her friend's eyes.

"Don't you even *try* to pull that with me. What were you thinking?"

"Oh, *fine*," Kelly said. "It crossed my mind that if this place is so perfect the bluebird of happiness might as well come down and land on our table."

"Ah *ha*!" Gemma said. "I told you so! Magic here is completely spontaneous. I'd be careful if I were you with my random thoughts."

"It wasn't a random thought," Kelly said, reaching for her coffee cup. "All magic, even the kind we are experiencing here, is intention based. My intent was to be convinced."

"Are you?"

Kelly paused to take a sip of her coffee before she answered. "Yes," she said finally. "I am. The magic here doesn't just feel different. It *tastes* different. Everything does. The air we breathe. The food we eat. Everything."

From behind her, Myrtle's voice said, "As it was in the days when my people dwelt in the Neverlands. That winsome creature was not the real Bluebird of Happiness, by the way, but he asked me to thank you for the bread."

One of the empty chairs slid back, making room for the aos

si to join them. Myrtle sat as the fabric of her dark cloak swirled around her.

"Good morning," Kelly said, "and why doesn't it surprise me that you talk to the birds and they talk back?"

Levitating a muffin across the table, Myrtle said, "You have the power to interact with all sentient beings as well, but the exchanges do not come as easily to you because you have spent your life in the human realm. On Tír na nÓg there is no need to summon such abilities. Here magic exists without taint, in its essential, virtuous state, joyously in union with all life."

"That's going to take some getting used to," Kelly admitted, "but Gemma's right. Tír na nÓg is wonderful. "Did you just arrive?"

"I did," Myrtle said, "and I have asked that Bronwyn and Katherine join us. There is news from Londinium we must consider together."

A current of warm wind swept over the table, lifting the napkins, which caught themselves, holding fast against the breeze before resettling in their owner's laps.

"Forgive me," Katherine MacVicar said, taking the remaining chair. "I tried to land gently."

Gemma shook her head. "You should have seen the first time your daughter blew into our lives. You baobhan sith do know how to make an entrance."

"Now why would a woman pass up the opportunity to turn heads if it is afforded to her?" Katherine asked, her crimson lips curving into a wicked smile.

"Honey," Gemma said, "you couldn't be ignored if you tried."

Katherine's green eyes danced with mirth. "Oh," she said, "we're going to get along well, Gemma Andrews. You say what you think."

"Generally when she thinks it," Kelly observed, "which typically spells trouble.'

The baobhan sith's smile deepened. "Trouble and fun travel the same road."

That made all the women laugh. "You are in fine spirits this morning, Katherine," Myrtle said. "From whence did you join us? You would not have used the flight of the baobhan sith had you been on Tír na nÓg."

Nodding at the coffee pot to fill her cup, Katherine said, "Londinium. My daughter is there, with the Witch of the Oak, the Water Elf, and Brenna Sinclair."

That announcement brought a look of alarm to Kelly's eyes. "Jinx is in Londinium? Why? What's happened?"

Bronwyn's approaching voice supplied the answer. "Reynold Isherwood has escaped the Tower."

Sweeping her hand over the scene, she made the square table round and added a fifth chair before continuing.

"Jinx and the others are at the British Museum coordinating search operations with Otto Volker."

Shoving her chair back, Kelly started to her feet. "We have to join them. They'll need all hands on board to re-capture Isherwood."

Myrtle's restraining hand stopped her. "No," the aos si said. "There are other things of which we must speak this morning. Other things that we must do before the sun sets tonight. Jinx is well protected in Londinium. We are not needed there."

Kelly settled back in her seat, but she didn't look happy. "What could possibly be more important to discuss than Isherwood being on the loose again?" she asked.

"Last night," Myrtle said, "Jinx experienced a vision while writing in her grimoire. She did not speak of the incident to me nor does she yet realize its significance. After she fell asleep, her pen came to me with the news."

"Her pen?" Gemma said sharply. "Barnaby and Moira enchanted that object for Jinx's personal use only. Violating her trust in that way should have broken the spell that animates it."

Myrtle laid a hand on her arm, gently soothing Gemma's anxiety as she had stopped Kelly's urge to run to Jinx's side.

"There was no violation of trust," the aos si said. "The pen and grimoire were enchanted to serve as Jinx's confidantes *and* protectors. As with all such objects, sentience is required for the fulfillment of their duties. The book and the pen discussed the vision and were sufficiently alarmed to seek me out when it became clear Jinx would not."

"That's a fine ethical distinction," Gemma insisted stubbornly, "but I know the method Moira used to create the bond between Jinx and those instruments. Are you sure they haven't been corrupted in some way? Maybe that vision is just another trick of Isherwood's. How do you know the pen is even telling the truth?"

"Because I know," Myrtle said simply. "There was no evil intent. The pen acted as any concerned friend would under the circumstances."

From across the table, Kelly said tightly, "What circumstances? There's more going on here than Isherwood escaping the Tower."

"There is," Myrtle agreed. "For the first time last evening, the pen's ability to record Jinx's thoughts merged with her psychometry. A most remarkable and somewhat disturbing sketch resulted. The pen created a copy for me."

Clearing away the breakfast dishes with a snap of her fingers, the aos si reached into the pocket of her cloak and brought out a single sheet of heavy paper. The drawing, depicting an ornate sword, had been executed with the skill of a master draftsman.

"That cannot be," Bronwyn said softly. "The blade Caledfwlch was returned to the lake from whence it was forged."

Kelly's face paled. "I only know one story about a sword and a lake. Are you telling us this is Excalibur?"

"Yes," Myrtle said, "the sword of Merlin, used to legitimize the claim of Arthur Pendragon to the throne of England and carried by the wounded king to Avalon, the Island of the Apple Trees, after the Battle of Camlann. What does Jinx know of Camelot?"

"Beyond seeing the musical?" Kelly said. "Only what Brenna told her."

Bronwyn leaned forward. "Can you repeat for me the account my daughter shared?"

As the group listened, Kelly described the conversation she witnessed between Brenna and Jinx. The sorceress had intended the tale to preface the revelation that she would have served as the Witch of the Oak had Reynold Isherwood not stolen her magic in infancy.

Brenna had spoken of the journey of Joseph of Arimathea from the Holy Land and his guardianship of a mysterious artifact, which human mythology styled as the Holy Grail. As a direct result of these events, the Order of the Knights Templar developed.

Human Templars, Brenna had explained, were devout Christians protecting pilgrims journeying to the Holy Land, but they were also Crusading soldiers in the papacy's ongoing war to reclaim the Biblical lands.

The Fae who joined the Templar ranks had an added responsibility: protecting the humans from the magical artifacts of the "Infidel" cultures. Such items, in the hands of humans with no understanding of how to wield them properly, could be dangerous beyond imagination.

"Brenna did not speak of Merlin or Arthur?" Myrtle asked.

"Not in any detail," Kelly said. "She did mention she didn't blame Guinevere for taking up with Sir Lancelot."

Bronwyn let out a short, sharp laugh. "My daughter is too young to have known them, but she no doubt picked up that feeling from her father. Henri found Arthur to have an insufferably good opinion of himself."

"What was *your* opinion of the king?" Kelly asked.

Bronwyn's eyes clouded with the mist of memory. As she talked, the contents of her thoughts drew themselves in the air over the table, first as faint outlines, then in living, animated color.

The women saw Camelot in the days before Joseph's arrival — a cosmopolitan town where humans and Fae mingled freely. Magic existed unquestioned — an accepted thread in the greater tapestry of creation.

"Centuries have passed since I walked those streets," Bronwyn whispered, her gaze taking in the familiar sights her mind and magic conjured. "Arthur was a man of vision, but that all changed."

The milling throngs on the projected streets altered slowly as more human faces replaced those of the Fae.

"Were the changes because of religion?" Gemma asked, her eyes following the figure of a stout monk as he strode across Bronwyn's memories and disappeared into the air beyond.

"No," Bronwyn said, "although Arthur and his knights became obsessed with the idea that the Grail was a lost holy cup, retrievable only by the solving of silly riddles and the accomplishment of meaningless quests."

The scene shifted to the interior of an alchemist's workshop. A tall, elderly man in robes argued with a figure that could only be the king himself.

The timbre of the wizard's voice sounded tinny in the morning air. "Arthur, all men seek the grail within their hearts. It is a *process*, an individual quest. A metaphor, not a reality."

In response, the king threw up his hands and stalked away,

swearing as he went. Merlin watched the stormy exit with sad eyes until a young woman joined him, touching the wizard lightly on the arm. The image froze.

"That man," Bronwyn said, "is Merlin, and the woman is Arthur's half-sister, Morgan le Fay. The new religion did not shatter the dream that was Camelot. Morgan did that, with her black, scheming heart. Morgan came to resent virtue in all its forms as the agent that took from her the dearest ambitions of her heart."

Kelly studied the suspended figures. "She and Merlin were lovers," she said quietly.

"How do you know that?" Bronwyn asked.

"Look at them," Kelly replied. "The way she touches him, with such casual intimacy. The expression in his eyes."

The figures came to life again, the Morgan of memory reaching her hand to caress Merlin's cheek before drawing his mouth to hers.

"Morgan was apprenticed to Merlin for the study of magic," Bronwyn said, "but she played on his vanities and emotions to her own ends. Merlin was a great and wise wizard, but he was also a man."

Gemma's mouth drew into a firm line. "Oldest story in the world," she said. "What was Morgan trying to accomplish?"

"She was jealous of her brother's throne," Bronwyn replied. "She worked in secret to engineer his downfall and that of his knights."

Katherine, who had watched and listened without reaction, spoke for the first time.

"Be fair, Bronwyn," she said. "Morgan would have been a far superior ruler to Arthur. Her jealousy was born of the same misogyny that plagued us all in those days. Histories written by men have an unfortunate tendency to blacken the name of any woman who sought to exercise her natural talents to their fullest. The aos si has lived longer than any of us and will bear out what I say."

Myrtle stared at the image of Morgan le Fay hanging before them. "I wish I could disagree," she said, "but I cannot. Morgan was a woman born to lead in a time when men would not allow it. But Arthur's presumed supremacy was not just a product of human culture. Even Fae men have been subject to this prejudice. Chesterfield and Isherwood both used Brenna as a convenient foil for many of their worst excesses."

A gray, monotone grittiness fell over the projection of Bronwyn's thoughts. The morning breeze caught the grains and blew them away toward the sea. Bronwyn watched the particles fly free, her throat working in a tortured effort to swallow.

"Much of that fault lies with me," she said hoarsely. "I answered the call of the Great Tree and abandoned my daughter to her father's cruelty. Had I ever thought Henri capable of such behavior, I would never have left Brenna in his care."

"Henri became drunk with power," Myrtle said. "He did not abuse Brenna until her magic failed to develop. Without her abilities, she could not be used to broker an advantageous marriage that would further solidify his already considerable holdings."

"An intoxication with wealth and influence that proved the downfall of the Templars," Katherine observed. "Human and Fae alike."

"I don't understand," Kelly said. "Weren't the Templars the good guys?"

Bronwyn shifted her gaze back to the table. "Another convenient recasting of history," she said. "Do you know the human phrase 'follow the money?'"

"I do."

"The Templars were the first international bankers. They built an empire that, in time, consumed them. Katherine, you dealt more directly with that aspect of their operation. Will you explain for our friends?"

Over the next few minutes, the baobhan sith described the evolution of the Knights Templar from an order of monks pledged to poverty to their ultimate status as financial power brokers.

"Understand," she said, "that only the human members donated property and monies to the order. Fae Knights like Henri de St. Clair made a show of their poverty and piety as a cover for their true mission. At the same time that they protected the humans from magical objects, they also amassed vast personal collections of manuscripts and artifacts."

As she talked, Katherine painted a vivid picture of the two classes of Knights whose interests closely intertwined. As the greed of the Fae Templars grew, so did the wealth of their human counterparts, a fact that did not escape either the attention or the jealousy of the papacy.

Nobles leaving for the Crusades entrusted their business affairs to the Templars. "The resulting status afforded the Templars put them squarely at the center of the emerging financial culture of Europe," Katherine said. "They began to issue letters of credit, practicing a system of deposits and withdrawals that presaged modern banking."

King Philip IV of France, heavily in debt to the Knights, ordered their arrest on Friday, October 13, 1307. His men seized the Order's holdings and executed its members. In response, the Church did nothing.

"That," Katherine said, "is the origin of the human superstition regarding any Friday that falls on the 13th day of the month. Seven years later, the Templar Grand Master, Jacques de Molay, was burned at the stake on charges of heresy. They lit his pyre in the shadow of Notre Dame."

The women sat in silence, digesting the details of the story until Gemma asked, "What happened to the Fae Templars?"

"They retreated to the Otherworld," Bronwyn replied, "and knights of a vastly different sort rose in their place — the Order of the Rodere."

"Rodere?" Gemma said. "Isn't that Latin for 'to gnaw.'"

"Your language lessons serve you well," Myrtle said, "but 'rodere' is also the root of another word — rodent."

12

R odney waited to stick his head out of Jinx's backpack until the elevator doors opened. When he did dare to have a look around, he found himself staring into the eyes of a stern-faced brownie in a crisp butler's suit.

The sight of the rat's furry features and luxuriant whiskers brought Siegfried to a screeching halt.

"*Stop!*" Siegfried shouted.

The line of bellhops immediately froze, forcing Rodney to dig his claws into the bag's fabric to keep himself from being flung out of his hiding place.

"*Who*," Siegfried said sharply, "are you?"

Twitching his pink nose, Rodney sat up straighter, smiled nervously and waved at the irate brownie.

Unmoved, Siegfried repeated himself. "Never mind an attempt at pleasantries. Who are you?"

Wilting a little, Rodney pointed to the backpack under his feet and then drew the symbol of a heart over his chest, hugging himself tight.

Siegfried silently considered the pantomimed statement before replying. Finally, he said, "If I am to interpret correctly, you claim to be a friend of the Witch of the Oak. Does she know that you have secreted yourself in her luggage?"

The rat shook his head.

"Which means she would disapprove of your presence," the brownie said. "I will have no choice but to apprise her of your actions."

Rodney held up one paw in the universal signal for, "Wait!" Then he executed a second complicated series of motions.

A thoughtful look came over Siegfried's face. "You are frequently forced to remain behind because Mistress Jinx regards you as too small to leave the safety of your home. Correct?"

The brownie let out a rueful snort when Rodney nodded.

"As a member of a vertically challenged race of Fae," Siegfried said, "I rather appreciate the annoyance such well-meaning condescension engenders."

Rodney grinned and held up his paw in solidarity. Glancing around to ensure none of the bellhops were watching, Siegfried used his index finger to return the high "five." Then, holding out his full hand, he allowed Rodney to scamper onto his shoulder.

"Gentlemen," Siegfried said, addressing his staff, "continue to your destinations and then return to your stations. You neither saw nor heard anything in this hallway. Am I understood?"

Six sets of heels clicked sharply as the bellhops answered in unison. "Yes, *sir*!"

"Excellent. Mr. Fulton, assume custody of this backpack and see that it is safely delivered to the Witch of the Oak's room. Look smart!"

Once they were alone, Siegfried turned to look at the rat on his shoulder. "We will speak in my office, but we must first cross the lobby downstairs. The management may not be amenable to the presence of one of your kind in our establishment. I have far too much to do today to take the time to deal with such ridiculous bigotry. Would you be so kind as to ride in the breast pocket of my jacket and save us both that experience?"

Giving Siegfried a thumbs up, Rodney dove under his lapel and disappeared.

Pulling his jacket taut, the brownie eyed the bulge on his left breast with open disapproval. "Flatter, if you please," he commanded, "You are spoiling the line of my suit."

As the lump obligingly evened out, Siegfried turned smartly and descended the nearby stairs with rapid, skipping steps. Traversing the lobby, he inclined his head politely, but not differentially to the manager behind the front desk.

Occupants of that overblown office came and went at Claridge's with the passing of the years, but Siegfried remained. No one, most especially not management, dared to question his movements inside the hotel.

Reaching his small, tidy office, the brownie majordomo closed the door and turned the key. Addressing his coat pocket, he said, "You may show yourself."

Rodney's head appeared from under the lapel.

Siegfried held out his hand. "Allow me to facilitate your movements," he said. "We have much to discuss."

The rat climbed onto the offered perch, then hopped onto the edge of the immaculate desk when Siegfried ferried him closer.

Sitting down in the leather desk chair, the brownie said, "Sir Rat, while you are quite skilled at the parlor game of charades, is there a more efficient way we might communicate? My time is valuable."

Rodney pointed at the closed laptop lying next to the blotter. When Siegfried opened the lid, the rat reached over the edge and put his paw on the touchpad, maneuvering the cursor until he found the notes app.

With a new window open, he climbed onto the wrist rests and leaned over the keyboard, selecting letters as Siegfried watched.

When Rodney finished, the brownie looked down at him over steepled fingers. "You cannot negotiate the streets of Londinium unattended. Something or someone will either consume or squash you. I assume you would find both rather unpleasant."

At that announcement, the rat's eyes grew round, and his head bobbed up and down.

"You are quite certain that the person to whom you wish to speak lives at this address?"

Rodney nodded again.

"Very well," Siegfried said. "I will arrange for you to be taken there and returned to me safely, at which time I will personally escort you to the portal that will return you to Briar Hollow."

Rodney reached over and tapped a few keys.

"No," the brownie said, "I will not tell Madam of your movements. Given the circumstances you've outlined, I understand why you chose this reckless, albeit necessary course of action. Wait here until I return."

As he rose from the chair, Siegfried reached to close the laptop, stopping when Rodney squeaked in protest.

"You may use the device in my absence, but do not attempt to purchase anything. I assure you that my credit card information is not stored within the machine."

Looking offended, Rodney pretended to reach into his pocket, take out a wallet, and flip it open.

For the first time, Siegfried laughed. "A rat with credit cards of his own. Whatever is this world coming to?"

Still chuckling, the brownie left the room and Rodney began to type.

Setting his paper aside, Lucien St. Leger walked to the window and stared out at the quiet Londinium street below. After several minutes lost in thought, he turned back toward the room, staring at the *Times* headline as he packed his pipe.

Isherwood Escapes Tower

The three words dwarfed the paper's masthead and consumed the entire page above the fold. Snapping his fingers to ignite a flame, Lucien puffed the tobacco to life, blowing out a cloud of smoke that he idly wove into an intricate Celtic cross.

"No one escapes the tower," he said. "Not even Reynold Isherwood. There is more afoot here than a clever jailbreak."

For weeks the *Times* had run stories detailing the changes in the realms wrought by the lifting of the Agreement. Photographs chronicled the construction of Shevington University, and then the momentous news of the re-emergence of Tír na nÓg.

Yggdrasil would not have allowed the Oak and the Rowan to forge an alliance or for a new tree witch to emerge unless a time of reckoning loomed. Clamping the pipe stem in his teeth, Lucien leaned down and retrieved the paper.

"Representatives of the reclusive coven headquartered in Copenhagen insist their order lives in seclusion, studying ancient and esoteric arts for purposes of pure research. They deny any connection with Isherwood, Irenaeus Chesterfield, or their crimes."

Why Copenhagen? That part of the story bothered Lucien. Copenhagen was Anna Koldings city.

He remembered the winter of 1589 so powerfully, a shiver passed over his body, sending him to warm his hands at the fire. Coal would not do in his house. He burned only oak logs given to him by the Great Tree herself, a perpetual flame that never required replenishment.

The fire went with Lucien to every abode he'd occupied since the old days when the humans lived in a world lit only by flame. It had been with him that winter when Anne of Denmark departed her homeland by ship to marry King James VI in Scotland.

A terrible storm almost sent the vessel to the icy depths of the North Sea. The captain managed to reach what was then the province of Norway, where they took shelter in Oslo.

James joined his wife-to-be for the wedding, but when the couple attempted to reach Scotland in the spring of 1590, violent weather once again menaced the voyage. It was then that Reynold Isherwood capitalized on the fear of witchcraft he had implanted in James' mind when the king was but a boy.

As a young monarch, James became convinced he and his wife were the victims of the black arts. That summer waves of witch hunting swept Copenhagen, the judges determined to find the source of the storms. Christoffer Valendorff, the Danish minister of finance, identified a coven that met in the house a weaver named Karen.

Valendorff claimed demons in her employ climbed the keels and swarmed the ships, intent on sinking the vessels and killing the royals. In the way of the accused and the desperate, Karen the Weaver named others, among them Anna Koldings, who, in the agony of her torture, called out five others.

Lucien shuddered at the memory, Karen the Weaver and Anna Koldings were not witches. They were humans suffering at the hands of other humans, speaking the words they prayed would end their torment and save their lives.

The angry mobs called Anna the "Mother of the Devil." She'd played to her increasing fame, trying to please her captors with repeated confessions and entreaties for forgiveness. It didn't work. They burned her at the stake anyway.

The events in Denmark inspired King James to begin his own round of witch hunting in Edinburgh, all under the direction of Reynold Isherwood. When the English queen, Elizabeth I, died and James assumed the throne in London, he brought his witch hunting with him — and Isherwood began to methodically work through his list of rivals and enemies.

"But those women in Denmark were not real witches," Lucien said, drawing contemplatively on his pipe. "If Isherwood did have allies in the northern lands, who were they?"

A sound at the door made him turn his head — a faint tapping accompanied by scratching. Getting up from his chair, Lucien called out, "Is someone there?"

In response, the scratching sound returned, only louder this time.

Opening the door, he found the passageway empty, but then something tugged at his pants leg. Lucien looked down and into the face of an old friend.

"Rodney," he said with a mixture of surprise and elation, "how did you get here?"

The rat held up one front paw, curling his fingers into a fist and gesturing with his thumb.

"You hitched a ride?" Lucien said. "With whom?"

Crossing his forepaws over his chest, Rodney simply stared, waiting for the light to dawn.

"Ah," Lucien said, "the Witch of the Oak has returned to Londinium. Come in, my friend, and warm yourself by the fire. Let us become reacquainted."

13

W e found the British Museum swamped with tourists. Rube, who left Claridge's ahead of us, said he'd "get in the joint a different way." Greer, Brenna, and I climbed the front steps. Normally I'd say we had to elbow our way through, but a few mumbled words from Brenna opened an easy path before us.

The baobhan sith and I were both wearing our IBIS badges, but their enchantment only masked us from the human surveillance systems, not from the milling throngs in the galleries. Brenna had a solution for that as well.

At the front of the Assyrian Gallery, the three of us paused and made a show of studying the winged bulls flanking the doorway. The entrance to IBIS headquarters lies under the belly of the statue on the left.

Brenna opened the guide book we'd bought in the gift shop. Running her finger down the page, her lips moved as she recited a spell. To the casual observer, she appeared to be reading laboriously.

By the time she was done, however, anyone who might have taken notice of us, no longer remembered we'd ever been there and not one eye blinked when we ducked through the secret opening.

In the hallway on the other side, the uproar in the main bullpen reached our ears long before our eyes registered the chaos. As we stepped into the space, an agent on the far side of the room yelled, "We have another sighting. This one is in North Africa. Do we have anyone in Casablanca?"

"Yeah," another agent called back, "hang on."

A sharp yelp punctuated the din, and I heard Rube's voice saying, "Pardon the claws, doll. My bad."

With a bounding leap, the raccoon sailed over one of the desks and landed at our feet.

"Geez, what took you dames so long?" he asked, taking a comb out of the pouch at what passed for his waist and smoothing back the fur on his cheeks.

Greer looked down at him tolerantly. "We do not all have the advantage of skulking through the sewer system, Reuben. Have you seen Lucas?"

"I ain't done nothing but dodge getting kicked in the kisser since I got here," he said. "Being short in a world of tall people don't equal no walk in the park, Red."

Glancing around, I spotted Jorge Castaneda and managed to catch his eye. The agent waved at me over the holographic map hovering above his desk, smiled, and shrugged. I got the message. No one had time to talk.

"Where's Lucas?" I mouthed.

When Jorge frowned, I repeated myself, exaggerating my silent enunciation.

Comprehension dawned on Jorge's face, and he pointed.

"Otto's office?" I asked.

When he nodded, I thanked him and turned to Greer.

"I heard," she said.

Vampires. I could have sworn Jorge, and I hadn't made a sound.

Hugging the wall to avoid getting run over, we made our way to the assistant director's office. Lucas and Otto were standing in front of a whiteboard while a floating black marker flew across the surface, dodging the eraser that went to work when the two men decided one of their ideas was out of order.

I knew at a single glance what they were doing: prioritizing the most likely sightings of Reynold Isherwood.

"What does a witch have to do to get a hello around here?" I asked.

The smile Lucas gave me when he looked over his shoulder put any thought of the outlaw wizard out of my head. "Jinx!" he said, coming over to embrace me. "You're here."

"I'm here," I echoed the sentiment, kissing him lightly. "And *here* looks like the middle of a hurricane."

"Have you ever been in the middle of a hurricane?" he asked softly, his face still near mine.

From the vicinity of our ankles, Rube said, "Geez, I'm glad I didn't eat lunch, 'cause I'd be losing it right about now."

Dropping his eyes, Lucas said, "You smell like a sewer."

"Likely 'cause I just walked through one," Rube answered cheerfully. "I ever tell you most days you smell like seaweed and old fish?"

"I missed you, too," Lucas said.

"Likewise, Elf Boy," the raccoon grinned. "So we going wizard hunting or what?"

Squeezing my hand and stepping away, Lucas said, "If we can figure out where to hunt. Isherwood got out of the tower without leaving so much as a trace of evidence. Otto and I have been considering the best leads, but none of them are very good."

"Hello, Otto," I said. "You look exhausted."

The assistant director of IBIS could have easily passed for a befuddled owl. A pair of round, gold-rimmed glasses rested precariously on the tip of his nose. He'd pushed his battered safari hat so far back on his head, the brim crowned an unruly fringe of gray, wispy curls.

"Hello, my dear," he said, scowling slightly as Rube scaled the corner of his desk and shoved a stack of papers out of the way to get a better look at the whiteboard. "It's been rather a long night."

Now standing on his hind legs, Rube said, "Poughkeepsie? You guys can't be serious. Isherwood ain't gonna fly the coop and land in Poughkeepsie. Or Bakersfield. Or the Galapagos. Now Vegas I'd keep on the list."

Greer, who was also studying the board, said, "I agree with Reuben. None of these locations with the possible exception of Las Vegas seems a likely destination for Isherwood to go to ground."

Okay, somebody had to do it. I took the bait.

"Why would he go to Vegas?" I asked.

Rube looked at me like I'd grown a second head. "Seriously, doll? You ever been there? There's a reason why they say what happens in Vegas stays in Vegas."

"There's a significant Fae presence in Las Vegas," Lucas explained.

I don't know why news like that continues to catch me off guard, but it did.

"Really? Is that why the satyr bartender from Cibolita thought he could crash that mixology convention?"

"Yes," Lucas said, "but the *nonconformi* aren't all that welcome with the pretty people."

That only perplexed me more. "Pretty people?"

"Elves," Rube said, putting an unpleasant inflection on the word. "The high falutin type. Sídhe."

"You've lost me," I admitted.

Otto took off his glasses and began polishing the lenses with a silk handkerchief. "High elves of the Old Court," he said. "Many of the glitterati of the human realm are either full or half-blooded Sídhe nobles. With their power of mesmerization, they can become famous quite simply and for no apparent cause."

Reaching behind him, he drew a book off the shelf, riffled through the pages, and handed me an illustration of the most elven looking elves I'd seen yet in my association with the Otherworld. Tall and lithe, with lean features and pointy ears, they could have been extras for the *Lord of the Rings* movies.

"You're telling me that a bunch of A-list celebrities are Fae?" I said. "How do they manage to pass as human?"

Rube reached up with one black paw and made a snipping motion at his ear. "You get the right plastic surgeon, doll, you can look like anything you want."

"They have mesmerization magic, and they still go in for plastic surgery?" I asked. "Why?"

"Physical alteration requires no unnecessary expenditure of energy," Otto explained. "The Sídhe who opt to remain permanently in the human realm prefer to direct the full brunt of their powers along more lucrative lines. Most find plastic surgery to be rather an amusing addiction."

Yeah, nip and tuck work is all fun and games until you wind up blinking your lips.

"So is the presence of these Sídhe elves the only reason you think Isherwood could be hiding in Vegas?" I asked.

Lucas picked up a tablet and brushed his hand across the surface, lifting an image into the air in front of the whiteboard. There, in full living color, was the face of someone I recognized — Fer Dorich, the Dark Druid, with his personal elven body-guard, Tarathiel in jet-black sunglasses hovering in the background.

"Jorge pulled this off the surveillance cameras at the Mirage," Lucas said. "It would seem that Fer Dorich has relocated his base of operations to Nevada since the Agreement was lifted. We need to check him out."

Greer disagreed. "*I* need to check him out," she said. "Fer Dorich and I have a long history. He will be more forthcoming with me than with an official presence."

From her place by the door, Brenna said, "And I would like to investigate the Tower myself."

"Why?" Lucas asked. "We've checked it out. There's nothing there."

The sorceress smiled. "I spent centuries evading attempts at detection. With all due respect to IBIS, my skills at obfuscation magic exceed your agency's resources."

Otto peered at her through his spectacles. "You're Brenna Sinclair," he said. "I'm afraid we did not have an opportunity to meet when last you were in Londinium."

Brenna inclined her head. "Dr. Volker," she said, "a pleasure to make your acquaintance. Your treatise on the feeding habits of the Filipino Aswang made for compelling reading."

The professor's cheeks colored with pleasure. "Why thank you," he said. "That was one of my more esoteric pieces of research. Gathering the primary data entailed ... "

Sensing that we were about to plunge into an academic, research-infused abyss, I cut him off smoothly. "Maybe Brenna's right," I said. "She practiced magic outside of conventional channels for years. Your people could have missed something at the Tower."

"But, of course," Otto said. "I will be happy to grant access to the crime scene to the entire special ops team."

After a little more back and forth about deployment details, we agreed to visit the Tower the next morning. Greer, however, left immediately for Las Vegas. I suspected she planned to take herself out for a liquid dinner before tracking down Fer Dorich.

The baobhan sith prefers to feed in crowded convention or party scenes where the menu of available humans has been well marinated in alcohol. It's not the taste of the booze she's after, but the compliance of her prey.

A sauced businessman disappearing upstairs with a knock out gorgeous redhead might raise the envy of his buddies, but it doesn't trigger unwanted attention about what's really happening.

Brenna accepted an invitation from Otto for a private tour of the museum after the doors closed to human visitors. I almost asked her if she could get back to the hotel on her own and then caught myself. Brenna had forgotten more about Londinium and every other major Fae city in the Otherworld than I could ever hope to learn.

Lucas and I asked Rube to join us for dinner, but he declined in favor of a trip to Lundenwic to dig up "scuttlebutt" in a dive called The Crooked Critter. Before he waddled off down the hall, however, the raccoon gave me an exaggerated wink.

With everyone else out of the way, Rube read the lay of the land and opted to give us an evening alone. Wise mouth or not, he's an okay guy.

Consequently, my spirits were high as Lucas and I stepped out from under the bull's belly and made our way through the now deserted museum. My work in association with IBIS allows me to enjoy the magnificent facility after hours without restriction, a job perk in which I delight.

As we meandered toward the main entrance, however, something unexpected happened. I spotted a painting that stopped me dead in my tracks.

"Who is that?" I asked, my voice coming out in a breathless whisper.

Lucas, who had stopped beside me, stepped forward and read the small plaque beside the canvas. "King Arthur," he said. "Why?"

"That sword," I said. "I was writing in my grimoire last night. My psychometry took over, and my pen drew that sword."

"Are you sure?" Lucas asked.

"Positive. The pen drew that sword."

"Honey," he said, "you might as well quit calling it 'that sword.' Your pen drew Excalibur."

14

Jeff Hamilton stretched his legs toward the fire in the lair. At his feet, his fishing dogs snoozed contentedly. Duke, the ghostly coonhound, happily snuggled with the pack.

"All I want to know is where I'm getting my Thanksgiving dinner," he said. "With everybody gallivanting around the realms, nobody seems to remember there's an important holiday coming up."

Looking up from the FaeNet terminal, Tori said, "Jeff, you do know there's a criminal wizard on the loose, a *nonconformi* migration problem, and university-induced growing pains in the Valley, right?"

"Yeah," he said, confused, "so what? Is it too much for me to want my wife home to make me my favorite chocolate pie for Thanksgiving?"

Tori took her hands off the keyboard, turned her chair around, and said levelly, "It is when his wife is the Roanoke Witch. Did it ever occur to you to learn to bake your own chocolate pies?"

Before Jinx's father could answer, Darby, who was sitting on the hearth watching Beau and Chase play chess, said eagerly, "I will bake a chocolate pie for you, Master Jeff, or teach you how to make the recipe. Whichever you would prefer."

"Good to know, Shorty," Jeff said warily, aware that he was on tenuous ground with Tori regarding the topic of domestic chore allocation. "A man ought to be able to feed himself. I'm looking forward to Kelly coming home . . . because I miss her . . . not her cooking . . . which I also miss . . . but . . ."

As he sputtered to a halt unsure what to say next, Tori took pity on him and laughed. "Evolution is hard, Jeff. You're allowed to miss Kelly's cooking."

"Oh thank heavens," he said, relief flooding his features, "because without Shorty here, I would have starved to death already. I can't even warm stuff up in the microwave without turning it to concrete."

Everyone laughed at his confession of hapless temporary bachelorhood. Glory, who was curled up on the end of the sofa with a copy of *People* magazine said, "Have you talked to Kelly since she's been in Tír na nÓg?"

"Yeah," Jeff said, "but it took me six times to get a connection on that danged mirror. I have an easier time figuring out my cell phone. I know she's doing important stuff in Tear Na Whatever, but our place sure is empty without her."

"Tír na nÓg," Tori said, getting up from the computer and joining the group around the fire. "Jeff, seriously, if you can't place a simple mirror call, you're not practicing your magic enough."

Groaning, Jeff said, "Here we go. I practice my magic plenty, okay? I enchanted two dozen of my Pheasant Tail variations just today to try on the brownies."

A horrified gasp from the hearth made them all jump. "Master Jeff," Darby said, "what are you planning to do to my people with bird tails?"

Jeff looked at him blankly. "Your people? Bird tails? What in tarnation are you talking about, Shorty?"

"You just said you plan to use the enchanted tails of pheasants against brownies," Darby said, his eyes wide and outraged. "How *could* you?"

Nobody wanted to laugh at Darby's earnest outrage, but his jumbled interpretation generated smothered grins all around.

"Slow your roll," Jeff chuckled. "I didn't mean *brownie* brownies. I meant brown trout. A Pheasant Tail is a great winter fly fishing lure."

Still eyeing him suspiciously, Darby said, "What did the brown trout do to deserve having feathered lures used against them?"

"Answer this one carefully," Tori counseled.

"Nothing," Jeff said, "fishing is kind of like a game."

"Not for the fish," the brownie countered stoutly.

Covering his eyes with his hands and shaking his head, Jeff said, "Shorty, we've been over this a dozen times. It's catch and release. I don't hurt the fish. Connor would have my head if I even thought about it."

Taking pity on him, Tori maneuvered to redirect the conversation. "The point I was trying to make," she said, "is that enchanting fishing lures isn't enough to help you develop your magic to its fullest potential."

"That's not all I do," Jeff said defensively, "I levitate the remote control off the coffee table all the time."

"Uh huh," Tori said. "Here's an idea for you. Use your magic and tell the TV to change the channel *without* the remote."

Jeff's brow furrowed. "I can do that?"

"Yes," she said, "and you could also manifest a gallon of ice cream at midnight when George and Irma are closed."

"I *could*?" he asked. "Any flavor?"

"Any flavor," Tori assured him, "*if* you'd do your homework and really master your powers."

Torn between the intriguing idea of using magic for late night snack runs and annoyance at being lectured, Jeff wagged an accusing finger in her direction.

"How," he said, "did we get from me wanting to know where my Thanksgiving dinner was coming from to my getting lectured about how I use my magic?"

"I'm talented that way," Tori grinned. "Don't worry about your Thanksgiving dinner. Jinx assured me before she left for Londinium they'd be back in time for the holiday, and Mom has sent me three shopping lists already."

Jeff's face brightened. "She's doing the stuffing, right?"

"*We* are doing the stuffing," Darby chimed in. "Mistress Gemma and I have had a lengthy discussion about spices. Also, Mistress Amity will be preparing candied yams with extra marshmallows."

"Okay," Jeff said, "I'm starting to feel better. We're eating down here, right?"

"Yeah," Tori said, "why?"

All three men answered at once. "Big screen TV."

Tori regarded the colonel with mock horror. "Beau Longworth, you're supposed to be a baseball man."

"While football may lack the elegance of baseball," Beau replied placidly, "there is a certain vigor about the contests I find appealing."

Festus picked that moment to come sauntering into the room. "We need to watch some rugby," he said. "Makes American football look like a game for sissies."

"Says the cat who spends his time tearing down Christmas trees," Tori deadpanned. "How was your time today?"

The old cat scowled. "Four point one seconds," he said. "I'm working on a better dismount. That hairless moron Aloysius has been training non-stop to defend his title. He's got brain mange if he thinks I'm gonna let that happen."

Hopping up on his desk, the werecat took a quick inventory of the GNATS drone feeds before calling up slow-motion recordings of his practice rounds.

"See," he said, "I've been doing a full trunk slam/spin combo dismount, but if the tree doesn't have the right amount of spring, I don't get the momentum I need to crush the packages *and* fling off the surviving ornaments. That's the wild card. Tree elasticity. Depends entirely on when they cut the danged thing."

Beau, Chase, and Jeff moved behind the desk and studied the footage.

"I think you're too high up on the trunk when you do the slam thing," Jeff commented, leaning forward. "You're not using your body weight to your full advantage."

"Huh," Festus said. "You might be right, but getting the proper position to execute the spin is critical."

Tori watched as Chase rotated his body and executed a back kick before she burst out laughing.

"Is something amusing?" Chase asked sounding slightly offended.

"Yeah, you guys," she said. "You're so sports addicted you're armchair coaching a *cat* about how to tear up a Christmas tree."

Festus curled his lip back. "They're discussing *technique* with an *athlete*. Something you obviously can't appreciate."

"I can appreciate that if you blow up any more ornaments in the interest of training, Amity is going to have your head," Tori retorted.

The werecat dismissed the comment with a wave of his paw. "That was Rube's doing, not mine. Besides, it gave the humans something to talk about."

"Which," Tori said, "is the one thing we don't need. You guys keep this up, and we're going to have those HBH brats sniffing around again. I'm going upstairs to clean the coffee grinder. No blowing stuff up during tonight's poker game."

"Pfft," Festus said, "we're not playing. Booger and Leon have some online multiplayer shooting thing they're doing, and Marty has a date. I figure me and Rodney will crash in front of the TV and binge something. Where is he, anyway? He usually comes to watch me practice."

"Beats me," Tori said. "I haven't seen him all day. Glory, do you know where he is?"

Guilt flooded Glory's features. "I don't," she said, "we really haven't been spending much time together. I think he's mad at me."

"*Wrong*," Festus said. "He's not mad *at* you, he's been hurt *by* you. You took up with this kid of mine here and dumped Rat Boy like yesterday's tuna."

"That's not true!" Glory cried indignantly. "It's not true, is it Chase?"

Looking like he would rather have been anywhere else in the world than confronting her question, he answered weakly, "It's kinda true."

"Chase!" she cried in dismay.

Buoyed by his son's agreement, Festus warmed to the topic. "Ah ha!" he said. "Answer me this. Why did you let all your *Words with Friends* games with Rodney expire?"

Glory's face crumpled. "I didn't know I did let them expire."

"I rest my case," Festus said smugly. "If Rat Boy isn't hanging around down here, it's probably because he doesn't want to be rejected again. When you were living life as a cocktail gherkin, Rodney was your best friend. Now you don't give him the time of day."

Her eyes filled with tears. "I'll make it up to him," she said. "I swear on Elvis and the Baby Jesus I will."

"Right," Festus said. "You're gonna have to find him first. Try *Heartbreak Hotel*. Thanks to you, he checked in weeks ago."

Two hours after Rodney appeared at his door, Lucien leaned forward and delicately refilled the rat's teacup. "This," he said, "has been a most illuminating conversation. You've changed, my friend. Dare I say they've domesticated you in Briar Hollow?"

Rodney's nose twitched as he sipped his tea. Then he pointed toward the fire before clasping his hands over his heart and smiling.

"Happy with home and hearth," Lucien said. "I'm both happy and sad to hear that. Happy that you've built a family with the Witch of the Oak and her compatriots, and sad that current circumstances demand your services."

With one paw Rodney drew the shape of a tree in the air.

"No," Lucien said, "I have not yet spoken with Yggdrasil, but given that Isherwood is on the loose, I will have no choice but to consult with the Great Tree. That will surely mean your recall."

Rodney shook his head.

"You cannot mean that," Lucien protested. "If Yggdrasil requires your service, you must come."

The rat held up one finger.

"Ah, I see. You will do this one thing and no more. Well, that you must settle on your own with Yggdrasil. We should hasten to Tír na nÓg as soon as possible . . . "

He stopped when Rodney once again shook his head, this time emphasizing the refusal with a firm stomp of his paw followed by a series of complicated gestures.

"You cannot disappear without an explanation," Lucien translated, "and you require me to go to Briar Hollow and tell your story. Of course, let me get my hat."

Rodney held up one paw and mimed writing a letter.

"A letter of introduction?" Lucien asked. "Why would we go to that length to arrange a communication when I can travel with you through the portal and be there in a matter of minutes?"

Trotting across the desk, Rodney patted Lucien's laptop. When his friend opened the device, Rodney carefully tapped out an address on the FaeNet.

Slipping his reading glasses on his nose, Lucien leaned forward. "Glory Green?" he asked. "Who on earth is Glory Green?"

Using his paw to open the notepad, Rodney typed, "Someone who needs to remember I'm important."

15

R odent. The word seemed to suspend itself in the air over the breakfast table like one of Bronwyn's projected memories.

"Rodent?" Kelly asked. "As in Rodney?"

"Yes," Myrtle said. "There is much more to our friend's history than simply having been abandoned in a cage on our doorstep."

"Excuse me," Bronwyn said, "but who is Rodney?"

Circling her hand in the space before her, the aos si brought into focus the image of a black and white rat dressed in medieval armor.

Gold engraved pauldrons covered his shoulders, creating an aura of power and control. His heavy, belted breastplate rested over a chainmail undergarment that extended past his waist and protected his haunches.

In one leather gauntleted paw, he wielded a short sword angled low, the point resting just above his high black boots. From the regal sweep of his whiskers to the proud look in his eyes, the rat radiated quiet authority and strength of purpose.

"This," Myrtle said, "is Sir Rodney de Roquefort."

Gemma almost choked on her coffee. "You are *not* serious," she said, "as in 'Roquefort cheese?'"

The corner of Myrtle's mouth quirked into a smile. "As in Roquefort-sur-Soulzon in the south of France. Cheese is one of the products of the region. The irony of the name is not lost on me, but I assure you our friend comes from a distinguished and noble line of Rodere knights."

"So why is he living with us in Briar Hollow?" Gemma asked.

"For his safety," the aos si replied. "There are few surviving members of his Order compared to the numbers they once commanded. The Rodere knights were ruthlessly maligned by their enemies and targeted for extinction with a unique and vicious weapon, the Black Death."

At the mention of the deadly Plague, Katherine's face clouded. "I well remember when the wretched contagion reached the shores of Europe in 1347," she said. "Be glad you were already here on Tír na nÓg, Bronwyn. The stench of the human dead in the streets will be with me to the end of my days."

"The Plague," Myrtle said, "was not a natural phenomenon. A shadowy coven of witches thought to exist in the Northern Lands unleashed the disease for one purpose, the extinction of the Knights of the Rodere. They very nearly succeeded."

Kelly paused to search her memory before she commented. "I think I remember the human history of the Black Death from high school. People blamed the Black Plague on the rats and killed them by the thousands."

"Correct," Myrtle said. "The real carriers of the disease, however, and of the spell that caused it, were the fleas with which the witches infested common, non-Fae rodents. It became impossible for the Rodere to travel in the human realm and to fulfill their mission as agents of Yggdrasil and the Mother Trees. They were forced to retreat to the Otherworld."

"Where in the Otherworld?" Bronwyn asked.

"Here," Myrtle replied, "on Tír na nÓg."

Bronwyn's face registered her shock. "That's not possible," she said. "I would have known."

"Only if Yggdrasil wanted you to know," Myrtle said. "You are aware of the tale of Ratatoskr?"

"Of course," she said. "Ratatoskr is a figure in the human Norse cosmology based on their understanding of Yggdrasil's role in the coherence of the natural order. The stories feature a squirrel named, Ratatoskr, who runs up and down Yggdrasil's trunk carrying messages."

Myrtle smiled. "A most winsome characterization," she said, "but incorrect. There are creatures that scamper in the shelter of the World Tree's branches, but they are not squirrels, they are the last of the Rodere."

"And this shadow coven of witches in the Northern Lands?" Kelly asked. "Are those the same Scandinavian witches implicated in Isherwood's crimes?"

"I believe they are," Myrtle said. "For reasons Yggdrasil did not reveal, she sent Rodney into hiding in Briar Hollow several years ago. He is next in line to serve as the Order's Grand Master and appears to be taking matters into his own paws at present. Jinx and the members of the special ops team are not the only residents of the fairy mound currently in Londinium. Rodney went there in secret, hidden in Jinx's luggage, to meet with the seneschal of the Order, Lucien St. Leger."

"How do you know that?" Kelly asked.

"The news was brought to me via the fairy mound herself, confirmed by a brownie of impeccable credentials, and augmented with intelligence from a most clever bird," Myrtle replied. "He will, in the space of a few hours, supply Jinx and the others with information that will cause Jinx to search her heart to discover the correct direction for their efforts. We will be waiting for her when she arrives on Avalon."

"And if she makes the wrong choice?" Kelly demanded. "What happens then?"

"That," Myrtle said, "would lead to disastrous consequences, but I have faith that Jinx will make the correct decision."

Gemma set down her cup. "Let me get this straight," she said. "Jinx had a vision about Excalibur. Rodney is descended from Medieval knights, and we're all going to Avalon, and if we don't, it's all going to hit the fan. Just for kicks, is King Arthur going to be there, too?"

"Where else would he be?" Myrtle asked placidly.

After a decidedly pregnant pause, Bronwyn said, "Then the stories are true. Arthur did not die after the Battle of Camlann."

"No," Myrtle said, "the King did not die, but he lives only so long as he never leaves the shores of the Island of Apple Trees. I have good reason to believe the Northern Witches will attempt to reach Tír na nÓg by going through Avalon. We must stop them there."

That news brought Bronwyn forward in her chair, "What do these witches want on Tír na nÓg?"

"To control virtuous magic," Myrtle replied. "According to my source, Morgan le Fay returned to Britannia, entered the Tower, and killed Reynold Isherwood as punishment for his incompetence."

At that news, Kelly's face flushed with indignation. "And you haven't told Jinx?" she asked heatedly. "What on earth are you thinking, Myrtle? You have to share this information with my daughter immediately."

Before Myrtle could answer, Bronwyn said quietly, "She cannot. The others must be led to Avalon by a pure impulse arising in Jinx's heart if she is ever to successfully wield Excalibur."

Wheeling on Bronwyn, Kelly said, "Jinx doesn't know anything about using a sword. That's preposterous."

"Just as it was preposterous when Arthur drew the blade from the rock and claimed his throne," Bronwyn said. "Remember, Excalibur was forged in the fire of Merlin's magic. We know not what it might do in Jinx's hand. That is between her and the sword."

Caught between their calm certainty, Kelly swiveled her head back and forth in frustration. "And in the meantime, we do what?" she protested. "Just sit here and wait? Isn't there anything we can do to help Jinx and the others *now*?"

"Your presence on Tír na nÓg is not without purpose," Myrtle said. "The five of us represent generations of magic that have been called to special missions. I have served as the mentor and teacher of the Daughters of Knasgowa. Bronwyn and Katherine have guarded this land against those who sought to subvert the natural order for their own purposes."

"And us?" Gemma asked. "What have Kelly and I done that can in any way compare to all that?"

The aos si reached for each of their hands.

"You," she said, "broke the line of succession and set in motion all that has transpired since the moment Jinx's magic awakened. The four of you are mothers. Your daughters are all integral to the task of protecting virtuous magic here to ensure its Renaissance in the realms. There is a great confrontation coming to these shores. Your daughters will have need of your wisdom and strength in that. Fear not, Kelly, the time for waiting is over. Now we will go to Yggdrasil and the Knights of the Rodere."

AN HOUR LATER, the women threaded their way through the

heavy boulders at the base of a jagged promontory far in the interior of Tír na nÓg. A thin mist softened the air, falling from a roaring waterfall hidden in the clouds surrounding the summit.

Bronwyn and Myrtle walked ahead, with Kelly and Gemma next, and Katherine bringing up the rear.

Struggling to keep a stable footing on the uneven ground, Gemma tossed a question over her shoulder at the baobhan sith. "Tell me again why you couldn't just fly us up this mountain?"

Katherine, who seemed to be handling the rough terrain effortlessly, said with evident bemusement. "Do you not think approaching the World Tree herself is worth some degree of effort?"

"Effort is fine," Gemma huffed. "Dropping from a heart attack is asking too much."

Catching her by the elbow with a steadying hand, the baobhan sith said, "Fear not for the health of your heart. It will beat long in your chest, as will yours, *Roanoke Pythonissam*."

Keeping her eyes on the path, Kelly said, "Good to know, but I'd rather you call me by my first name."

Extending her other hand as a counterbalance, Katherine said, "Greer has told me of the refreshing informality you all share. She used a most unusual word for our kind, 'family.'"

"Greer is part of our family," Kelly said. "She's a steadfast friend and a dedicated DGI agent. I always feel better knowing she's with Jinx."

"Then," Katherine said, half-lifting the other woman over a particularly rough patch of ground, "you must not be concerned about what road carries Jinx to Avalon. My daughter will not allow her to come to harm."

Kelly looked up long enough to give her a grateful smile, "Thank you for saying that. You know how it is. Mothers worry."

Katherine's brow crinkled. "To be truthful, I do not," she admitted. "Children are a rarity among the baobhan sith."

"You don't worry about Greer?" Gemma asked, the words punctuated by her labored breathing. "With all the dangerous things she does?"

"We have not had direct contact for at least a hundred years," Katherine admitted. "It would appear I have much to learn about my daughter."

"Get to know her again," Kelly suggested. "She's pretty damned impressive."

In spite of her overall reserved manner, something like pride moved through Katherine's eyes. "I look forward to discovering that for myself," she said.

Ahead on the path, Bronwyn called out, "The terrain grows smoother ahead. Then our true climb begins."

Looking up toward the misty summit, Gemma muttered, "I can hardly wait."

16

"Mindy, would you give an inch already!" Kyle said. "There is no way you can say an *earthquake* in North Carolina is *normal!*"

Typing rapidly on her laptop, Mindy quickly scanned the screen and read, "We're roughly 160 miles from the Eastern Tennessee seismic zone. We'd feel the effects of an earthquake in roughly one minute."

Kyle stared at the webpage. "Yeah, for a magnitude 6. It says right there that the biggest quake on record in the zone was a 4.6 in 1973. Was there some big disaster-movie earthquake in Tennessee I missed?"

"Fine," she said, crossing her arms over her chest, "then it must have been illegal fracking."

Kyle's forehead creased with confusion. "I don't even know what that is," he admitted, "unless you're dropping a *Battlestar Galactica* reference, which would mean you're way cooler than I thought you were."

Slapping the table in frustration, Mindy groaned, "Oh my *God! Battlestar Galactica*? Really? Fracking is a serious environmental issue. Natural gas companies want to pump millions of gallons of water and toxic crud into the ground as part of their drilling operations. There's a huge push to keep fracking out of the state because it's causing *earthquakes* in places like Texas where it's legal."

"Oh yeah?" he shot back. "Do they have glitter shooting out of the gutters in Texas?"

As much as she might have wanted to, Mindy had no counter-argument for *that*.

"Gotcha!" Kyle cried in triumph. "Take a look at this."

Shoving her laptop out of the way and spinning his around to give her a full view of the screen, Kyle cued up a video of the courthouse square at night.

The instant the scene came into focus, Mindy's tone grew serious. "What is this, Kyle?" she asked. "I thought we agreed you weren't going to be taking any more video or still photos of The Witch's Brew."

"I'm not," he said defensively. "We are still supposed to be investigating ghosts, right? This camera is pointed at the Confederate Monument, which is supposed to be haunted, but look at what I captured a little after 4 a.m."

Doubt still etched on her face, Mindy watched the video. Midway through she frowned, hit the pause button, stared at the scene, and then replayed the whole thing.

Finally, she said, "What is that?"

"I wanted an answer to that question, too," Kyle said excitedly. "I went down there and took pictures before those people in the store could hide the evidence."

Hitting a couple of keys, he switched programs, filling the screen with a color photo of the pavement in front of a storm drain. Green and red glitter covered the asphalt in a conical plume shooting out from the sewer.

"Huh," Mindy said, sitting back in her chair. "That is weird, but I don't see how it could have anything to do with the earthquake. *If* it was an earthquake."

"It could if there's something going on *under* the store," Kyle said. "When you worked there you said Tori and the other lady were always going down in the basement. What if it's like their secret base of operations or something?"

Mindy stared at him slack-jawed. "I'm sorry, did you say you were photographing glitter or smoking it?"

"Why is that such a crazy idea?" he pressed. "Tori has to keep her supercomputer somewhere out of sight."

"I'm starting to worry about you," Mindy said. "Tori Andrews doesn't have a supercomputer hidden in her basement. She uses a MacBook."

Dragging one of the chairs out from the table, Kyle flopped down. "That's not what GhostFish says, he . . . "

"Don't!" she ordered. "That's a perfect example of why this is all just, plain *wrong*. You're listening to somebody on the Internet claiming to be the ghost of Dead Mayor McAlpin and building a massive conspiracy theory off of what he says. Ghost-Fish is probably some 13-year-old kid who watches our YouTube channel and is getting a huge laugh out of pulling one over on you."

"But what if he's not?" Kyle asked seriously. "What if he really is Mayor McAlpin and he was murdered, and there is something going on in that store. When did we stop being investigators, Mindy?"

Momentarily uncertain how to answer him, she finally said, "We didn't stop, we're just looking for conventional paranormal evidence."

"That's one of those oxy things," Kyle argued.

"You mean an oxymoron?"

"Yeah, what's 'conventional' about paranormal evidence?"

"As much as it pains me to say this," Mindy replied, "that's a good question, but how is glitter paranormal?"

"It's not," Kyle said, "but it is out of the ordinary — plus, that storm sewer is the one right in front of The Witch's Brew."

Mindy stared at the screen for several seconds and then said, "Okay. Now you've got my attention."

GREER DIDN'T bother to look into the shadows as she came out of the British Museum. "Good evening, mother," she said, without breaking stride.

In a blur of motion, Katherine was at her daughter's side. "I assume the IBIS crowd is on high alert to locate Isherwood."

"They are," Greer replied. "I would have thought you would be guarding the approaches to Tír na nÓg."

The older baobhan sith stopped at the front gate, forcing her daughter to halt as well. "I am on my way back to the sanctuary," she said, "but I wanted to see your first."

"Why? Has something happened?"

Katherine hesitated slightly. "No," she said finally. "I was in town to speak with Hilton Barnstable on Bronwyn's behalf, and he mentioned that you and the others had arrived from Briar Hollow to take part in the investigation. I simply wanted to say . . . hello."

Greer regarded her mother with disbelief. "You altered your plans and tracked me down at the British Museum to say nothing more than hello?"

"We have to begin again somewhere, daughter," Katherine said, shifting uncomfortably. "Will you at least afford me some credit for making an effort?"

Looking more than a little discomfited herself, Greer tried to think of an appropriate response, settling at last for, "Hello . . . mother."

Accepting the two-word response as encouraging, Katherine asked, "Where are you going in such a hurry? Do you have a lead on Isherwood?"

"Perhaps," Greer said. "Fer Dorich has moved his operation to the human city of Las Vegas. I am going there to speak with him and to . . . dine."

The moon breaking through the clouds fell on Katherine's features just as green embers stirred in her eyes. "Do give the Dark Druid my regards," she said in an unmistakably sultry tone.

Greer processed the implication in her mother's words in a split second. "Please tell me that you and Fer Dorich were not involved."

"Why would I . . ." Katherine started and then stopped as realization struck her as well. "You and Fer Dorich?" she asked.

"It was centuries ago," Greer hedged, adding quickly, "and I have no desire to trade stories about the Dark Druid with my mother."

"A point well taken," Katherine said, "but may I still offer you a bit of advice?"

"So long as you keep your phrasing neutral."

"Do not 'dine' until after you meet with Fer Dorich," Katherine said. "He would never admit it, but he fears our hunger. Go in with fire in your eyes and the edge of appetite to your manner. He'll tell you whatever you want to know."

As GREER WALKED through the lobby of the Mirage, Katherine's words came back to her. She had to give her mother credit. The woman knew how to direct an entrance. Greer found a path through the crowd opening up before her on the sheer force of her magnetism alone.

Normally she would never have gone among humans with her appetite on such a razor's edge, but tonight she found her effect on the boisterous chaos of the casino enthralling.

Nature designed the hunger of the baobhan sith to lure unsuspecting men, to lower their defenses, and to deepen their preoccupation with the moment. Oblivious to the consequences, any of them would have followed Greer had she so much as looked in their direction.

But she did not look. She simply moved — like a stalking cat, languid in an ebony mandarin jacket, with gold threads woven through the fasteners and diamonds studding the buttons. Floating through glittering prisms of reflected light, Greer allowed her hunger to bank the smoldering embers of her power, well aware of the effect she had on those around her.

As she approached the door to a private room, a man in dark glasses barred her passage, but she saw the heavy swallow that constricted his throat as she drew nearer.

"Tarathiel," Greer said, the elven name flowing from her lips like honeyed wine. "Don't be tiresome. I do love what you've done with your tips."

The elf ran a finger self-consciously over his newly rounded ears but said nothing.

"Surely Fer Dorich has not become so incapable of wielding his magic that he required you to submit to physical mutilation rather than be detected by the humans?" Greer purred. "That would aggrieve me terribly."

From beyond the door, a man's voice said, "Let her in, Tarathiel, if you can still remember how to use a doorknob."

Grimacing, the bodyguard held the door open for Greer to pass, inhaling sharply when she trailed one manicured nail over the lapel of his jacket.

Inside the room, the baobhan sith found the Dark Druid playing cards with four Sídhe nobles. Inclining her head, she spoke to them in Elvish. Without hesitation, the men folded their cards, collected their chips, and left.

Sighing, Fer Dorich threw his hand down on the table. "I wish you hadn't done that," he complained. "You scared off my opponents when I had a winning hand. Shall I order dinner for you? Maybe a nice software engineer from the convention next door?"

"No thank you," Greer said, claiming one of the empty chairs. "I prefer to select my own cuisine. Do you know what the humans call the combination of cards you are holding?"

Fer Dorich fanned out aces and eights in front of him. "No," he said. "What do they call it?"

"A Dead Man's hand."

He let out a sharp laugh. "An ironic bit of information coming from a hungry baobhan sith," he said. "To what do I owe the honor of your company, Greer MacVicar?"

"I've come to inquire about your relocation to Las Vegas."

"Have you now," he said, his smile taking on a dangerous edge. "Is this a matter of personal interest or the consequence of your tedious job in law enforcement?"

"Call it a mixture of both."

Leaning back in his chair, the Dark Druid spread his hands wide in an exaggerated gesture of innocence.

"I am an open book," he said. "Surely you can understand that after my extended sojourn in the Middle Realm I find the energy of Las Vegas invigorating. Not to mention how good this place is for business. So many opportunities for gainful entertainment."

"When did you lower your standards sufficiently to do business with the Sídhe?" Greer asked. "There was a time when you did not tolerate their supercilious natures."

"Their checks cash," Fer Dorich said pragmatically. "Beyond that, I don't care what they think of me. If you do not wish to dine, would you care for a drink? A dram of the Dalmore 64 Trinitas, perhaps?"

Inclining her head slightly in acceptance, she said, "That would be lovely. There were only three bottles of that Scotch ever produced."

"I know," Fer Dorich said, taking a cellphone out of the breast pocket of his suit. "I own two of them."

He spoke into the handset, and in mere seconds a well-dressed woman appeared carrying a silver tray bearing a single bottle decorated with a silver stag's head and two Baccarat tumblers.

As he poured the mahogany whisky, Fer Dorich said, "I assume you are here on behalf of the tiresome agency for which you are employed."

Taking the glass he held out to her, Greer said, "I am. *Slàinte.*"

"*Do dheagh shlàinte,*" he replied.

A single sip of the Scotch sent a flickering tendril of green fire across Greer's eyes. Fer Dorich saw it and chuckled. "Good, isn't it?" he asked.

"Magnificent," she replied.

For the space of several minutes, they enjoyed their whisky in silence until Fer Dorich sighed again.

"Let us cut to the chase, as the humans say. I am not hiding Reynold Isherwood nor is anyone else in Las Vegas. He's dead, and the person who killed him should be your primary concern."

Greer's face betrayed no trace of reaction. "Do tell," she said, "and how do you know this?"

"Every bird loves to hear himself sing," Fer Dorich replied. "Discretion forbids me to say more than that."

"If Isherwood is not our enemy, why does it stand to reason that the one who killed him works against us?"

The Dark Druid tilted his glass and watched the play of the room's lights across the fluid surface.

"I see you remember your *Arthashastra*," he said. "'The enemy of my enemy is my friend.' Alas, that wisdom does not apply in this case."

"Fer Dorich, say whatever you have to say. I grow weary of these word games."

Raising the tumbler and knocking back the remaining whisky, the Dark Druid sat the glass down in front of him with an authoritative thud.

"As always, Greer, you want the arrow pulled from your chest without benefit of anesthesia," he said. "Very well. Morgan le Fay killed Reynold Isherwood, and before she is done, she will kill every living soul who stands between her and the Vessel of Pure Magic."

~

RUBE SLAPPED his paw on the bar at The Crooked Critter to get the bartender's attention. "Yo! Barkeep! Can we get another round here?"

"Keep your fur on, mate," the barman growled, drawing a fresh pint for the raccoon and another for the lemur sitting beside him.

While they waited for their drinks, the monkey's gold eyes began to water, and its black nosed quivered uncontrollably.

"Aw, man," Rube said, edging farther down the bar. "Don't you dare sneeze, Sam. You fling snot worse than a Spanish ribbed newt."

"I warnthed you I had a coldth," the lemur wheezed. "I'm cogesthed. Gib me a breakth."

Fishing in the pouch at his waist, Rube pulled out a mostly clean handkerchief and slid it down the bar.

"Yeah, yeah. I know. You've got a cold, and all you want to do is go stick your head in a eucalyptus bush. You told me that part already. Tell me the part about the big black bird again."

17

Lucien and Siegfried faced off in the mirror, each frowning at the other with an almost identical mix of consternation and amusement. Neither was prepared to yield their position.

When the impasse stretched beyond the point of comfort, Lucien broke and made the first move, infusing his words with reason and good humor.

"Siegfried," he said, "I understand that you feel a personal responsibility to the Witch of the Oak, but Rodney and I have enjoyed a long association."

"I do not doubt that sir," Siegfried said with forced patience, "but the conditions of the agreement I struck with Rodney call for him to return to Claridge's after his meeting with you and from here to go home to Briar Hollow."

Rodney, who was sitting at Lucien's elbow, raised his paws, nodded sheepishly, and shrugged.

"Obviously he confirms your interpretation," Lucien said to Siegfried, "but things have altered in the interim. As soon as we receive a response from a communiqué I dispatched via Pixie Post to Briar Hollow, I will personally escort Rodney home."

Siegfried opened the middle drawer of his desk and took out a small pamphlet. The cover read "Pixie Post Schedules and Rates."

After thumbing through the pages and studying one in particular, he said, "Pixie Post from Londinium to Briar Hollow requires overnight transit."

"Yes," Lucien agreed, "it does, which is why we are proposing that Rodney spend the night here. You have my word of honor that he will be completely safe with me."

The brownie's face wrinkled in stark disapproval. "I do not appreciate having been excluded from the determination of this plan," he said. "I should have been consulted rather than face approving a unilateral decision."

Lucien responded with a deferential nod. "A most unfortunate breach of manners on my part for which I apologize sincerely."

Siegfried fixed his gaze on Rodney. "Do I have your word that you will return to Briar Hollow in the company of this gentleman when you receive a response to your message?"

Rodney sat up on his haunches, crossed his heart, and held his paw up in the Boy Scout salute.

The corners of Siegfried's mouth threatened to quirk into a smile, but he managed to maintain his stern demeanor.

"I take you to be a rodent with a sense of honor," he said. "Do not disappoint me. If you have not returned to Briar Hollow by this time tomorrow evening, I will have no choice but to speak with Madam Hamilton."

The surface of the mirror faded back to silver. Lucien looked down at Rodney, who instantly clenched his jaw and extended his limbs in a pantomime of rigor.

Chortling, Lucien said, "Rigid is a good way to describe Siegfried, but he has quite the reputation as a fixer. Even though he rarely leaves Claridge's, he knows everything of importance that happens in Londinium. Now! We have the evening to ourselves. Are you hungry?"

Rodney nodded and patted his stomach.

"Do you still have a fondness for Stilton cheese?" Lucien asked. "I have fresh bread from the bakery on the corner and a bottle of Chateau Montrose 2005. For one night, it will be like the old days, yes?"

The words brought brimming tears to the rat's eyes. Swallowing hard, he pointed toward the fire.

Lucien snapped his fingers, and the flames rose higher, crackling merrily. A faint aroma of wood smoke mixed with the earthy scent of the outdoors filled the room.

"There," he said. "Not quite a campfire with the fellows, but a fair enough approximation. Now, make yourself at home, and I will get our food."

❧

MUCH LATER IN THE EVENING, Rodney nibbled on the last piece of buttered bread and bit into the final crumb of the pungent cheese. He sighed as he reached for the wine glass that fit perfectly in his paw.

Even though he had nice things in Briar Hollow, eating with dishes made especially for someone his size was a rare treat. Dabbing at his whiskers with a damask napkin, he looked across at Lucien dozing in his leather chair.

His friend had started to nod off on the second glass of wine. Half-way through the third, his soft snores intermingled with the crackling of the fire.

Rodney finished the wine and jumped from the desk to the bookcase. He'd spotted a familiar volume earlier in the evening and intended to ask Lucien to take it down for him, but rather than wake his friend, Rodney would retrieve the book on his own.

Running along the edge of the polished wood, he spotted the calfskin spine decorated with a gold embossed miniature of the de Roquefort family crest. Working his way between the volume and its neighbor to the right, Rodney went to the back of the shelf and pushed.

Just as the album started to topple, he darted forward, standing quickly and catching the cover at its uppermost edge. Then, having broken the book's momentum, he dropped it flat with a faint thud.

Lucien stirred in his chair, but only enough to snuggle deeper into his cardigan. After waiting for a minute or two, Rodney shoved the album to the widest part of the shelf. Then, working carefully, the flipped the cover back revealing the book's interior.

On the first page, he found a picture of himself in full armor, taken when he was a young rat on Tír na nÓg. As he looked at the portrait, Rodney glanced down to appraise the size of his belly. Even stuffed with bread and cheese, he was in pretty good shape for a rat just shy of his 664th birthday.

How Rodney wished his father could have seen him grow to adulthood. He barely remembered the jet black and imposing Robert de Roquefort, but his gentle-voiced mother was a different matter.

If Rodney closed his eyes, he could still feel her soft paws stroking the fur between his ears. Solange's pristine white coat glowed in her son's cherished memories of the nights when she sat beside his bed reading him to sleep.

But then the Black Death came in 1345 and with it the rat catchers. Robert and Solange allowed themselves to be caught so that their son might live. As frightened voices and panicked squealing rose in his memory, Rodney closed his eyes and shook his head.

He couldn't let the bad pictures rise in his mind. He'd worked for centuries to drive them away, and since he'd been living in Briar Hollow, Rodney hadn't thought about those dark days even for a minute.

The night his parents died changed his life in ways far beyond leaving him an orphan. When his grandfather, Sir Reginald, found him hidden deep in the shadows between the foundation stones of the castle, Rodney hadn't answered even one of the old rat's questions.

When days passed, and he still refused to speak, Reginald summoned the Rodere healer to examine his grandson. They didn't know Rodney overheard their conversation.

"It would not be wise to force him to speak of that night, Sir Reginald," the doctor whispered. "He saw terrible things. Let him have the peace of his silence. His mind is sharp and his body strong. Words are not everything. If Rodney speaks again, it must be his decision."

In all the many years that had passed since that night, he had never felt the need to make that choice. His silence became an accepted part of his identity. Rodney didn't need his voice to get his point across and to him it seemed that when people spoke less, they heard more.

Reginald had led the surviving Rodere through the portal to Tír na nÓg where Rodney began his training as a Rodere knight. He grew to adulthood in the roots of Yggdrasil, but unlike the old warriors who sat around the fires at night, he hoped the day of the Order's recall would never come.

Now, slowly turning the album's pages, Rodney remembered the sunlit warmth in the World Tree's branches as he and his friends frolicked high in the canopy. Fearless and surefooted, they'd climbed to the place where the leaves met the clouds to watch the dragonlets in the skies over the Never Wood.

Rodney loved so much about Tír na nÓg. Would it really be such a terrible thing to return there? To take up his place with the Rodere and to become the Order's next Grand Master? He knew there was no dream dearer to his grandfather's heart.

Going to the window, Rodney leaned against the pane and watched the carriage traffic on the street below. At this hour, the town square in Briar Hollow would be completely deserted. But here, in Londinium, people were on their way to dinners in beautiful restaurants or plays in the city's theaters.

His grandfather had allowed Rodney to spend time here in the city with Lucien as part of his education. Rodney loved the cosmopolitan atmosphere of the metropolis sprawling along the Thames. How many times he'd gone out tucked in Lucien's pocket or under the collar of his coat!

Not because he'd needed to hide, but because his body was little in a world that was large. But for all that, Rodney had never been made to feel small until Jinx and Tori took over the store.

He understood that his friends were being protective, in part because he'd played his role too well. They thought his intelligence and ability to communicate had grown under their tutelage. Was it any wonder they kept him out of harm's way even when he'd proven his capabilities time and time again?

But then Glory had come to live in Briar Hollow, and he'd had someone his size as a companion and friend. She treated his sign language as a great game of charades, consulting him about her convoluted problems and understanding his answers every time.

When she mixed up the potion that returned her to normal size, nothing about their friendship changed — until Jinx broke up with Chase and Glory set her cap for the werecat next door.

After that, in Glory's eyes, Rodney ceased to exist.

But it wasn't just her. They were all guilty of ignoring and discounting him.

That was the problem with humans. More times than not, they missed what was happening right under their very noses.

The only person who saw Knasgowa take Rodney aside to entrust him with the eighth wand was Festus, and it didn't seem to occur to the werecat that the rat wasn't up for whatever task he'd been given.

Later that night in the storeroom, the old werecat had said, "Something you want to tell me, Rat Boy?"

Feigning innocence, Rodney shook his head.

"Uh huh," Festus said, "like I didn't see Knasgowa take you off in the stacks."

Rodney put his paw to his lips and made the motion of turning a lock and throwing away the key.

"Promised to keep quiet, huh?" Festus said. "Okay, I get that. But answer one question for me. Is trouble on the way?"

The rat's eyes turned solemn and round as he shook his head and shrugged.

"When you do know, will you tell me?" Festus asked.

Rodney had nodded, which meant he'd made a promise.

That was one of the reasons he had to go back to Briar Hollow before anything else happened — to keep his word to Festus.

Knasgowa had made him, Sir Rodney de Roquefort, the guardian of the eighth wand.

Rodney wasn't sure that even she realized the wand's true significance or in whom she'd placed her confidence, but that didn't lessen his determination to fulfill his mission.

The eighth wand was Merlin's wand.

Now Jinx had experienced a vision of Merlin's sword.

The wand and the sword. The symbols of fire and air.

Could water and earth be far behind? And who would know

how to unite the wizard's tools but Merlin's apprentice and lover, Morgan le Fay?

If the Morgaine had returned, Rodney knew the Knights of the Rodere would be needed. A de Roquefort, he told himself, does not wait to be called. He seizes the moment.

But at the same time, if Rodney could also make his friends understand that he was far more than what they imagined? Well, what was the harm in that?

18

S hifting her gaze from the 16th and 17th-century mechanical clocks in the case, Brenna caught Otto Volker's eyes reflected in the glass. He was studying her, not the display, with keen interest.

When Volker realized he'd been caught, he coughed self-consciously. "The clocks are elegant, are they not?" he asked. "Ornate, but functional. An intriguing combination."

"I knew men who built such devices," Brenna replied. "The human desire for advanced technologies amuses me. We Fae are feared for our magic, yet in the name of science, they create mechanical enchantments."

"For as fond as I may be of humans, they can be a study in contradictions."

"True," the sorceress agreed, "but my granddaughter, Tori, has become fascinated with a merging of the alchemical and the technological. Imagine, Dr. Volker, what marvels could be wrought were human and Fae culture ever to mingle freely again."

Grimacing good-naturedly at the formality of his title, Volker said, "Would it be forward of me to propose we place our association on a first name basis?"

"Not at all, Otto."

He beamed at her acceptance. "Thank you, Brenna. Allow me to apologize for staring just now. It was rude."

"Was it?" she asked, with a speculative tilt of her head. "I am aware of my popular status as a curiosity."

Volker's bushy eyebrows shot toward his hat brim with alarm. "Good *heavens!*" he said. "That is not at *all* what I was thinking."

"Then what were you thinking?"

The assistant director blinked rapidly, unsure how to answer the question. Finally, stammering over the words, he said, "I was admiring your great beauty and thinking that the descriptions I have read of you do not do you justice."

Brenna's relaxed demeanor never faltered, but something in her eyes softened, offering a nuanced revelation of a tightly held inner fragility. The window onto those reserved depths closed as quickly as it had opened, but when she spoke, her voice was warm and deep.

"No gentleman has paid me such a sincere compliment in a very long time," she said. "Thank you, but I dare say you've also read less appealing accounts of my *behavior*."

Volker shrugged slightly. "If I am to be honest," he said, "I found the details of your exploits oddly compelling. You followed no rules but your own. However, have you managed to adjust to life in an arguably pedestrian human village?"

"Long before I was the terror of Europe, I was — arguably — rather a pedestrian girl," Brenna said. "It comforts me to have a family again. I treasure both their forgiveness and their acceptance."

Volker opened his mouth to ask a question, then shut it

almost as quickly, a reaction that drew a bubbling laugh from Brenna.

"Come now, Otto. You are an academic," she said. "It is in your nature to ask questions. I do not mind. What is it that you wish to know?"

Choosing his words carefully, Volker said, "The subject of human ethics fascinates me. They can be a sublimely kind people on the one hand and utter barbarians on the other. You were, twice in your life, and for extended periods, a prisoner."

"Yes," the sorceress said. "I was. First in the Orkneys and then when I was bound to the grave of the Cherokee witch, Knasgowa."

"And you were alone."

"I was."

"The humans have crafted a set of rules for the ethical treatment of prisoners called the Geneva Convention. It states that severe and extended isolation is a form of torture. I am curious . . . . I mean it interests me . . . "

Taking pity on the man's cautious reticence, Brenna finished the thought for him.

"You wonder how a Fae mind bears up under such circumstances," she said.

The flatness of the statement dismayed Volker. "I am not handling this well at all," he said regretfully. "To hear the words spoken aloud makes me realize the ghoulishness of my query."

"On the contrary, Otto," Brenna said with perfect equanimity. "I find your frank interest refreshing. Many have probed for details of my transformative experience in the Middle Realm, but none, not even my family, have asked about what those years of isolation did to me. To discuss that time openly would be a relief."

Offering her his arm, he said, "Then let us walk. I have found that ambulation can facilitate even the most difficult conversation."

Linking arms, they walked quietly through the displays until Brenna began to speak.

"The cave was, in many ways, the better of my two prisons," she said. "The Druid, Skea, cast his binding spell with cunning and skill. No light or sound reached me in those first days. There, alone in the dark, I raged against the loss of my freedom and also that of my child."

Brenna's voice grew rough, and her arm tightened in Otto's. They passed through two quiet, shadowed galleries in silence before she could continue.

Pausing before the Rosetta Stone, she said, "Finally the day arrived when I had to choose between creating an existence for myself or going mad. Fae prisoners, especially those who are Creavit, are at a considerable disadvantage to their human counterparts. For us, suicide is not an option."

She gestured toward the etched tabled. "I was not yet in my second prison when Pierre-François Bouchard saved this stele from destruction in Egypt, and I was still a free woman in 1822 when Jean-François Champollion deciphered the hieroglyphs. By 1853, I had been consigned to limbo. Imagine, Otto, leaving a world where the decoding of an ancient text is one of man's greatest achievement only to reemerge in the 21st century where humans have gained the power of flight."

"I cannot imagine," he said. "In a way, you are a traveler through time."

The sorceress laughed bitterly. "Many humans seek to halt the passage of time," she said. "In those prisons, I learned how immortality can be more a curse than a blessing. In the cave, my magic remained intact, but in limbo, I had no means to create a comfortable existence. I was condemned to watch the passing of the living world through the shadowy, filtered light of a sun under whose rays I could never walk. I watched many a human go to their peaceful graves and envied them the oblivion of death. When Jinx accidentally released me, she did, perhaps, set loose a mad woman on the world."

"But you are not a mad woman now," Volker said. "Jinx and the others speak of you with open admiration and love."

This time, Brenna made no effort to stop the tears that filled her eyes. "That is the gift of redemption I did little to earn, but work so hard to deserve."

In a tone filled with compassion, Otto said, "Your Creavit magic did not rob you of your conscience."

"It did not," Brenna admitted. "I have no interest in attempting to clear my name or in enhancing my reputation after all these centuries even though many of the crimes ascribed to me belong to Irenaeus and Reynold. Having said that, I am no innocent, and I still live with my guilt."

To her surprise, the cryptozoologist reached across the space between them and caught hold of her hands.

"Do not," he said. "You are not now who you were then. Guilt carries a weight heavier than any substance on earth. Your redemption has stirred admiration in the hearts of many."

A small shudder ran through her. "I do not wish to be admired, only to live now in a useful way. That is why I want to examine the Tower and help to apprehend Reynold if he has indeed escaped."

Otto looked at her sharply. "What do you mean 'if?'"

"Frankly," Brenna answered, "Reynold lacks the cleverness to plan an undetectable escape. More is afoot here. I have felt it since the day we set foot on Tír na nÓg."

"But we have used every scanning device at our disposal including the new RABIES technology," Otto protested. "There is no suggestion of any unauthorized personnel in the facility."

"No matter how thorough your investigation, Otto, it cannot

penetrate the dark currents of magic I know to exist in this world because I have practiced them. I cannot tell you what we will find in the Tower, but I do not expect it to be evidence of an escape."

19

The brief encounter with King Arthur's portrait unnerved me for a reason I wasn't ready to share with Lucas. Since our visit to Tír na nÓg, something inside me had started to change. Remember my reaction to the Christmas tree coming through the portal?

I wrote the whole thing off to exhaustion and nerves. That's not the truth. Every day my senses seemed to grow sharper. It was like standing in the middle of one of those old radar screens from a World War II movie. A new sensitivity extended outward from my mind in a growing circle of awareness I could no longer deny.

Yes, the sword in the painting caught my eye, but what compelled me forward was the overwhelming desire to reach into the scene and lift the blade from the canvas. I had to ball my right hand into a tight fist to keep myself from doing just that.

My greatest fear was that had I tried, I would have succeeded in lifting Excalibur into three-dimensional life. At the same time, a wild urge to freely unleash that animating power threw itself like a wild animal against the solid wall of my apprehension.

Something Myrtle once said rose in my mind on a frightening wave of recognition.

I hear and feel life in all its forms, Jinx, even its residue, but some imprints are so tiny and faint they do not register in my awareness unless I direct all my focus on locating them.

On Attu, I'd felt Eugene's presence long before we located him by conventional means. I *felt* the pain of his confused memories of the war and his fierce need to protect himself and his beloved island from potential harm.

In Russia, at Lake Brosno, I *felt* the beating heart of the dragon *and* the pulsating life of the lava buried deep within the volcano.

And still, I said nothing.

In all the adventures we've taken together, I've never shared with you my current perspective as narrator. I don't want to ruin the telling of the tale, but I can say that I am now in a position to guide younger witches who have, in the way of the precocious, asked me why I didn't do this or that at certain points in my evolution.

"Why didn't you ask Myrtle?"

"Why didn't you try to learn faster?"

When I answer those questions, I point out that in the same way that there is a difference between the brain and the mind, there is also a subtle dividing line between volition and denial.

From day one, I tried to manage my powers, to slow the pace of my progress to match my emotional ability to accept who and what I am.

That night in the museum you may think I should have turned to Lucas or that when we went back to Claridge's I should have gotten on a mirror and called Brenna, or Myrtle, or Mom.

"Should" is an easy word to use when you're on the outside looking in at someone else's life.

That night I did what I *could* do. I went back to the hotel with Lucas, my mind working overtime all the way. I was trying to come up with half-truths to share with him that might, in the telling, give me the courage I needed to be genuinely honest.

Thankfully my stomach intervened and bought me some time. The instant we stepped into the lobby, it growled — loudly.

Going for the obvious, Lucas asked, "Would you like to get something to eat?"

"I guess it's either that or we need to hire a lion tamer for my gut," I answered. "Do you think we can get a table?"

Out of nowhere, Siegfried appeared at my elbow.

"I have a table reserved for Madam and the gentleman in a quiet corner if you will be so good as to follow me."

"How do you do that, Siegfried?" I asked as we trailed after him.

"Do what, Madam?"

"Anticipate our every need."

I couldn't tell if my question made him frown or if his expression reflected his perpetual state of exasperation with the world.

"Madam," he said, with courteous patience, "I *am* a brownie."

Well, there you go.

Siegfried showed us to a lovely and fairly romantic table tucked into a corner nook of the restaurant. The pleasantly dim lighting soothed my nerves. The tight band of tension around my chest loosened so I could breathe again.

We had a full view of the other diners, but still enjoyed a sense of cozy privacy. Since I hadn't seen Lucas for almost two days and we were probably going to discuss sensitive subjects, the setting couldn't have been more ideal.

Lucas ordered a bottle of wine and an appetizer to take care of my complaining belly until the main course arrived. Even though I wasn't ready to talk about what just happened at the museum, Lucas willingly answered my questions about Morris Grayson.

"So you've seen your uncle?" I asked.

"Twice," Lucas said. "The first time was Otto's idea. Dinner and diplomacy. Uncle Morris values his reputation too much to have been nasty in front of Otto, but he made it clear he doesn't approve of the special ops team or my being in Briar Hollow."

Trying not to clench my teeth, I said, "And by extension, he doesn't approve of me, either."

"Honey," Lucas said, "the two of you didn't exactly hit it off."

"He said, and I quote, that your 'future prospects will not be furthered by taking up with any witch that comes along.'"

Lucas reached over the table and caught hold of my hand. "From where I'm sitting my 'future prospects' look just fine, not to mention that you showed Uncle Morris you're not just any witch."

"Harumph," I grumbled. "How about the second meeting?"

"That one was all business," Lucas said. "Uncle Morris wants Reynold Isherwood back in the Tower as quickly as possible."

Before I could answer, Siegfried returned with our appetizer. He slid two gorgeous, toasty warm pieces of bruschetta onto my plate. The aroma, redolent with garlic and basil, was more intoxicating than the wine.

The brownie doesn't work in the dining room on a regular basis, but he served us that evening with elegant attention. If I hadn't had so much on my mind, and skipping my annoyance over Morris Grayson, the evening would have been perfect.

Lucas waited until the appetizer had disappeared and I was on my second glass of wine to bring up what happened at the museum.

"Are we going to talk about 'that sword,'" he asked, smiling at me over the candles in the center of the table, "or are we still officially in avoidance mode?"

"Very funny," I responded. "Yes, we're going to talk about 'that sword,' but I honestly don't know where to start. Other than movie references and high school reading assignments, I don't know anything about King Arthur and Camelot."

That much was absolutely the truth.

Lucas held up the bottle tipping it slightly in my direction. When I nodded, he filled my glass again.

"Don't take this the wrong way," he said lightly, "but you're thinking like a human again.

"Thirty-year habit," I quipped, "and what does that have to do with anything?"

"If you had a vision about Excalibur that can only mean that the sword itself or some aspect of its power will touch your life. Probably sooner than later."

Sometimes I forget I'm dating an investigator — a good one.

"I guess we can't sell that as a coincidence?" I asked hopefully.

When he shook his head, I asked, "Do you think my vision has something to do with Isherwood's escape?"

"That's hard to say," Lucas admitted. "At the moment, I can't see how it would, but I don't know enough about possible links between the sword, Camelot, Arthur, and Tír na nÓg to say for certain. At the very least, we have to take this up with Otto."

Ignoring the last part, I said, "Tír na nÓg? Why would there be a connection between Excalibur and Tír na nÓg?"

"I don't know that there is," Lucas said, "but there have been three major events in rapid succession that have rocked the Fae world."

He ticked them off on his fingers: the lifting of The Agreement, the disclosure of Isherwood's crimes, and the revelation of Tír na nÓg.

Just as Siegfried arrived with our dinner plates, Lucas said, "The Fae world hasn't been in a state of chaos like this since the Reformation. I'd be shocked if there *wasn't* a link."

Like all professionals in his line of work, Siegfried seemed to be completely oblivious to the conversation, but I knew the brownie was listening when Lucas continued.

"After we visit the Tower in the morning, we should go straight back to IBIS headquarters and talk to Otto about the sword."

At those words, I detected the merest hint of a reaction from Siegfried.

"Is there something you'd like to contribute to our conversation?" I asked him.

Presenting me the best blank face I've ever seen, he replied, "I am sorry, Madam, but I have no idea to what you are referring."

"Don't give me that," I said. "You know exactly to what I'm referring. Do you know something about Isherwood's escape from the Tower? Or what it might have to do with a sword?"

Moving to refill Lucas' water glass, Siegfried said, "Rather than offering a direct contribution, I might venture to make an observation."

"Which is?"

"Consider, Madam, that your efforts might best be focused on identifying the person who does not wish to see Isherwood stand trial rather than on the wizard himself. Think also on the words of Lucius Annaeus Seneca."

With the mention of that name, Siegfried had my full attention. "The Roman philosopher or the raven?"

"The philosopher," the brownie said. "'A sword never kills anybody; it is a tool in the killer's hand.'"

"Meaning?"

"Why, Madam," Siegfried said. "I should think that would be

clear. Never let a sword fall into the hands of one who intends to use it for an ill purpose."

THE NEXT MORNING, we opted to walk, strolling across Tower Bridge like tourists enjoying the crisp, bracing air. Well, Lucas and I enjoyed the air. Rube, who was nursing a hangover after his evening at The Crooked Critter, complained every step of the way until we crossed through the Tower's main entrance and over the dry moat.

There, just inside the gate, the sun seemed to disappear from the sky. The growing sense of hyper-awareness that had crept up on me for days sprang at my throat with the ferocity of a ravening wolf. Sounds pushed in on me from all directions and the air seemed to be sucked from my lungs.

The restraining spells used to contain Isherwood had been lifted, but I heard the echo of their presence in the stone walls. Whispers rose from the lapping waves beneath Traitor's Gate, carrying to my mind the plaintive voices of those who had entered the prison never to leave again.

Disoriented and confused, I stumbled, forcing Rube to dive to the side before I ran right over him. Lucas caught my elbow, but his touch sent the world swimming around me. The acrid taste of saltwater filled my mouth, and the roar of the ocean flooded my ears. On instinct, I pulled away sharply.

Lucas looked at me with shock and surprise.

"It's not you," I said, choking on the words. "There's something . . . here. Something in this place."

Lucas reached for me again but stopped himself for fear of causing another negative reaction. Shoving his hands in the pockets of his leather duster, he said, "What did you see?"

"I don't think it was a vision," I said, taking deep, slow breaths. "I tasted saltwater and heard the ocean."

"But that's still your psychometry, right?" he asked.

"I don't know," I admitted. "It's never happened with another person, only inanimate objects — and there's more. I hear voices in the walls."

Rube, who was leaning against the nearest wall watching us, jumped away and stared over his shoulder at the stones. "What voices, doll?" he asked. "I don't hear nothing."

"Neither do I," Lucas said, never taking his eyes off my face. "Do you think it's Isherwood?"

"No," I said, "I think I'm hearing *all* of the people who have been imprisoned here. If his voice is in there, it's mixed up with the others."

Lucas' eyes tracked over my shoulders. Without turning, I said, "Brenna, what's happening?"

The sorceress came up next to me, blanketing me in a cool envelope of soothing energy. "Do not fight the awareness," she counseled gently. "Open yourself to the images. They come from your magic. They, like it, are yours to control."

In the shelter of her supportive powers, I was able to breathe again and center my focus. The voices receded and with it, the wild hammering of my heart.

"Let's go," I said. "Take me to the spot where Isherwood was last seen. It's time we got some answers."

20

Glory sat slumped in her chair staring disconsolately at the mountains of correspondence piled on the blotter. From across the room Festus stared at her for several minutes before rolling his eyes, jumping down, and padding over. When he sprang onto the desk, creating an avalanche of envelopes, she didn't even move.

"Pickle," the werecat said, "you gotta snap out of it. You're going green around the gills. Literally."

Tears rolled down Glory's cheeks. "I know," she sniffed, holding up one arm. The sleeve of her sweater drooped loosely over her hand. "I'm shrinking, too. I just can't help it. I'm so upset about what I've done to Rodney. Have you found him yet?"

"No," Festus said, "because I haven't been looking. Rodney's a big boy. If he needs some time to himself, that's his business. I suspect he has a rat man cave in the wall between the storeroom and down here. I think that's where he goes when I forget to put in my dental appliance, and the snoring gets bad."

To Festus' complete horror, Glory burst into a storm of hiccupping, watery gasps. "Please, Dad. Can't you call down to him? Or up to him? Or something? I have to apologize. I just *have* to."

Looking around quickly to make sure they were the only ones in the lair, Festus reached out and patted her arm awkwardly with his paw.

"For Bastet's sake, Pickle," he grumbled, still managing to make the words sound kind. "Stop that caterwauling."

Without warning, Glory threw her arms around him, the sound of her sobbing rising to levels that made the werecat's ears go flat.

"Okay, okay, not into the hugging," Festus said, trying to keep his voice level as he worked to squirm out of her grasp. "Turn loose, Pickle. You're getting my fur wet."

"Oh!" Glory wailed, grabbing a handful of tissues. "I'm so sorry. Let me dry you off."

When she began to scrub at his fur, Festus swatted at her hand, but he didn't extend his claws.

"It's fine. It's *fine*," he assured her. "Just *stop* already. You need those tissues more than I do. Wipe your nose."

Uncertain, but obedient, Glory dabbed at her face. "I'm sorry," she said. "I'm just a total mess."

Working his mouth in barely contained annoyance, Festus said, "Would you please stop apologizing. I get it. You're sorry you hurt Rodney's feelings, and you're sorry you got my fur wet. Message received."

Struggling to regain her composure, Glory said, "What am I going to do, Dad?"

Narrowing his eyes in consternation, Festus asked, "Did you have a father?"

Glory blinked. "Of course I had a father. How else would I have gotten here?"

Drawing on every ounce of patience he could command,

Festus said, "I'm not talking about biology, Pickle. Did you have a *father*?"

"Oh," Glory said, wilting even more. "Not really. He didn't like me very much."

"Why not?"

"He thought I was silly and kind of useless."

The werecat's whiskers twitched. "Okay," he said sternly. "First, your old man sounds like a first class jerk. Second, you are silly, but you're not useless."

Glory's eyes went round with astonishment. "What did you say?"

"Don't make me repeat myself," the werecat said crossly. "Getting it out the first time was bad enough. You are not useless. You do first-rate work with Beau here in the archive. Those columns of yours are . . . not unreadable. You're good for my boy, and well, you're kind of the heart of this family. And don't you *dare* tell anyone I said that or even *suggest* that I read that drivel you spew."

"I won't," Glory said, bobbing her head back and forth earnestly. "No one would believe me anyway."

In spite of himself, Festus chuckled.

"Good one, Pickle," he said. "Now look. Calm down about Rat Boy. You got all wrapped up in a new romance and ditched him for a while. It's nauseating as hell, and you do owe him an apology, but it happens."

Festus turned his head at the sound of Chase's voice somewhere in the stacks. *"Let's get these boxes back to the lair, Beau. I'll come back for the third one by myself."*

Swiveling toward Glory, Festus said, "Wipe your face. Buck up and get back to work. Show my kid what you're really made of — and I mean it, not one word about this conversation or I'll swear up and down you've lost your damn mind."

"But what about Rodney?" Glory whispered.

"If he doesn't show up before bedtime, I'll see what I can do," Festus promised, "but in the meantime, no more crying."

Hopping down from the desk, the werecat loped across the lair on three legs and was lounging nonchalantly on his desk grooming when Chase and the Colonel came in, each carrying heavy boxes of documents.

"Hey, honey!" Chase called out happily. "Wait until you see these scrolls. Barnaby requested them for his *Intro to Magical History* class. These things are ancient."

Hastily putting on her glasses to help hide her red, swollen eyes, Glory said, "I can't wait to look at them, but I have to finish these letters first."

"Are you okay?" Chase asked with concern. "You look at little . . ."

"Green," she sighed. "I know. I think I'm getting a cold. Every time I sneeze I shrink at least an inch. I'm going to talk to Tori about it when she comes down. This is chess club night so she has to keep the store open late."

"Do you want me to go up and ask her for a remedy now?" he said. "I don't mind."

Flashing him a radiant, if damp smile, she said, "I can wait. You all go ahead and start cataloging that stuff. I'll be done here in a little bit, and then we'll work on those documents together."

With that, she reached for a letter opener and plucked the first envelope out of the mess Festus had created. She paused to run her finger over the stamp bearing a portrait of Queen Elizabeth II in profile. Even as upset as she was about Rodney, Glory felt a thrill of excitement knowing she had readers all the way over in England!

Slitting open the thick paper, Glory pulled out a single sheet and started to read. She'd barely finished skimming the words before she shoved her chair back and said, "Oh my goodness gracious, you all need to hear this."

"What?" Chase asked. "Something in that letter?"

Glory nodded. "Yes. Listen to this."

Dear Miss Green,

A few years ago I left a friend named Rodney in Briar Hollow. I am led to believe you are a close personal acquaintance of his. Rodney has been in contact with me, and upon his request, I will be making the journey to the fairy mound within roughly one hour of the time you read these words. The letter has been enchanted to apprise me of its receipt, thus triggering my departure.

As I am not authorized to enter via your portal, please be prepared to grant me access. If you require references regarding my character, I refer you to Siegfried at Claridge's.

I look forward to meeting you and to discussing with you Rodney's history, which he believes must now be communicated to you and your associates.

Best regards, Lucien St. Leger."

When she finished reading, Glory looked up with wide eyes. "*Now* I think you better go get Tori," she said.

Without saying a word, Chase put down the scrolls he had been sorting and disappeared through the passageway to the cobbler shop. After about 20 minutes, he and Tori came down the stairs together.

"How much time do we have before this guy shows up?" she asked from the landing.

Beau took out his pocket watch and stared at the face. "By my best calculations, approximately half an hour."

"Then let's get Siegfried on the line," Tori said, coming down the last few steps and rolling the standing mirror away from the wall. "Festus, you've met him. You make the call."

Festus jumped from his desk to the back of the couch. "I'm

warning you," he said, lifting his paw to start the dialing incantation, "this guy is one uptight brownie."

When the connection coalesced on the silver surface, Festus went out of his way to start the conversation with the most annoying greeting possible while the others listened out of Siegfried's line of sight.

"Siggie!" the werecat cried with overblown enthusiasm. "Long time no meow!"

Other than a slight muscle spasm in one cheek, the brownie's face remained carefully neutral. "Mr. McGregor," he said, "is there something I can do for you?"

"Yeah," Festus said. "We just got a letter from a guy named . . ."

He glanced at Tori off-screen.

"Lucien St. Leger," she said, stepping into the mirror's field of view. "Siegfried, my name is Tori Andrews. I work with the Witch of the Oak."

Unlike his stilted reaction to Festus, Siegfried nodded his head differentially toward her. "I know of you, Madam Andrews. I can vouch for Mr. St. Leger."

"Can you tell me anything about him?" she asked.

The brownie's eyes remained blank. "I think Mr. St. Leger would prefer to explain his position to you in person," he said smoothly. "Is there anything else with which I may assist you this evening?"

His words left no doubt that in his mind, the conversation was over.

"Do you know if Jinx is in the hotel?" Tori asked.

"She is not, Madam," Siegfried replied. "The Witch of the Oak, Mr. Grayson, and that raccoon with whom they associate left this morning to investigate the Tower of Londinium. They have not returned."

"Really," Tori said. "What time is it there anyway?"

"It is 11 p.m., Madam. Do you wish me to convey a message on your behalf?"

"No, thank you, Siegfried. I'll call her later."

"As you wish, Madam."

Festus stuck his head around Tori's elbow and waved a paw. "Quick question before you go, Siggie. Are you still stuffing your own shirts or are you sending them out?"

The brownie's cheek muscle rippled again. "Droll as always, Mr. McGregor," he deadpanned. "Good evening."

Just as the connection was breaking, the words "undisciplined lout" wafted through the mirror.

21

As the women continued to climb, the whole of Tír na nÓg spread out before them. In the skies to the west, flights of dragonlets staged mock battles over a densely wooded forest. The creatures' iridescent scales flashed in the morning air along with the occasional burst of good-natured fire.

"Look at them," Kelly said. "I've never seen so many drag-onlets in one place."

"That is the Never Wood," Bronwyn explained. "The forest is home to the dragonlets and to many other fabled creatures who are neither Fae nor *nonconformi*. It is a place of playful enchant-ment and endless surprises."

"You make it sound like a page from a children's storybook," Gemma said.

Bronwyn laughed. "In many ways it is," she said. "We have no children on Tír na nÓg, but if we did, I imagine it would be quite hard to keep them away from a place as joyously wondrous as the Never Wood."

The group followed the sheer rock face for several minutes

longer. The roaring of the waterfall had grown so intense that conversation was no longer possible. When the trail opened onto a boulder-strewn clearing, the women saw the grandeur of the cascades for the first time.

White plumes poured through Yggdrasil's massive roots turning them into gnarled, living sculptures. The river's thundering voice seemed at odds with the delicate rainbows whispering through the misty clouds.

From their vantage point, which was still low on the cliffs, the group couldn't see the World Tree's trunk, but its massive canopy extended well over the canyon's rim.

Gemma craned her neck upward, shouting to make herself heard. "That," she said, "is one hell of a big tree."

Bronwyn gestured toward the falls, instantly muting their sound.

"Did you just turn off a waterfall?" Gemma asked, glancing over her shoulder toward the river. "Or half of one, at least?"

The preternatural silence surrounding them amplified her words so powerfully, even Katherine flinched.

"No," Bronwyn replied quietly. "I erected a barrier through which the sound may not pass. We still face a considerable climb. I saw no reason to waste our energies shouting at one another."

"Good point," Gemma agreed, looking up again. "So, how big *is* Yggdrasil?"

Bronwyn's gaze followed hers. "No words can do the World Tree justice," she said admiringly. "She is the beating heart of Tír na nÓg, indeed of all the realms. Each of the Mother Trees sprang from her life force. They sprouted in the soil of this island and dwelt together in a grove atop this mountain before the Great Dispersal."

Wiping the sweat from her brow, Gemma asked, "How does

that work, exactly? Yggdrasil is an ash tree. If the Mother Trees are her children, how can they all be different species?"

Myrtle, who had taken a seat on one of the flat rocks, answered. "The energy embodied in Yggdrasil is the source of the infinite diversity of creation," she said. "The expression of that impulse knows no limits. Each of the Great Trees echoes an aspect of the elemental World Tree made manifest."

Kelly's impatient voice interrupted their conversation.

"Look," she said. "I have as much reverence for Yggdrasil as anyone, but that tree up there isn't going anywhere. We can visit her anytime. Why aren't we heading straight to Avalon to meet Jinx and the others?"

Myrtle answered with patient kindness. "Avalon is not a place that can be approached lightly," she said. "Perpetual mists separate the Isle of the Apple Trees from all other realities. The elf queen, Argante, rules there in concert with Viviane, the Lady of the Lake. None but Yggdrasil can grant our access."

The aos si's answer wasn't enough to satisfy Kelly. "If that's true," she said, "then how will Jinx get to Avalon?"

"In the way of the seekers of old," Bronwyn said. "She must go to Glastonbury Tor and enter St. Michael's Tower. If her intent to reach Avalon is pure, she will emerge from the tower into a watery world filled with impenetrable mists. There, a boat will await her steered by no hand she can see. The craft will ferry her to Avalon."

Rather than calm Kelly's maternal instincts, Bronwyn had unwittingly made them worse.

"You mean she'll be alone and unprotected?" Kelly asked. "What about Lucas and the others? She needs them."

This time when Myrtle spoke, her voice carried a note of gentle rebuke. "Enough, Kelly," she said. "You must stop thinking of Jinx as a child. Your daughter is a witch with depths of power she has not yet begun to tap. There is no circumstance under which she can be unprotected."

A storm of conflicting emotions filled Kelly's eyes. "I know about the discovery of true power," she said tightly, "but I also know the crippling effects of self-doubt. You are supposed to be her mentor, Myrtle. How can you just stand by and let her go into an unknown land alone?"

"As her mentor," Myrtle replied. "I understand that Jinx has moved beyond the time when she requires any instruction save the impulse of her heart. Inner wisdom will guide her to Avalon, and that steadying force will put Excalibur in her hand at the moment when she has the greatest need of the weapon."

Kelly threw her hands up in frustration. "How many times do I have to say this?" she cried. "Jinx doesn't know anything about using a sword!"

"You must not limit your thinking," Bronwyn counseled. "We cannot know how Jinx will call Excalibur to her service. The enchantress Viviane gifted Merlin with his magic and forged the blade for him. He used the sword as a means to bring Arthur to the throne, not as a weapon of war. Do not fall into the human trap of equating the most powerful magic with violence. Even a trickle of water will, over time, wear away stone."

Drawing in a steadying breath, Kelly said with forced calm, "Neither one of you have answered my question. Will Jinx travel to Avalon alone?"

"Only one may pass through St. Michael's Tower to seek Avalon's shores," Bronwyn answered. "Jinx will be alone."

Kelly started to say something, but Gemma stopped her.

"Okay," Gemma said to Myrtle, "so Glastonbury Tor is the front door to Avalon, does that mean we're coming in by the back door?"

"It does," the aos si replied, "and that is a door to which only Yggdrasil holds the key."

That information seemed to galvanize Kelly. "Finally!" she said, striding across the clearing to the point where the path continued. "An answer I can live with. Come on. Let's get going."

Gemma looked at Myrtle. "Sorry," she said. "Roanoke Witch or not, she's still a mother."

The aos si nodded, "I, too, am worried about Jinx, but I also have faith that she will reach Avalon unscathed. Once she is there, we will all fight by her side."

"Good," Gemma said, "but for right now, let me see if I can catch up with Mother Hen up there and get her to simmer down."

As Gemma started after Kelly, Bronwyn gestured toward the waterfall, and the roaring of the cascades filled the canyon once again.

Except for whatever private words Kelly and Gemma exchanged, the group didn't speak until they covered the last few steps of the climb and emerged onto a sprawling meadow covering the summit.

A single tree dominated the landscape, one whose scope did, as Bronwyn had warned them, defy both description and imagination. The highest reaches of the leafy crown touched the soft, wispy clouds overhead, while the branches shaded the whole mountaintop. The trunk wrapped into an intricate, swirling braid that conveyed Yggdrasil's great age as well as her indomitable strength and wisdom.

"Wow," Gemma breathed, "you weren't kidding."

"I was not," Bronwyn said. "No matter how many times I cast my eyes upon her, Yggdrasil still takes my breath away." Then, looking more closely, she added, "I believe we are about to receive our official welcome."

There, nestled among the thick roots at the base of the tree lay a medieval city in miniature. Smoke rose from the chimneys of the buildings lining the deeply ridged wood, and lights twinkled in the windows. As the women watched, the gates swung open and the Knights of the Rodere emerged.

They advanced in regimental order, stately rats astride winged fairy horses that stood twelve inches at the shoulder. In the lead, on a chestnut mount a head taller than the rest rode a rat whose shining silver fur glistened under the mid-day sun.

His white muzzle and whiskers betrayed his age, but he sat erect in the saddle, his tail looped regally over one elbow. The shield he held bore a coat of arms with two wheels of blue cheese on the upper left and lower right and fleurs-de-lis in the remaining squares.

As the rat neared the women, he drew his steed to a halt. The miniature horse spread its wings and rose to eye level with Bronwyn.

"Lady Bronwyn," the rat said, "you honor us with your presence. Sir Reginald de Roquefort at your service."

"Sir Reginald," Bronwyn said, "we are here to seek Yggdrasil's guidance on a matter of great importance. We must journey to the Isle of the Apple Trees."

The rat studied her with aged eyes. "Has she returned?" he asked. "Does Morgan le Fay once again assault the forces of virtuous magic?"

"She does," Bronwyn replied. "On Avalon, we will stand with one who possesses the strength to stop her."

Nodding gravely, Reginald said, "The witch, Morgan, and her sisters decimated the ranks of my men with the curse of the Black Death. Long have we dwelt in peace within the roots of the World Tree, but our weapons have not dulled with the passage of time."

Then, turning in the saddle, he called down to his men. "What say you, Knights of the Rodere? Go we this day into battle by the side of the Lady Bronwyn?"

They answered with their voices and with their upraised

swords, as one after another the fairy steeds took to the air until the whole of the Rodere army floated amassed at their leader's back.

"Lady Bronwyn," Sir Reginald said, "the Rodere are yours to command."

22

Kyle sat cross-legged on the couch with a remote control box in his hands. "Okay guys, check this out. Keep your eyes on your computer screens."

On the floor in front of him, a robotic vehicle with tank-like treads sprang to life. "Little Geek is on the case!" Kyle crowed as he manipulated one of the joysticks.

"Hippy," Nick said automatically, "you're going to give that rat a disease."

Mindy glared at them both. "You're just doing that because you think I've never seen *The Abyss*, but you are both wrong."

"Okay, okay," Kyle said his eyes glued to his laptop screen. "Mindy racked up cool points. Go you. Now *watch*."

The ROV lumbered across the living room and disappeared into the hallway. On their screens, the trio watched through the machine's cameras as Kyle guided the vehicle remotely through the downstairs rooms of the Pike house.

"We have a serious dust bunny issue in this house," Mindy said, leaning forward to get a better look as the ROV trundled past a bench in the hall. "Either of you two geniuses ever vacuum *under* the furniture when it's your turn to do the floors?"

Kyle looked up. "Why move the furniture?" he asked seriously. "It's not like we're walking under that stuff."

Rolling her eyes, Mindy said, "Never mind. You've proved to us this ROV thing works. Now explain to us why you blew our budget buying the darn thing without even asking."

Steering the ROV back into the room, Kyle looped the vehicle through a series of slow doughnuts before bringing it to a stop at Mindy's feet.

"This," he said triumphantly, "is the official HBH Sewer Rover."

Nick started at the ROV thoughtfully. "You want to send it down in the storm drain in front of The Witch's Brew to find out where that glitter came from, don't you?"

"Exactamundo!" Kyle said. "Am I brilliant or what?"

Before Nick could answer, Mindy said, "I vote for 'or what.'"

"Come on!" Kyle whined, looking crestfallen. "How can this *not* be a good idea?"

"How *can* it be a *good* idea?" she demanded. "These people almost sued us for invasion of privacy, defamation of character, slander, and a whole boatload of other scary legal stuff because you got all snap happy with your camera."

"I know that," he said, "but the storm drain belongs to the City of Briar Hollow and Howie says it's fine."

Mindy's jaw dropped. "You think this is a good plan because the *dead* mayor gave you permission? That's assuming that GhostFish *is* the dead mayor."

"Well, yeah," Kyle said. "He said he still has the authority. Let me read you the email."

Digging his phone out of his pocket and thumbing through his messages, Kyle read, "'I was never voted out of office. Since I was murdered, all subsequent elections are null and void. Dead or not, I am still the only duly elected chief executive of this town.'"

"Lord," Mindy groaned, "if that is the ghost of Howard McAlpin, he really is dumber than dirt. He's *dead*, Kyle. Dead wins over elected. Trust me on this one. Back me up here, Nick."

Instead of answering her immediately, Nick stared thoughtfully at the ROV. "At most, the city might hit us with a fine," he said slowly, "and it would be really interesting to figure out the source of that glitter."

"Oh my God. You, too?" Mindy said. "Am I the only one around here who isn't certifiable?"

Nick looked at her and grinned. "You know you want an answer as much as we do, you just think you have to be the responsible one. Newsflash. You don't."

In spite of her best efforts not to, Mindy grinned back. "Well," she said, going for an *Abyss* line. "'It's not easy being a cast iron bitch.'"

"Yes!" Kyle said, pumping his fist in the air.

"*One* time," Mindy said. "We put that thing down in the storm drain *one* time. Under cover of darkness — and if we get caught, I don't know either one of you."

BRENNA WALKED beside me as we moved toward the prison's interior. I could feel her stabilizing magic wrapped around me like a protective cloak.

"Not that I'm complaining," I said, "but what are you doing to me?"

"Allowing you the opportunity to find your equilibrium," she replied, "by allaying your fear of drowning in the flood of sensations you just experienced."

Even the mention of the words "drowning" and "flood" triggered a fresh surge of panic, which I drove back with a series of deep, slow breaths.

"I've never been hit with that much information in a vision," I told her. "I think it's because visiting Tír na nÓg did something to me."

The sorceress studied me keenly. "Have you experienced other changes in your magic since returning?" she asked.

Coming clean about everything suddenly seemed like a far better option than risking another techno-color trip into an alternative reality.

"I had a spontaneous vision when I was writing in my grimoire night before last," I said. "My pen drew a highly detailed image of a sword. I wasn't touching either the pen or the book when it happened."

Brenna came to a full stop. "What kind of sword?" she asked with more urgency in her voice than I liked to hear.

"Judging from a painting Lucas and I saw in the British Museum last night," I said, "it was Excalibur."

In response to that news, the sorceress muttered something that I could have sworn was "catfish witch."

Figuring the last thing I needed to deal with were wand-waving channel cats, I pressed for more details.

"Excuse me?" I said. "What did you say?"

Brenna repeated the word, which still sounded like "catfish witch" to my ears. Now I know that what she said "Caledfwlch."

It's the Welsh name for Excalibur, but instead of clearing up my confusion, Brenna made it worse in the next breath by calling the sword "Merlin's blade."

"Hold on," I said, "didn't Excalibur belong to King Arthur?"

"The elves of Avalon forged Caledfwlch and crafted its scabbard under Merlin's direction long before Arthur's birth," she explained. "In Arthur's hand, the sword could not be broken and so long as he wore its scabbard he would not bleed from wounds sustained in battle."

Far back in the dim shadows of my awareness an innate

knowledge of Excalibur stirred from slumber and whispered, "*There's more.*"

"What else can the sword do?" I asked.

Brenna looked at me curiously. "That can only be answered by the one whose hand grasps its hilt," she said. "The magic marries itself to the power of the sword bearer. In what setting did your pen place Caledfwlch?"

"It didn't," I said. "The drawing was only the sword, nothing else." Then, pausing for a beat, I dropped my voice a little and asked, "Have you felt any change in your magic since we went to Tír na nÓg?"

"No," Brenna said, "but my abilities stabilized centuries ago. Yours are still in flux, so naturally, you would be more susceptible to the effects of exposure to the island's intuitive atmosphere."

I'll admit I had no idea what she meant by that, but I could feel Lucas' worried eyes on me as he listened to our conversation.

Resolving to take the topic back up with Brenna later, I grinned at him and said, "If you keep frowning like that, your face will freeze, and I'll have to get another boyfriend."

That was all the opening line Rube needed.

"Just say the word, Doll," he chimed in, "and I'll fix you right up. You ever thought about dating a leprechaun? I know they're on the short side, and they got a thing for rainbows, but you could do worse than hooking up with a short dude who banks his gold in pots."

Lucas took a swipe in Rube's direction, which the raccoon dodged with a drop and roll. "Whoa!" he said, springing up on his back paws and dancing playfully. "Down low! Too slow!"

High-level special ops team or not, there are those moments when I feel like I've been dropped into a low budget movie about Fae frat boys. But they make me laugh, which is exactly what I needed at that moment.

"Okay, you two. Knock it off. You," I said, pointing at Lucas, "stop with the worrying, and thanks but no thanks on the leprechaun. Let's get back to business."

First, we questioned the gargoyle guard who had been on duty during the escape. He offered to take us to Isherwood's cell and then to the courtyard via the same route he'd used that day with his prisoner.

There was nothing remarkable about the adjoining rooms where Isherwood had been confined: a spartan cot, writing table, and armless chair by a meager coal grate. A few books sat lined up along the windowsill along with a portrait of a woman in a small, oval frame.

When I picked up the personal memento to have a closer look, Lucas said, "That's his wife. Thomasine Isherwood. She's been in seclusion since his arrest."

"A possible accomplice?" I asked.

"No," Brenna replied. "I know Thomasine. She is a gentle woman who has suffered long at the mercies of her husband's ambitions. Whatever happened here, Thomasine had no hand in it."

We followed the guard down a narrow hallway that stopped at an oak door. The gargoyle took a ring of keys from his belt and put one in the blacked iron lock.

In the movies, the hinges would have squealed dramatically, but instead, the heavy door swung open smoothly. The Tower might look ancient, but the facility was well maintained.

The instant I stepped into the inner courtyard, a raven cawed on the wall over my head. When I looked up, the bird refused to meet my eyes, skittering quickly out of sight.

Siegfried's words came back to me.

"Consider, Madam, that your efforts might best be focused on

identifying the person who does not wish to see Isherwood stand trial rather than on the wizard himself. Think also on the words of Lucius Annaeus Seneca."

I was almost certain the brownie wanted me to talk to a particular raven in Blackfriars, not take up reading Roman philosophy. Seeing the big black birds perched in strategic spots around the Tower seemed entirely too coincidental given that piece of advice.

"Rube," I said, "are you too hungover to climb up there and have a chat with our feathered friend?"

The raccoon stabbed at his chest with his paw and staggered melodramatically. "You wound me, Doll. I ain't never been *too* hungover in my life. I'm a professional sauce hound."

"Duly noted," I said. "Please go find out why that raven is so nervous."

23

As Siegfried's face faded from view, Festus cracked up laughing. "Man," he said, wiping at his eyes with his paw. "I *love* getting to that guy. Rube and I had a *blast* giving him crap when we were in Londinium. Do you know he uses a freaking *comb* to make sure the rug fringe is straight?"

"You two must have done a real number on him judging from the 'undisciplined lout' crack," Tori said.

The werecat snorted. "He'd never admit it, but I'm telling you, Siggie thought we were great. Who wouldn't love the stinking gutter rat and me? We're the life of the party!"

"We've all seen your idea of being the life of the party, Dad," Chase said. "You're usually not happy until you pass out on the pool table with your paws in the air."

"Says the guy who gets excited about a game of chess," Festus said, rolling his eyes. "You never saw the day you could hold your booze like your old man, and you know it."

Chase shrugged. "You've got me there, but no one has ever seen *me* hanging my head over the litter box begging Bastet to take me and relieve my suffering either."

"*That*," Festus said, "is a total lie. I do my barfing in the house plants."

Tori held up her hands in the "time out" sign.

"I, for one, don't want to sit here debating the location merits of cat barf," she said. "Let's get back on track. Where's Rodney? He should be here when this St. Leger guy arrives."

Casting a sidelong glance at Glory, Festus said, "We haven't seen him since last night."

Tori's eyes went wide. "You haven't seen him. At *all*? Why didn't you go looking for him?"

"Because he's a grown rat and he's entitled to his own life," Festus retorted. "Besides, he's got a beef with the Pickle, and we think he's just taking some time for himself."

At that, Glory broke into hiccupping sobs as bilious green waves undulated over her complexion and her sweater seemed to grow two sizes.

"Okay, okay, calm down," Tori said hastily, taking a seat on the couch beside the sobbing woman. "Chase, get me a glass of water and look in the cabinet behind my work table. Bring me the blue bottle on the top shelf. The one labeled '*Viridi et Abierunt.*'"

Beau repeated the Latin words silently to himself and then said, in a puzzled voice, "Green Be Gone?"

"I had to call the potion something," Tori said. "I used Latin because in English 'green be gone' sounds like weed killer."

In response, Glory wailed at the top of her lungs, "I *am* a weed. A terrible, horrible, awful, weed choking out the pretty flowers. A big old bunch of grass burrs is a better friend than me."

Completely perplexed by the outburst, Tori looked at Festus. "Translation?" she asked.

"Pickle ditched Rat Boy without so much as a kiss my

gherkin when she took up with my kid, and now she feels bad about it," the werecat replied.

Chase came back with the water, and the bottle as Glory's sobs increased in volume and intensity. Handing both to Tori, he sat down on Glory's other side and put his arm around her shoulder.

"Honey," he soothed, "you have to stop crying. We'll fix everything with Rodney. I promise."

Looking over at Tori, he added, "Will that stuff take care of the size issue, too?"

"It should," she replied, "as long as she doesn't get any more upset."

Uncorking the bottle, Tori carefully poured two drops of the potion into the water, looked at Glory, and poured two more. The liquid bubbled and a thin tendril of smoke curled off the surface.

She held the glass out to Glory. "Drink this," she ordered. "All of it."

The overwrought woman did as she was told, pausing between swallows to take shuddering breaths. By the time she finished the glass, the green waves had retreated behind her ears, which also began to fade to normal.

"Better?" Tori asked, reaching for the glass.

Glory nodded. "Greenwise, yes," she said, "but I'm still an awful, awful, *awful* person."

Chase tightened his arm around her shoulders. "No, you're not. We'll both have a talk with Rodney. I owe him an apology, too. I'm just as guilty as you are."

Festus, who had disappeared up the stairs during Glory's de-greening session, came padding back down. "I checked the storeroom," he announced, pushing off the last step and jumping onto his desk. "No Rat Boy."

Addressing the air around her, Tori called out, "Darby?"

The brownie popped into view. "Yes, Mistress Tori?"

"Have you seen Rodney, today?"

"No, Mistress," Darby said. "I haven't seen him since he left with Mistress Jinx and the others for Londinium."

Stunned silence greeted his announcement.

"There is no way Jinx let Rodney go with them to Londinium," Tori said.

"Oh, no," Darby replied brightly. "Rodney hid in her backpack before they stepped through the portal."

"And you did not think it wise to mention this to any of us?" Beau asked.

Darby's face fell. "If I have made an error I am sorry, Mistress," he said, looking earnestly at Tori. "I did not realize Rodney was not allowed to lead his life as he pleased.

Tori put her head in her hands. "Nobody is saying Rodney can't lead his life," she said, slowly and with emphasis, "and no, you're not in error. We're just worried about him."

Glory sniffed loudly. "If Rodney isn't here," she said, "and Jinx doesn't know he's there, where is he?"

Ignoring her convoluted phrasing, Beau said, "Were I to hazard a guess, I would say he will be arriving shortly in the company of Mr. St. Leger."

"Which is what we should be concentrating on," Tori said. "Festus, do you know anything about how Rodney came to Briar Hollow? You were the first person to find him, right?"

"Yeah," the werecat said. "It was a Sunday morning. I went out to take a sunbath, and there he was in his cage on the front doorstep."

"Was there a note?"

"No. " the werecat replied. "Fiona came out to get the paper, took one look at Rodney, went all gaga over him, and adopted him on the spot."

Behind them, the warning bell on the Londinium portal sounded.

"Okay then," Tori said. "Showtime."

They all moved to stand in in a loose semi-circle a few feet in front of the opening while Glory remained in the lair.

As Tori spoke the final word of the welcome incantation, a trim, gray-haired man in an antique, double-breasted greatcoat stepped through the pulsating membrane with Rodney perched on his shoulder.

"Good evening," the man said. "Are you Miss Glory Green?"

"No, I'm Tori Andrews. This is Chase McGregor, Colonel Beauregard T. Longworth, and Festus McGregor."

Bowing from the waist, the man said, "Lucien St. Leger, at your service." Then, looking beyond the group and into the lair, he added, "Miss Green, I assume?"

Glory answered in a squeaky voice. "That's me."

"Sir Rodney speaks highly of you," Lucien assured her. "He was most insistent that I come here and discuss his situation with you."

"Let's sit down," Tori said. "Welcome home, Rodney."

Answering with a wave of his paw, the rat ran down Lucien's arm. The man bent and allowed Rodney to jump to the floor where he went straight to Festus and held up his paw.

The werecat returned the "high paw" with a grin. "Gone walkabout, did you?"

Rodney nodded and pointed to the cat's shoulder.

"Sure," Festus said, "you can have a lift. No fur pulling."

In the lair, the werecat went to his favorite place on the hearth, allowing Rodney to step off on the bricks first.

"Hi, Rodney," Glory said, already on the verge of tears. "It's nice to see you."

Although he chose to stay by Festus on the hearth, Rodney gave Glory a half-hearted wave. A single tear rolled down Glory's face, and she shrank back into the circle of Chase's arm when he joined her on the sofa.

Lucien, who had taken one of the leather wingback chairs, said, "Rodney visited me in Londinium because he feels the time has come for all of you to understand the truth about his origins. As the seneschal of his order, he felt I was in the best position to tell the story. Are you aware of the existence of the Knights of the Rodere?"

An hour later, when he'd finished his narrative, the group in the lair sat in complete silence until Festus slapped Rodney on the shoulder with his paw and said, "Six hundred and sixty-four? You don't look a day over 450."

Ducking the blow, Rodney grinned and stuck out his tongue at the werecat.

From the sofa, Glory said, "Oh, Rodney. The way you lost your parents. I'm just so, so sorry. About everything. About the way I just let myself forget about you. About *everything*. Can you possibly forgive me?"

He crossed his paws and stared at her as if considering the question.

"Come on Sir Rat Boy," Festus said. "Let the Pickle off the hook."

Rodney's whiskers twitched, and then he did a swift Elvis move, ending with questioning eyes trained on Glory.

"An Elvis movie?" she said hopefully. "I would *love* to watch an Elvis movie with you. Anyone you want. And we'll do pizza and popcorn. Burgers. Hot dogs. You pick."

The rat pointed at Chase and raised his eyebrows.

"I'm invited, too?" Chase said. "Really?"

Launching off the hearth, Rodney landed on the sofa and held out his paw to Chase, who shook it delicately.

"So we're good?" Chase asked.

Rodney nodded and gave him the thumbs up.

"I think we all owe you an apology, Rodney," Tori said. "We completely underestimated you. Why didn't you ever try to tell us before?"

Lucien cleared his throat. "I believe I can answer that question," he said. "Rodney regards you all as his family. He's quite happy here and wishes to remain in Briar Hollow, but first, he must go to Tír na nÓg and confer with Yggdrasil."

"That doesn't sound good," Tori said. "Does this have something to do with Reynold Isherwood?"

"Only indirectly," Lucien replied. "The greater threat lies with Morgan le Fay."

Festus, who had been grooming his whiskers, stopped in mid-lick.

"Oh *crap*," he said. "That's the part that isn't good. Now we've got problems."

24

Bronwyn accepted the Rodere's pledge of fealty with gracious dignity. "You honor me, Sir Reginald," she said. "Surely we will not fail in our purpose with such gallant knights by our side. Now, time grows short. We must speak with Yggdrasil."

"Allow me to personally escort you to the audience chamber," the rat offered.

He shifted his weight in the saddle, forcing the fairy horse to flap its wings vigorously to remain level. Reginald's whiskers quivered in the breeze.

Raising his voice, he called to one of his lieutenants. "Mandrake, post sentries at the approaches to the World Tree."

A sleek black rat pulled on the reins of his mount. The horse reared and wheeled in place. "On me, my lads!" he called. Then, spurring his steed forward, he shot across the plateau as groups of the Rodere peeled from the ranks and flew after him.

Sir Reginald remained at Bronwyn's shoulder as the women advanced toward the World Tree.

"There has to be a punch line in this set up somewhere," Gemma whispered to Kelly.

"What do you mean?" Kelly whispered back.

In a bad Groucho Marx voice, Gemma said, "A flying rat, a vampire, and two witches walk up to a tree . . ."

Myrtle and Katherine heard the remark. The baobhan sith laughed outright, but Myrtle said wistfully, "Julius was a lovely man."

Gemma and Kelly exchanged a puzzled look.

"Who?" Gemma asked.

"Julius Marx," Myrtle said. "Groucho was such a silly stage name, but he and his brothers were quite the comedic sensations in 1930s Hollywood."

Thunderstruck, Kelly said, "*Wait.* You're telling us you were hanging out in Hollywood during the Golden Age? You know we're both crazy about that period. Why haven't you ever told us this before? Who else did you know?"

With teasing good humor, Myrtle said, "A lady does not divulge the details of her assignations."

Gemma looked like she wanted to choke. "*Assignations?* With Hollywood movie stars? Myrtle! Come on! *Talk!*"

As she spoke, a dense curtain of shade fell over the group.

"We will have to resume this conversation at a more apropos time," Myrtle replied. "We are now beneath the canopy of the World Tree."

"You are not getting out of this," Gemma warned. "We *are* going to finish this conversation."

"Yes," Myrtle agreed, "we will, but a more important exchange lies before us."

Sir Reginald gestured toward Yggdrasil. "In a crevice at the base of the trunk, you will find a room where you may commune with the spirit of the Tree in complete privacy. Pose your questions. Air your concerns. Wait for Her wisdom to enter your minds."

"Thank you," Bronwyn said. "We hope, in short order, to begin a journey to Avalon."

The rat's face betrayed no reaction, but one paw came to rest reflexively on the hilt of his sword. "My men and I will be ready, Lady Bronwyn."

With that, he flew toward the Rodere city leaving the women alone to cross the remaining yards to the World Tree.

Standing outside the dark split in the trunk, Gemma said, "We're supposed to just walk inside a tree?"

"No harm will befall us in the heart of Yggdrasil," Bronwyn said, "but if you wish, you may remain here."

Gemma shook her head. "No, I'm good. A little claustrophobic, but good."

Bronwyn moved into the opening first, with the others following in single file. They crept forward in total darkness for several seconds before emerging into a circular chamber illuminated by an otherworldly glow.

Roots rose up from the floor to greet them, weaving themselves into chairs cushioned with verdant, thick leaves.

At a nod from Myrtle, they each claimed a seat. The light in the room changed as an ancient, wise, and innately benevolent presence made itself felt. In the center of the space, an image of the World Tree in miniature formed.

A resonant voice asked, "How fares the aos si?"

Myrtle allowed her full powers to flow freely. Golden light suffused her form, and her face took on the ethereal radiance of eternal youth. "I fare well, Mother of All Trees," she said, "and I am overjoyed to be with you once again."

"Many seasons have come and gone since you were born in the roots of my Daughter Oak," Yggdrasil said. "We are glad you are once again restored to your natural form. What seek you?"

"Permission to enter Avalon," Myrtle replied.

The scent of apples filled the air. "With the reemergence of

Tír na nÓg in the consciousness of the Fae, old ambitions stir," the Tree said.

"They do," Myrtle agreed. "The Wand of Merlin lies safely hidden, but Morgan le Fay thinks to gain the wizard's sword on Avalon. She will come here next in search of the cup."

Yggdrasil breathed a heavy sigh. "Long did Morgan study with Merlin, but like her brother, she failed to understand."

"That ignorance will drive her to assault the peace of this sanctuary," Myrtle warned, "but forces align to send the Witch of the Oak to Avalon. If her heart is true, she will find a way through the mists, and we will meet her on the Isle of the Apple Trees."

"Fear not," Yggdrasil answered. "Already she travels across the smokey waters."

No longer able to contain her anxiety, Kelly asked, "What does that mean?" Then remembering herself, she added, "Forgive my forwardness, Mother of All Trees. I fear for the safety of my child."

"Do not still your voice, Servant of the Rowan and the Oak," The Tree replied. "I know well the cares of a mother. Your daughter travels through the mists that shroud Avalon. She is safe and well."

"Then may we join her?" Kelly asked.

"Yes," Yggdrasil replied. "Sir Reginald and his knights will lead you to the place of passage. The Witch of the Oak will face a test on the shores of Avalon to which you must all play witness."

With that, the abiding essence of the World Tree retreated. When the women stood, the leaves and roots sank back into the floor leaving them in an empty room.

"Guess that's our cue to get a move on," Gemma said.

As they exited the audience chamber, Bronwyn said, "The Knights of the Rodere will lead us to St. Gabriel's Tower, the gateway to the shores of the lake on whose waters we will reach Avalon."

"Can you explain these towers to me?" Kelly asked. "Jinx went through St. *Michael's* Tower. Now we're going to Gabriel's Tower. Both of those names belong to archangels."

"In the human Christian cosmology, that is true," Myrtle said, "but Michael and Gabriel, like their brothers Raphael, Uriel, Selaphiel, Jegudiel, and Barachiel are powerful beings who guard places of transition."

Counting on her fingers, Gemma said, "Does that mean there are five more gates to Avalon?"

"It means there are seven towers," Myrtle said, "but where they lead relates directly to the journey in need of completion. In this instance, the path wends to Avalon."

A few feet from the gate of the sprawling Rodere city they stopped to admire the rows of orderly homes arranged on the terraced roots of the World Tree. From their vantage point, the women could look down into a bustling city market where rats of all ages plied their goods from carts and canopied stalls.

Some of the city's residents turned their heads to look up at the visitors looming over their home, but none showed any sign of fear or apprehension. In an open field in the center of the city, young rats chased a ball through an intricate maze. Beyond that, knights drilled on a parade ground and fairy horses stirred in their corral.

"I've never seen anything like this," Kelly said. "There must be hundreds of them."

"Thousands," Katherine corrected her. "I hear the beating of their hearts. There are many more of these creatures deep within the roots of the tree and in the ground below."

As they watched, Sir Reginald emerged from one of the houses accompanied by a female rat with soft gray fur and white ear tips. She touched noses with the grizzled old warrior and held his paw in hers for a long moment.

When they parted, Reginald walked to his horse without looking back, swung into the saddle, and lifted into the air. He climbed toward where the women stood, reining up in front of Bronwyn.

"Are we ready, m'lady?" he asked.

"We are," she replied.

"The distance is not great to St. Gabriel's Tower," Reginald said. "We do not anticipate trouble along the way and in Avalon, your powers will take precedence over our skills. My primary concern lies in guarding the World Tree. The bulk of my troops have been assigned to that task. We will be accompanied by my second in command, Sir Cedric Wingard and his adjutant Sir Forest de Winter. They will meet us beyond the city where the road forks. Shall we?"

He gestured to a path that led past the Rodere city and away from Yggdrasil. As the group began to walk again, Bronwyn said, "Was the lady of whom you took your leave your wife?"

Reginald smiled. "Yes. My Millicent. It has been many centuries since we have been forced to part from one another on the eve of a perilous mission. She was not happy to learn that I am going to Avalon."

"We have every good intention of returning you to her safely," Bronwyn replied.

The rat smiled. "Do you know the writings of Saint Bernard of Clairvaux?" he asked.

"*L'enfer est plein de bonnes volontés ou désirs,*" Bronwyn quoted with a droll smile.

"*Exactement,*" Reginald agreed as they both laughed.

"How about a translation for those of us who didn't pass French in high school?" Gemma asked.

Myrtle answered, "I believe the modern translation would be 'the road to hell is paved with good intentions.'"

"Oh, great!" Gemma muttered. "Just what I wanted to hear."

Beyond the fork in the road where they were joined by Reginald's officers, the group walked for half an hour before a lone tower appeared on the horizon. It looked like the ruined remnant of a medieval church, with sky showing through the windows. There was no roof, and the single open entry was mirrored on the opposite side by an identical exit.

A smooth clearing encircled the structure. The women and the rats stopped there and studied the building.

"What now?" Kelly asked. "Are we going to open a portal?"

"No," Myrtle said. "We will pass straight through the Tower and emerge in a shadowed place far different from this sunny plain. Are you all ready?"

"Why not?" Gemma said, stepping up first to enter the tower. As she passed under the door's lintel, she said, in a sing-song voice. "Follow the yellow brick road."

25

A fter Rube went off to talk to the nervous raven, I looked at Brenna. "Take down your cloaking magic," I said. "I need to experience whatever happened here."

"Jinx, are you sure about this?" Lucas asked. "You don't know how to control this aspect of your psychometry yet."

"I don't want to control it," I told him. "I want to set it free. If Isherwood escaped, I should be able to see how. If something else went down, we need to know what. It's not like I'm trying this alone. If I get in trouble, Brenna will pull me out, right?"

The sorceress nodded. "Correct," she said. "I do not like the experiment either, Lucas, but it will be the fastest way to get to the truth. My senses tell me that powerful magic has been worked in this courtyard in spite of the dampening spells that guarded Isherwood."

From the way Lucas shoved his fedora back on his head and scrubbed at his forehead, I knew he wasn't happy. We run the special ops unit as a team of equals, but when you get right down to it, as one of the Women of the Craobhan, I outrank Lucas in just about every way possible — but then there's the matter of our relationship.

As my boyfriend, he could have asked me to stop, which would have put me in a horrible position, but we both knew he wouldn't do that. Lucas is a fast learner. He'd watched the mistakes Chase made with me and had no intention of repeating them.

When I held out my hand to him, Lucas intertwined his fingers with mine. "I have to find out," I told him quietly, "and you have to let me, so let's not do this, okay?"

"Okay," he relented, tightening his grasp, "but for the record, I am not happy."

"Duly noted," I said, bringing our joined hands to my lips and kissing his knuckles.

He released me and moved several steps away. Brenna raised a questioning eyebrow. When I nodded, she dropped the soothing blanket of magic that had been protecting me from the impressions stored in the prison's stone walls.

My vision dimmed to gray before resetting in disjointed sepia tones. Reynold Isherwood stood facing a woman who wore a black cloak. I could feel pulses of fear mixed with a sort of wary arrogance vibrating from the wizard. He was afraid of the woman, but still believed he could gain the upper hand with her.

When her crimson lips curved into a seductive, menacing smile, I couldn't deny her beauty, but unlike Brenna and Greer whose appeal pulsates with an undercurrent of life and vivacity, I knew instantly the figure in my vision had ice water in her veins.

An impression that completely fit with her eyes — eyes so blue, I could have been looking into the faceted depths of twin sapphires.

She seemed to issue an order to Isherwood. He reluctantly began to walk beside her, and I followed. I didn't find out until later that I did start moving around the courtyard while Brenna and Lucas shadowed me cautiously.

I couldn't hear what the two figures in my vision were saying, but I did hear the woman laugh. The sound echoed — a lilting knife's edge of pitiless mirth that made me cringe in tandem with the image of Reynold Isherwood standing just a few feet away.

He stepped back, but there was nowhere to run. The dampening spell worked against him, but it didn't stop the woman who casually summoned a ball of energy in the palm of her hand. When she hurled it at her victim, an envelope of flame engulfed the renegade wizard.

That's when I lost control.

The heat wrenched a choking cough from my throat and seared my skin. Crying out, I fell to my knees, writhing against the flames. My lungs hovered on the brink of exploding when a cool rush of water swept over me. I felt Brenna's hands on my shoulders.

"Jinx," she said urgently, "whatever you are seeing it is not real. Release the vision!"

The strength of the command woke me up. I found myself on my knees staring into Brenna's searching gaze.

"There you are," she said. "Breathe slowly. Allow the energy to dissipate."

Over her shoulder, I saw Lucas. He stood rigid with his hands balled into fists by his side.

"I'm fine," I told him, meeting his eyes. "It's all right. I'm not hurt."

He nodded tightly, forcing himself to set his personal concerns aside and tend to business. "What did you see?"

"Isherwood," I replied, letting Brenna help me to my feet. "There was a woman here, with black hair and ice-blue eyes — and a long black cloak. She killed him. She killed Isherwood."

Behind me, paws scampered over the flagstones. "According to the ravens, she fried that guy like chicken for Sunday dinner," Rube said, looking up at me. "You good, Doll?"

I nodded and answered in language the raccoon would appreciate. "Five by five."

A toothy grin split his face. "Primo," he said, "cause you gotta talk to this bird. Name of Munin. Jumpy. Uncomfortable in his feathers, but he's got a story to tell. Them birds just sit up there all day watching what goes on. He saw everything. All of 'em did, but he's the only one willing to squawk."

"Why is he willing to talk to me?" I asked.

"'Cause he's got instructions to talk," Rube said. "That Seneca guy over in Blackfriars told him you'd come to the Tower looking for answers."

Lucas, who had now jammed his hands in his pockets, said, "Do we have any reason to believe this Munin?"

Rube danced back and forth a couple of times weighing what he was going to say next.

"It's possible I *might* of got a lead in Lundenwic last night," he admitted, "that corri-ob-er-rates what this raven is saying."

"Corroborates," Lucas said.

"What?" Rube asked. "We got an echo in here? I said that already."

Rolling his eyes, Lucas said, "Go on."

"Well," the raccoon continued, "If I *did* talk to someone at The Crooked Critter, which I ain't confirming I did, it's possible that what that imaginary person told me points us in the same direction."

So, all roads lead to Seneca in Blackfriars.

"Let's talk to this Munin," I said. "Preferably here on the ground."

Rube turned around and put his fingers in his mouth, letting out an impressive whistle. Above us on the wall, one of the ravens fidgeted indecisively on his perch.

"You know who I am," I called out, "and I am *not* having a good day. Believe me when I tell you that you don't want to make me climb up there. I think there's a recipe for raven soup in my grimoire."

The bird stopped his anxious pacing and appeared to make a decision. Spreading his broad black wings, he glided smoothly downward and nailed a perfect landing in front of us, immediately dipping his beak toward the grass.

"Witch of the Oak," he said. "I am your faithful servant, Munin."

"Tell her what you told me," Rube prodded.

The bird's black eyes flitted toward its compatriots on the ramparts. "My friends believe I should keep my silence. They fear the Goddess of the Crows."

"Let me guess," I said. "Blue eyes, black hair, black cape, black heart?"

The raven nodded nervously. "She killed Reynold Isherwood," he said. "Breaking with our tradition, I left the Tower and carried the news to one who knows the story far better than I. You will find him in . . ."

I finished the thought for the bird.

"A key shop down a dark alley in Blackfriars."

Lucas wanted to go back to IBIS headquarters and check in with Otto. I didn't.

"Whoever this Goddess of the Crows is," I said, "she doesn't know we're on to her. If we tell Otto, he tells your uncle, who tells Hilton Barnstable, and then the whole Fae world knows. We'll completely lose the element of surprise."

We were standing just outside the main gate of the Tower. Rube had scaled the chest high wall so he wouldn't have to crane his neck to talk to us.

"I like the way you think, Doll," he said. "We got like autoimmunity with the special ops team, right?"

Shaking his head, Lucas said, "I think you mean autonomy."

"Whatever," the raccoon replied, "we don't got to ask nobody permission to do nothing, right?"

Lucas nodded — reluctantly.

"Then we find this crow dame and put her out of commission," Rube said. "We come out smelling like heroes."

"Roses," Lucas said, "we come out smelling like *roses*. Do you have to mangle words and mix metaphors?"

Completely nonplussed, Rube said, "I ain't never met Phor, much less mixed with her. I'm trying to talk English here, Elf Boy. Work with me."

"Let's just save the grammar lesson for later," I interjected. "Rube and I are in agreement. What do you say, Brenna?"

The sorceress shook her head. "I am not a member of the special ops team."

"You are on this mission," I said. "You get a vote."

"All I will say for the moment is that I do believe we should talk to this raven, Seneca," the sorceress answered. "There is only one being known as the Goddess of the Crows. If she is the one with whom we are dealing, I do not know what our next course of action may be."

It wasn't like Brenna to withhold information. Since her return from the In Between, she had insisted on complete transparency in her dealings with us on all levels.

"You know who this woman is?" I asked.

"I *think* I know," she corrected me, "and I do not wish to say until we speak with Seneca."

We took that as our cue to go talk to a bird.

Nothing about the shop had changed since my last visit. The buildings in the dark alley still threatened to topple into one another. No bell rang when I pushed open the door. But one thing was the same.

Seneca sat on the counter obviously waiting for us.

"So," he said, turning his head to focus on us with one obsidian eye, "you've found your way back to me. I assume you have not, however, found Reynold Isherwood."

"No, we haven't," I said, "but you knew that already. Can we just skip all the double-talk and get to the point?"

Behind me, I heard the door open and felt a familiar surge of power. "Hi, Greer," I said, still staring at the raven. "How was Vegas?"

"Illuminating," the baobhan sith answered. "Fer Dorich told me Reynold Isherwood is dead. He prefaced the information with an intriguing statement. He told me 'every bird loves to hear himself sing.'"

Seneca hopped from the counter to the top of the cash register and said, "Ravens do not sing."

"But you do talk," Lucas said, "and we'd appreciate it if you'd *talk* about someone called the Goddess of the Crows."

"She does not like that name," Seneca said, "but exercising control over the lives of others? Morgan le Fay revels in that."

26

The Key Man was nowhere to be seen, so we followed the raven into the shop's backroom. The light from the fire caught the bottles and tools littered across the benches and stacked on the shelves.

Lurid, distorted shadows played across the walls while the steady beat of a sudden downpour against the windowpane provided a rhythmic bass line to Seneca's story.

Rube took one look at the setting, and I saw that thieving look in his eye. Raccoons are natural born acquisitors. Leaning down, I whispered in his ear, "No pilfering. Anything you shoplift out of here might turn you into a toad, and that's looking on the bright side. Keep your paws to yourself."

Caution and self-preservation won out over greed. He promptly backed himself up to the hearth, sat down, and listened to the conversation without saying a word. That didn't keep his eyes from roaming around the room, but he behaved himself.

Seneca and I sat down on opposite sides of the worktable. The raven talked. I listened.

Even after the things he shared with us that day, I can't say that I know Seneca's true identity. I can almost guarantee, however, that he didn't start life with feathers and a beak.

You see, he was there. In Camelot.

He knew them. All of them.

Arthur. Guinevere. Merlin.

And a jealous, over-achieving royal half-sister with ice blue eyes named Morgan le Fay.

It's hard to know where to start with her story.

Morgan wasn't just the king's jealous sibling, she was Merlin's lover, and the woman who engineered the collapse of the kingdom with a traitor named Mordred — who may have been her nephew. That one's up for grabs.

Thankfully, Seneca listed *him* as killed in action, which was good since we already had complications coming out of our ears.

Morgan is one of nine sisters. The others are Moronoe, Mazoe, Glitonea, Gliton, Gliten, Tyronoe, Thiton and Thiten. These women comprise the mysterious "Scandinavian" coven implicated in all of Isherwood's schemes.

After the fall of Camelot and Merlin's disappearance, death or eternal imprisonment (accounts vary), Morgan briefly ruled the island of Avalon. When she was driven out by the elf queen, Argante and Viviane, the Lady of the Lake, Morgan gathered up the family and headed north.

"The layers have been peeled away," Seneca said. "Chesterfield led you to Isherwood, and now Isherwood gives way to the real villain, the one who has been working against the virtuous expression of magic for centuries — Morgan le Fay."

That information begged the million-dollar question, which I posed. "What does she want?"

"She seeks the tools of Merlin," Seneca said. "The sword, Excalibur; the wand crafted from the wood of the World Tree, the vessel in whose depths virtue will flower, and the pentacles that will pay the price for the use of them all."

My first thought was, *"Here we go again. A magical bad guy trying to assemble artifacts to make even more bad things happen. Been there. Done that. Got the t-shirt."*

Seneca, however, blew that blythe and cynical assumption right out of the water. When I asked him what those objects could do in combination, his answer surprised me.

"Their combination is irrelevant, but when they are assembled, they will give Morgan access to all of Merlin's vast knowledge. He crafted the objects as a cipher to safeguard his notebooks, wishing the material to pass only to one who would further his work."

"Morgan was his pupil," I said. "Why didn't he leave his life's work to her?"

Seneca's beak clacked as he spoke. "Merlin's great dream was the perfection of the relationship between magic as a pure element of the universe and its unique expression through the filter of individual practitioners. We do not speak of a treasure that can be measured in monetary worth or gauged solely by its ability to create or destroy. Morgan is driven by hatred and ambition. She does not deserve to receive Merlin's legacy nor can we say what she would do with the material were she to obtain it."

Lucas, who was standing at the hearth staring into the fire said, "Why was she working with Isherwood?"

The bird's answer made my blood run cold.

"It has been said," Seneca replied, "that The Vessel of Virtuous Magic is not an object, but a Fae child yet to be born. By helping Isherwood perpetrate the Creavit heresy, Morgan ensured that the brightest children, those with the greatest potential, would be drained of their pure magic. In time, each was offered the return of a shadow of their gifts through dark design, thus making them enemies of virtue as well."

On one level the explanation made a ruthless degree of sense, but it also seemed counterproductive to Morgan's goals. "But why sabotage all the potentials," I asked. "Morgan needs the vessel of virtuous magic to break Merlin's cipher."

"Yes," Seneca agreed, "but to use the material she would then gain, she must be in complete control of that vessel."

I couldn't believe what I was hearing. Morgan had been culling Fae children until she found one she could use as a pawn in her grand scheme to abscond with Merlin's legacy. It was beyond monstrous.

Across the room, Brenna sat by the fire opposite where Lucas was standing. The flickering flames lit her face in profile, highlighting the strain of the attention she paid to Seneca's words. The sorceress might be sitting with us in a strange shop tucked away in Blackfriars, but her mind and her feelings must have been drawn back into her stolen youth.

Brenna had been one of the children Isherwood drained. He took not just her natural gifts, but the safety and warmth of her home. He stole her future as the Witch of the Oak and lured her with an unnatural bargain to become one of the most hated and feared women in all the realms.

Had her hereditary magic not been restored by accident, she would be Creavit still. Every day she struggles to come back from what she had been, to make amends for the crimes of her heart and spirit. This woman, who had humbly asked my forgiveness for her past misdeeds had fought by my side with the courage of a lioness, but sitting there by the fire, her face etched with memory, I saw the wounded child she had been.

Brenna must have felt my eyes on her because she looked over at me. In the long, silent moment of communication we shared, we made a promise to one another. Our common purpose required no words.

We couldn't let one more child be harmed by the ruthless ambitions of beings like Reynold Isherwood and Morgan le Fay.

Which is why when we left the shop in Blackfriars, Greer carried us to Somerset, to a place called Glastonbury Tor and to the crumbling remains of an ancient church known as St. Michael's Tower.

Long regarded as the gateway to the hidden island of Avalon, it pointed the way to the first of Merlin's tools, to the one that seemed to be calling directly to me — Excalibur.

Lucas went on the record again. He still wasn't happy, but he did agree that tipping Morgan off that we were on to her wasn't a good idea.

When we landed in Somerset, he confirmed the terms of our deal one more time. "We're going to Avalon, getting the sword, and taking it straight to Otto at IBIS headquarters. Right?" he asked.

"Right," I said for the tenth time. "Trust me, Lucas, I have zero desire to take on some centuries old virtue-hating badass witch and her eight sisters. We get in. We get the sword. We get out."

St. Michael's Tower sits alone atop Glastonbury Tor, a hard cap of exposed sandstone with terraced slopes. The ruined building has no roof and an arched doorway that seems to lead straight through to the other side — or at least that may be how most people walk into and out of the building. I was about to have a different experience.

Lucas, Greer, Brenna, and Rube made it to the lip of the seventh terrace with me, but there they met an invisible barrier. It took me several steps to realize they were gone. Looking back, I saw my friends standing in a row pressing their hands against what I saw as thin air.

"What is it?" I called back.

None of them answered me or even seemed to realize I'd spoken at all.

I heard Lucas say, "Jinx was right here not five seconds ago. How could she be gone just like that?"

Brenna closed her eyes and laid her hands flat against the wall of energy that separated us. Her palms glowed against the invisible surface, and I felt the merest whisper of her mind trying to reach mine.

Moving to stand directly in front of her, I tried to put my hands against hers, but what I felt could have been a cold sheet of glass.

Since my voice likely wouldn't penetrate the barrier, I closed my eyes and opened my mind. "Brenna, I'm here."

She answered, calling to me as if we stood at opposite ends of a long tunnel. "Are you safe?"

"Yes," I replied. "Nothing has changed. I can see all of you and hear you. Lucas is going to put what I'm about to say on his 'I'm not happy' list, but I don't think we have time to try to break through this barrier. I'm going on alone."

"What do you wish us to do?" Brenna asked.

"I'm not sure," I admitted. "Any suggestions?"

"Yes," she said, "my mother knew Morgan le Fay. If we cannot accompany you, I think we should go to Tír na nÓg and consult with her."

Calling in the magic cavalry sounded like a great idea. Especially since Myrtle and *my* mother were on Tír na nÓg. "Perfect," I said. "Do that. I'll get there myself or find a way to contact you as soon as I can."

"Be safe, Jinx," she said, her voice beginning to fade. "Trust your instincts. They will not lead you astray."

The thin connection broke, and I was left standing there looking at the people I loved over an invisible chasm. I saw

Lucas react to Brenna's account of our conversation. It wasn't good.

First, he shoved his fedora back on his head, and then he threw it on the ground. I think he would have stomped on the innocent hat if Rube hadn't snatched it out of harm's way.

Resting my hand against the barrier again, I tried to reach Lucas with my mind, sending my love along with assurances that I could handle whatever lay ahead.

For just an instant, he turned his head, seeming to listen to my voice. Then, grabbing his hat back from Rube and shoving his hands in his pockets, Lucas started back down the terraces of Glastonbury Tor with long, swinging strides.

With more resolution than I felt, I turned and climbed the last terrace to St. Michael's Tower, took a deep breath, and walked through the doorway.

I left a world lit by the warm rays of the afternoon sun and emerged in the misty half-light. Following the sound of lapping waves, I reached the edge of what could have been a lake or a sea. The deepening fog obscured my vision too much for me to know for certain.

A small rowboat rested at the water's edge. Brenna told me to trust my instincts, so I did. I got into the boat — which promptly slid off the rocks. The oars righted themselves in their locks and began to work with no hands to guide their motion.

"Don't guess you're going to tell me where we're going?" I asked, recoiling when the words echoed in the stillness.

My question went unanswered, leaving me with no choice but to sit back and enjoy the ride. Lost in those mists, I had no sense of the passing of time or distance. We could have been rowing for an hour or a year, over a gentle pond or crossing the ocean itself.

The rhythmic dig and pull of the oars against the water left me hypnotized in a dreamlike state, my mind wandering over scattered scenes from my life. I meandered through the sunlit days of my childhood, felt again the complacency of my years working at Tom's Café, and then I heard Aunt Fiona.

You have the most wonderful heart, Jinx. You always have. And that's where being a good witch starts, with a good heart.

That's when I smelled the apples.

27

"Wait a minute," Tori said. "Morgan le Fay? As in King Arthur? Knights of the Round Table? *That* Morgan le Fay? How is that possible?"

Lucien spread his hands. "I have no direct knowledge of Morgan's current whereabouts or about what she intends to do," he said, "but according to Rodney, the Witch of the Oak was given a vision of Excalibur before she went to Londinium."

Tori looked at the rat. "How do you know that Rodney?" she asked. "Did Jinx tell you? For that matter, does she even know you hitched a ride in her backpack?"

Looking properly guilty, Rodney shook his head.

"Yeah," Tori said, shaking a finger in his direction. "That's what I thought. I'm not bailing your fuzzy butt out on that one. You get to tell her yourself that you pulled that stowaway routine again. Now, what about the vision?"

The rat mimed a book opening.

"Jinx's grimoire showed up?" Tori frowned. "Is it allowed to do that?"

Rodney shrugged and pretended to open the book again.

"Okay," Tori said, "I'll take your word for it, but what does seeing the sword mean?"

"That," Lucien said, "is what we must go to Yggdrasil to discover. Rodney believes he was shown the sword because he has knowledge of another of the tools belonging to the great wizard, Merlin."

Tori's eyebrows went up. "Guess I should have known he was going to show up, too. What tool are we talking about here?"

The rat crossed his heart and held up one paw.

"You promised someone you wouldn't tell?" Tori interpreted. "All right. No one expects you to break your word. If you need Yggdrasil to tell you what the sword means, are you going to Tír na nÓg from here?"

Before Rodney could answer, a warning claxon went off at Festus' desk.

"For the love of Bastet," the werecat grumbled, "now what!"

He jumped from the hearth to the back of the sofa and onto the desk where he began touching controls on one of the iPads.

After scrutinizing the screen, he let out with a long string of profanity, ending in, "What the *hell* are those brats up to now?"

Shrugging into his headset, Festus pawed the mic and said, "GNATS 5, zoom in on the subject seated next to the Confederate monument."

"Roger that, Big Tom," the pilot said. "On approach now."

The others crowded behind the desk as Festus manipulated the display, diverting the feed from the drone to cover nine of the tablets mounted on poles in front of his workspace.

"Ooohhhh," Glory said. "That's pretty! It's like one of those big pictures they make with itty bitty tiles."

"Mosaic," Festus growled, "and so *not* the point, Pickle."

As the group watched, the drone circled the bench and Kyle's face came into full view.

"What's that thing in his lap?" Glory asked.

"It's a control box for some kind of remote vehicle," Tori said. "Like the one that just rolled out from under the bench."

The drone gave them a clear view of Kyle's movements as he maneuvered the ROV past the statue and onto the pavement in front of the courthouse. It was too late in the evening for there to be any traffic on the streets, but he still glanced up and down the square before sending the robot zooming across to the storm drain in front of The Witch's Brew.

Tori leaned in for a closer look. "Why on earth is he interested in the sewer system?"

"Good question," Festus asked. "GNATS 5, stay on that robot. You good to maneuver underground?"

"Roger that, Big Tom. We are five by five for sewer recon."

As the ROV tumbled into the drain, the GNATS drone followed. The vehicle landed firmly on its treads. Rings of red lights sprang to life around its twin "eyes" signaling that the cameras had gone to infrared viewing.

The picture from the GNATS drone, however, remained in sharp, vivid color — which is when they saw the red and green glitter.

"Holy *hairball!*" Festus said. "That's it. When Rube gets back, I'm making a coonskin cap out of his worthless hide."

Tori retrieved her laptop from the worktable and sat down beside Festus. "Where do you store the GNATS drone footage?" she asked.

"Ironweed set us up with an account on the Fairy Cloud," he replied. "My username is BigTom1, and the password is KatzPaJamz."

Rolling her eyes, Tori logged in to the server and began typing strings of code in a terminal window. "What are you doing?" Chase asked.

"Writing an algorithm to search the files for the timestamp

of the big ornament blast," she said. "I think I know what happened out there."

She finished the last few lines and hit the enter key. The screen filled with streaming characters until the search triggered a video window, which opened with footage showing the front of The Witch's Brew. The storm drain was visible at the bottom of the frame just above the timestamp ticking off the seconds.

At a little after 4 a.m., the buildings on the square shook and a jet of glitter shot out of the sewer system.

"Okay," Chase said, "that tells us how the glitter got there, but how did the HBH kids find out about it?"

"That's how," Tori said. She zoomed the footage to show a video camera mounted on a tripod pointed at the Confederate monument. "Look how the lens is angled. They probably got a better view of the glitter plume than the GNATS drone shot."

"Shouldn't all of the glitter have stayed inside the fairy mound?" Glory asked. "I mean I know you were covered with it, Dad, but how much glitter could Rube possibly have packed into a bunch of Christmas ornaments?"

Festus didn't have to answer. The fairy mound did it for him, letting out with a coughing sneeze that showered the entire lair with glitter.

Blowing the shining particles off the keys of her laptop, Tori looked up at the ceiling. "We could have done without the demo," she said. "We get the idea. Let's see what Kyle has been up to online."

While Beau explained the HBH situation to Lucien, Tori hacked into Kyle's email and uncovered his conversations with GhostFish.

"If Howie wasn't already dead," she muttered darkly, "I'd kill him myself. He's obsessed with catching his murderer, but I don't think that has anything to do with Kyle's sewer cam."

Looking up again, she addressed the fairy mound, "You're

not going to let that ROV see anything it's not supposed to see, right?"

The lights blinked off and on.

"Good," Tori said. "Then let the HBH kids explore the sewers all they want."

Festus, who had been looking over her shoulders reading the emails said, "Hang on a second. I think I've got an idea."

"What kind of an idea?" Chase asked suspiciously.

It was the werecat's turn to address the fairy mound. "Can you keep that ROV busy for a while?" he asked the fairy mound. "Get it lost or something?"

The lights dimmed and then brightened.

"I'm going to take that as a 'maybe,'" Festus said. Craning his neck toward the tree house, he hollered, "Booger! You up there?"

A black-masked face appeared through the leaves. "Yo, bro!" the raccoon yelled back. "What's up?"

"You feel like perpetrating a little breaking and entering?"

The coon's eyes lit up. "B&E? Suh-well! I'll be right there."

Chase held up his hand. "Slow down, Dad. Breaking and entering where exactly?"

"The evidence locker at Sheriff John Boy's office," Festus said placidly. "We're going swordfishing."

When Booger lumbered into the lair, Festus laid out the details of the plan.

"All you gotta do is get in the evidence room and find a brass swordfishing trophy. I don't think there will be more than one, but make sure the plaque says 'Howard McAlpin,'" the werecat said. "Break the tip off the fish's bill with something. Can you manage that?"

Booger rummaged in his fanny pack and produced a multi-tool, which he flipped open to a pair of wire cutters. "Piece o'cake, bro," he said. "What do you want me to do with the thing when it's busted?"

"Put the trophy back where you found it," Festus said. "Take the broken piece and get into the sewers, find that ROV, and drop the tip of the bill right in front of the damn thing. I looked up the model of ROV this HBH idiot is driving. It has a robotic arm. Don't leave until you're he's retrieved the evidence. But you gotta make this fast, Booger. Half an hour, tops."

The raccoon held up his paw and high-fived the werecat. "No sweat, bro," he said, grinning happily. "Booger is on the case."

As Tori watched him waddle away, she looked at Festus, "You're a genius," she said admiringly.

"Like this is new news?" Festus asked.

Groaning, Chase said, "Do not encourage him. For the non-geniuses in the room, what, exactly, are you trying to accomplish here, Dad?"

Festus pawed at Tori's laptop and highlighted one of the GhostFish emails.

"Howie gave me the idea," he said. "Right here in this email, he says our dumber-than-dirt Sheriff ruled the good mayor's death as a probable accident even though he had the murder weapon bagged and tagged."

"Okay," Chase said, "I'm with you so far."

"So," Festus said, "if Howie 'accidentally' killed himself with a brass swordfish, and Kyle here finds the tip of said swordfish in the sewers, how did it get there *unless* . . . "

"*Unless* the killer ditched it there to hide the evidence," Chase said. "It pains me to say this, Dad, but you are a genius."

Glory held up her hand.

"You got something to say, Pickle?" Festus asked.

"Won't the sheriff realize that the tip of the swordfish wasn't broken before?" she asked.

Festus made a scoffing sound. "That's assuming he paid any attention to it in the first place, which he didn't, because everybody was so glad Howie croaked, they couldn't wait to close the case. Now we're giving His Honor the Mayor what he wants, a reopened investigation. One that should keep the HBH kids occupied and off our backs."

"My heavens," Lucien said, "you seem to grapple with the most interesting problems here."

"You have no idea," Tori said. "No. Idea."

"As interesting as this all is," he said, "Rodney and I should be on our way to Tír na nÓg."

From across the lair, Lucas' voice interrupted their conversation. "I'd hold up on that if I were you — whoever you are — we have a situation on our hands."

28

Beyond the boat's bow, the mist lightened. The oars instantly picked up the pace, propelling the craft over the water with eager anticipation. As we broke into clear air, I saw an island covered in apple trees, some in bloom, others in full fruit.

The aroma of the trees mixed with the clean scent of the water awakened me from my dream state. As my vision and awareness sharpened, I spotted an unexpected welcoming party on the shore.

Mom, Gemma, Myrtle, Bronwyn, and Katherine stood on the narrow beach waving. Something seemed to be hovering around their shoulders. Squinting, I could just make out . . . rats?

On winged horses?

"Why not?" I thought.

In my world, anything is possible. Literally.

The boat glided out of the water and onto the smooth sand allowing me to step off without getting my feet wet. I'd barely managed to get my bearings before Mom reached me and pulled me into a tight hug.

"You're here," she said in a choked voice.

We hadn't even been apart for a week, but I felt the emotion of our reunion as much as she did. "I'm here," I agreed, the words muffled against her shoulder, "but what are you doing here?"

"Your pen and grimoire shared with me your vision of Excalibur," Myrtle said. "Do not be outdone with them. They feared for your safety. I carried that concern to the others on Tír na nÓg. We sought Yggdrasil's permission to journey here to, as Tori would say, watch your back."

Turning loose of Mom, I gave Myrtle a fierce hug. "I love it when you say stuff like that," I laughed.

Gemma held out her arms next. "What about me, kiddo?" she asked.

"Hi, Gem," I said, embracing her. "Keeping my Mom out of trouble?"

"Trying," she said, "and failing. Same old, same old."

As we parted, I held out one hand to Bronwyn and the other to Katherine MacVicar, who took it somewhat awkwardly. The warm undercurrent of her power reminded me of Greer. When I smiled, the baobhan sith smiled back in a way that was almost shy.

Over her shoulder, I saw a trio of rats astride miniature flying horses waiting patiently for their turn to greet me. The one I took to be the leader inched his mount forward when he realized my attention had turned in his direction.

At a tug of the reins, the horse, still airborne, went down on one knee and bowed its head, while the rat drew his sword and held the blade upright before his face in salute.

"*Quercus de Pythonissam*," he said, "I am Sir Reginald de Roquefort. My life and my sword are yours to command. These are my men, Sir Cedric Wingard and Sir Forest de Winter."

The other knights dropped their horses into kneeling positions and raised their swords in the same manner.

"Thank you . . . gentlemen," I managed. "I, uh, appreciate that."

As the rats pulled their mounts back upright, Bronwyn came to my rescue with an explanation.

"Sir Reginald and his officers command the Knights of the Rodere," she said. "They are the sworn protectors of Yggdrasil and our boon companions."

Even though my medieval slang wasn't up to par, I'd seen enough old movies to understand that "boon companions" meant good guys.

"You know, it's funny," I said thoughtfully, "but one of my dearest friends is a rat."

"I know, m'lady," Reginald replied, "Sir Rodney de Roquefort is my grandson, sent to dwell among you in Briar Hollow for his protection."

A million questions popped into my head, but before I could ask any of them, a man stepped out of the trees and spoke to Myrtle.

"Fare thee well, aos si?" the newcomer asked.

Myrtle moved toward him and held out her hand, "I do, Your Majesty," she said. "How fare thee on the Isle of Apples?"

"Well," he said, "but I live here as a common man, not a king. In this place, I am Arthur, a loyal subject of Queen Argante and servant of the Lady of the Lake."

As Festus would say, *holy hairball!*

I was standing not ten feet from King Arthur. *The* King Arthur!

For all his protestations of being an ordinary guy, my hand still trembled when Myrtle introduced me to the legendary monarch.

"M'Lady," the king said, still holding my hand but going down on one knee, "long ago did I pledge my fealty in service to the Trees and to the Women of the Craobhan. I am Arthur, your humble servant."

I've always had a problem with Fae formality, but usually, I can navigate the fancy manners. This situation left me completely stumped.

"I, uh, I'm Jinx," I stammered. "You can call me Jinx."

Arthur stood, towering over me by a head. "Thank you, Lady Jinx," he said. "Under normal circumstances, we would have time for pleasantries, but Queen Argante sent me here as her messenger. She has taken her elves far into the interior of the island for their safety. My sister, Morgan le Fay, approaches through the mists."

Great.

"Is everybody up to speed on Morgan?" I asked the group.

"She's his sister," Gemma said, pointing at Arthur. "She had an affair with Merlin, pretty much wrecked Camelot, got kicked out of Avalon, and has been hanging out with the Vikings up north. She killed Isherwood, and she's after Merlin's stuff starting with the sword. Did I miss anything?"

Only Gemma could make me laugh standing on a beach with a living king peeled straight out of the pages of mythology while we waited for his lunatic sister to come charging out of the fog.

"That pretty much covers it," I agreed. "The special ops team was headed here to get Excalibur before Morgan could snatch it. The idea was to take the sword to IBIS headquarters for safe-keeping. I'm the only one who made it to the top of Glastonbury Tor though. The others were stopped by some kind of invisible barrier of energy."

Arthur explained the significance of that unexpected hurdle. "If St. Michael's Tower would not let your compatriots ascend with you," he said, "the quest is yours alone to complete."

I can't even begin to tell you how I cringe when people start tossing around words like "journey" and "quest."

"Which means what?" I asked.

"That you must face Morgan alone," he replied.

The only word that describes my mother's reaction to that would be "eruption."

"Absolutely not," she declared stoutly. "I don't care if you are King Arthur. You're out of your mind if you think the five of us are just going to stand here and watch while my daughter takes on your whack-job sister."

Arthur thought about that last part for a minute and then said, "While your language is strange to my ears, I believe you are asserting that Morgan is insane. My sister is not a raving mad woman, but rather a calculating creature of evil purpose and studied intent."

"Which doesn't make me feel better in the slightest," Mom snapped. "I know you and your knights have this whole hero's quest thing going, galloping around looking for the Holy Grail, but I am not going to abandon my daughter."

Myrtle moved beside my mother and said quietly, "Kelly, do not consider what is about to occur as abandonment. Arthur is correct. If the Tower allowed no one else to reach the top of Glastonbury Tor, then Jinx is the one who must face Morgan and win Excalibur.

Mom may not be a big woman, but when she's defending me, I swear she's ten feet tall. "I've always respected you, Myrtle," Mom said, "but this time I refuse to do what you say."

Bronwyn spoke quietly. "In that refusal, you may condemn Jinx to death. We find ourselves in a world surrounded by water, a substance that in its flow seeks levels other powers cannot reach. Water nurtures life without conflict. It has been said that the expression of the supreme good can only occur in the absence of struggle. If we quarrel among ourselves, Morgan has already won."

Before Mom could bristle again, Gemma caught hold of her hand. "When we were young, women and the girls were just babies crawling around on the floor we said we weren't going to be the kind of mothers who suffocated them. You know as well as I do that Jinx and Tori have outgrown us. Don't get in Jinx's way now, Kell."

Mom looked at me. "Norma Jean?"

"Do as Myrtle says," I answered. "When my pen drew Excalibur, I had an overwhelming sense that my destiny was tied to the sword. If I'm meant to take it up, it won't fail me."

Arthur nodded approvingly. "Spoken as one who possesses the purity of heart to wield the blade."

"So where is it?" I asked. "Where do I find Excalibur?"

The king shook his head. "You cannot summon Merlin's sword to do your bidding, *Quercus de Pythonissam*. The weapon must come to you of its own free will."

"Then it better hurry up," Gemma said. "We're about to have company."

Following her line of vision, we saw the prow of a Viking longship split the fog. There wasn't much chance Morgan le Fay and I were going to come to some peaceful agreement anyway, but an entrance like that didn't improve our chances.

Avalon sent *me* a rowboat, and *she* comes riding in on a Norse warship? People who show off like that set my teeth on edge before they fling a single lightning bolt.

Which was the next thing Morgan did.

The blast struck the earth between Katherine and me, melting the sand with enough heat to leave a crater of glass in its wake. The baobhan sith's eyes filled with green fire and she raised her hands.

"Stop," I commanded. "Get out of here, now. All of you."

As I spoke, Morgan fired again, unleashing a cloud of icicles sharp as daggers. On instinct, I raised my hand and met them with a wall of fire. My reflexes were good, but I could have been faster. The water from the melting ice drenched us all as it fell to earth.

Mom grabbed my arm. "Please, Norma Jean, let me stay."

I heard my voice. I knew it was me speaking, but I didn't sound like myself at all.

"Enough. Go. This is not up for discussion. This is my battle, not yours."

Beside us a second blast hit, kicking up a spray of sand. Annoyed more than frightened, Mom flicked her hand in a tight circle and covered us in a shield of energy. The next splattering of sand bounced off the barrier in a glittering shower of sparks.

The incantation bought Mom the time she needed to wrap her arms around me and whisper in my ear, "you've got this. I love you," before she joined the others beside Katherine who carried them to safety on the flight of the baobhan sith.

That left me, standing alone on the beach.

The longship was less than a hundred yards from shore now. With my mother's barrier spell broken, I stood exposed and defenseless; a state Morgan exploited with a bigger volley of ice shards that careened toward me on a frigid blast of air.

This time the enchantress was too fast for me. I ducked and rolled, but not before one of the missiles glanced off my shoulder, tearing through my shirt and leaving a bleeding gash behind. Hissing at the sudden pain, I scrambled behind the rowboat for cover. Morgan thought that was the funniest thing she'd ever seen.

"The mighty Witch of the Oak cowering like a frightened rabbit," she jeered. Throwing her head back, she laughed — just the kind of laugh you'd expect from an arch-villain with a serious case of self-regard.

While she was busy enjoying her moment, I stood and fought back, unleashing twin bolts of energy from my outstretched hands. The left bolt blew the dragon figurehead off the longship and set the deck on fire; the right blast cut through the port oars.

Before the starboard oars could correct, the ship veered drunkenly, throwing Morgan off the side. She caught herself just above the water's surface, levitating into a standing position to hover over the waves.

"That," she said, "was tedious and unnecessary."

"Don't tell me your problems," I shot back. "You started this fight."

"And I will be the one to finish it unless you give me what I seek," Morgan said. "Turn over Excalibur now, and I may be convinced to let you live."

Let's pause here to consider the scene.

One wet, bleeding witch covered in sand standing by herself on a beach behind a rowboat.

One immortal enchantress hovering over the water against the backdrop of a burning Viking ship.

Do I even need to mention how good her hair looked blowing around her face like a black thundercloud?

Put my hair through wind like that, and I'd be combing out the tangles for a week.

This would be the point in the battle where I went with the tactic called "taunt your enemy and hope it works out."

The taunting part was a success.

The working out part? Not so much.

Morgan hit me with a solid wall of energy that felt like a freight train. It threw me off the beach and slammed me into the trunk of one of the gnarled, ancient apple trees. I fell to my knees as the edges of my vision grew dark and ragged.

I was still in that position trying to clear my head when

Morgan's shadow fell over me. That was enough to get me to my feet. If I was going out, it would be standing up.

"You look worse for wear *Quercus de Pythonissam*," Morgan purred. "Why will you not capitulate and save yourself?"

It took two tries before I could get enough air into my lungs to answer. "You drained magic from children," I rasped. "That doesn't fly with me, lady."

"I drained them of their pathetic virtue," Morgan said, "and gave them back stronger magic than they would ever have commanded. You could have that gift, too, Jinx Hamilton. Creavit magic will put fire in your veins and harden your heart to a level of invincibility you dare not imagine."

"Pass," I coughed.

"What a pity," she said. "For a weakling, novice witch you have acquitted yourself well today, but I grow weary of toying with you."

She never touched me, but I still felt the vise-like grip of her fingers on my neck. My feet left the ground, and she held me suspended, fighting for every breath. I tried to summon my magic, but the sensation of choking shattered my concentration.

"Now," Morgan said, "be a good little witch and tell me where I can find Excalibur."

"Even if I knew," I gasped, "I wouldn't tell you."

"A small matter," Morgan said. "Avalon was mine once. The trees themselves fear me. If I have to burn every living thing on this island to a cinder, I will find what I want."

Her grip on my throat tightened, and my vision swam with black spots. I'll be honest. I wanted to give up.

In what I believed to be the last moments of my life, I thought about my parents, about Lucas, about Tori, and everyone else I cared about. Some people say when you're dying you see a bright light. I didn't.

Darkness descended around me, and I fell into a dark,

bottomless pit. Some inner sense told me that when I did find the bottom, my fight would be over.

But that's not what happened.

Instead, my spiraling descent slowed until I found myself suspended in a state of limbo. The overpowering scent of apples returned, and then he was there.

An elderly man. The very picture of what you'd expect a wizard to look like. He didn't have to tell me his name. I knew who was with me — Merlin.

"She's killing me," I said simply.

"No, child," the wizard said, "she is *trying* to kill you. The spark of life has not left your soul, nor will it this day. You carry a bright note that must live to sing in another time. Call to Excalibur."

"I don't know how."

"Your answer lies not in knowing," Merlin told me. "The answer lies in *feeling*. Call with your heart, Jinx Hamilton, and reclaim your life."

My life.

My plans.

All the things I wanted to do. The things I didn't want to give up.

The love I didn't want to lose.

That was the thought that saved me. The love — pouring into my soul from every river and source of caring that filled my world.

It was exactly what Bronwyn had said back on the beach. Water finds a way into unknown crevices. I felt carried along on a river of love, a current that buoyed me up through that black hole and threw me back into the light.

The force of the awakening loosed Morgan's grip on my throat, but I didn't fall. My magic held me aloft as I put out my hand and closed my fingers over the hilt of a sword. Excalibur's energy fused with my being in an exhilarating rush of pure power.

I saw Morgan's ice blue eyes widen in alarm as I swung the blade toward her chest. Everything around us exploded, but instead of being swept away on the hot wind, this time I rode the storm.

When it cleared, I stood alone at the base of the apple tree with Excalibur in my hand.

Morgan le Fay was gone, and the Sword of Merlin was mine.

29

"Wait, wait," Festus said, choking on this nip beer. "You gotta see this part. Watch. Okay. There's Booger. He comes right up to the ROV and drops the swordfish bill in front of the camera. Then the stupid human backs the camera up and . . . *BAM* . . . Booger slaps the ROV in the kisser and makes the moron look again. Man, I could watch this thing a million times."

I shifted in my chair to get a better view of the screen as Merle, Earl, and Furl crowded around Festus on the surface of the desk. The four of them made quite a picture. The triplets with their Scottish fold ears and trim bodies next to Festus sporting a more . . . "well-fed" look.

As I changed positions, I hissed in discomfort. Even though Brenna had applied her healing magic to the cut in my shoulder, the muscle still pulled if I moved too fast. A voice next to me said, "You good there, Doll?"

Looking down, I met Rube's black eyes, now anxious with concern. "Five by five," I assured him.

"Suh-wheet," he said, scaling the leg of the desk and taking his place with the werecats.

Festus hit the play button on the iPad again. We watched as the robotic arm on the ROV extended and gingerly picked up the slender piece of brass.

"You mean to tell me that Kyle took that thing to Sheriff Johnson and got him to re-open the case?" I asked. "On the day before Thanksgiving?"

"Yep," Festus said. "That part was icing on the cake. No way Sheriff John Boy was going to let anything get between him and his dinner. Here's the GNATS footage from inside the Sheriff's department when the HBH brat showed up with the evidence."

The next video showed Kyle triumphantly entering the office with the tip of the swordfish bill in a plastic bag. There was some argument back and forth and Sheriff Johnson finally said, "Fine. I'll show you the damned trophy and prove to you that brass toothpick you've got there has nothing to do with Howard McAlpin's death."

Johnson disappeared into a back room and came out with the fishing prize, which was in serious need of polishing. The moment the Sheriff appeared back on camera, we could see the slightly sick expression on his face.

"Let me see that thing," he grumbled, sticking his hand over the counter in Kyle's direction.

Without taking the fragment of metal out of the bag, the Sheriff lined up the two edges. "Well," he said, "I will just be damned. It *is* the tip from McAlpin's fish trophy."

"*See!*" Kyle said. "I told you so. If Mayor McAlpin accidentally killed himself, how would the tip of the trophy wind up in the storm drain?"

The sheriff had no answer for that question, nor did either of them care to dwell on the fact that the evidence had been hand delivered by a raccoon.

This series of events led to the Thanksgiving edition of *The*

Briar Hollow Banner coming out with a headline dominating most of the space above the fold:

Sheriff Re-Opens McAlpin
Murder Investigation

Tori assured me that she'd chewed Howie out six ways from Sunday and yanked every means he had of sending or receiving an email, but the ghost of the late mayor was still elated. Finally, someone believed that his death was not an accident.

While Festus grabbed another nip beer and cued up the Booger footage so he and his buddies could watch it yet again, I wandered over to the chip and dip table where Tori was filling her plate.

"Hey," she said, "how's the arm? I caught that look on your face when you scooted closer to the desk."

"Still sore," I admitted, "but otherwise okay. I'm just glad we made it back in time for Thanksgiving dinner."

"Me, too," Tori said. "Look, Jinksy, I'm sorry I wasn't there for you on Avalon."

"It's okay," I assured her. "The gateway to St. Michael's Tower set the whole thing up. Nobody could have helped me, and believe me, Mom tried."

Spooning out a generous helping of French onion dip on her plate, Tori said, "I know. My mother told me about the whole thing."

After Katherine whisked the group away from the scene of the battle, she deposited them on the high ground overlooking the beach. My mother was forced to watch helplessly as I dueled with Morgan le Fay.

From what I'd been able to piece together when the enchantress raised me off the ground in a chokehold, it took Gemma *and* Katherine to restrain my mother.

"Mom says Excalibur just materialized in your hand," Tori said.

"It did," I said. "Merlin himself had to kick me in the butt and remind me to fight, but when I got the message, the sword was there for me."

"You gonna tell me where you stashed it?" she asked.

"Nope," I answered, munching on a nacho. "You're safer not knowing."

As I reached for a second helping, Tori nudged me with her elbow. "Speaking of swords," she said, "check that out."

I looked toward the hearth where Rodney and his grandfather were mock fighting with broadswords. Glory sat cross-legged on the floor clapping in delight every time Rodney scored a point on the older knight.

"Can you believe Rodney's story?" I asked as Tori and I walked over to claim a couple of the folding chairs Darby had scattered all over the lair.

"It's pretty amazing," she said. "After you all got back from Tír na nÓg, I told him to ask as many of his family for Thanksgiving as he liked, but I didn't expect a regiment of rats."

Beau pulled up a chair and joined us as she spoke.

"Miss Tori," he said, "a regiment would consist of more than 1,000 troops. There are fewer than 50 of the Rodere Knights here today."

The lair seemed to be crawling with rats in medieval finery, whose horses were peacefully grazing on an impromptu field outside Myrtle's front door thoughtfully provided by the fairy mound. Rodney assured us that all the rats were his first or second cousins — and I thought *I* had a big family.

We also had a good number of spirits from the cemetery enjoying the semi-corporeality afforded them by the fairy mound. Hiram Folger and my Dad were playing catch at the base of Rube's treehouse. The raccoons from Rube's wrecking crew lolled in the branches watching and offering unsolicited and unwelcome advice on Hiram's pitching form.

"Beau," Tori said, "not to be nosey, but how did you deal with Linda Albert's invitation to join her for Thanksgiving?"

The colonel looked momentarily uncomfortable, but then said, "I had coffee with Miss Linda this morning and explained that though I am flattered by her interest in me, I still and always will see myself as a married man. I believe she was somewhat hurt in the beginning, but we have agreed to be friends and genealogical research partners."

"That conversation must have been hard for you," I said, "but it sounds like you handled it as well as you could under the circumstances."

"I do hope so," Beau said. "What I told her was not an untruth, as I certainly could not explain the real facts of my existence to her."

"We all have things we have to hide from our human friends," I assured him. "Don't think of it as lying."

Seeing the three of us talking, Lucas wandered over balancing a plate of hors-d'oeuvres on top of his wine glass. "Your mother," he said, sitting down beside me, "should get a job with the Brown Mountain Guard as a drill sergeant."

He pointed toward the main table. Mom and Darby, clipboards in hand, were checking off the menu items and consulting with one another about quantities.

"Well," I said, "Ironweed is perched over there on Festus' desk, talk to him about it. But honestly, I think my mother is too much even for the elite fairy commandos."

"You could be right," Lucas agreed. "She got worried that there wasn't enough butter, so she sent Darby out for more. The poor little guy was so scared he wouldn't bring back enough to suit her, he showed up with six dozen sticks."

We all laughed at that and Tori said, "That should be just

about enough congealed cream to clog every artery in a 25-mile radius. Isn't Darby supposed to be helping Bart practice for the dusting competition?"

"He is," I said, "but the fairy mound is pitching in until Darby can break free. It keeps coughing up more glitter for Bart to clean up. Personally, I think the mound is just using him to get its sinuses clear."

That comment set off a fresh round of mirth that attracted my brother Connor's attention. He excused himself from the conversation he was having with Moira and walked over to us.

"What's so funny," he asked, taking the empty chair next to Tori and putting his arm around her shoulder.

"Glitter eradication, brownies, and *your* mother," I replied.

"*My* mother?" Connor grinned. "She's only *my* mother when she's done something excessive. So, Sis, tell me. Does the whole Excalibur thing mean you're a Knight of the Round Table now?"

That got him a punch in the arm. "No," I said, but then I caught myself. "Wait a minute. You don't think the knights are still alive, too, do you?"

Lucas bit into a pig in a blanket and chewed contemplatively. "Do we really want to go there, honey?" he asked.

"Good point," I said, stealing the last nacho on his plate before he could catch me.

"Seriously," Connor said, "can we get word to Arthur that the descendants of his stallion, Hengroen, are safe in Shevington? I think he'd like to know that."

I assured my critter whisperer brother that I'd talk the matter over with Bronwyn who would take it up with the World Tree. Even though I agreed with Connor that Arthur would like to know about the horses, there was a protocol about the hidden island of Avalon we had to follow.

Before we left there and after Katherine had brought

everyone back to the beach, Arthur had asked to hold Excalibur one last time.

Standing against the backdrop of the apple groves, the king looked like what he was — a man out of time and place. "Excalibur will serve you well," he said wistfully, handing the weapon back to me.

"You could come with us," I said. "Back to Tír na nÓg, or even to Shevington."

Arthur shook his head sadly. "I cannot," he replied. "My life force is tied for eternity to the Isle of the Apple Trees. Were I to leave this place, I would cease to exist, but thank you *Quercus de Pythonissam*. Even to be asked to rejoin the world at large is a great thing."

We had returned to Tír na nÓg via St. Gabriel's Tower and then back to Briar Hollow where Lucas greeted me with such a crushing embrace I thought my ribs would crack. Then he saw the blood on my shirt.

He'd been more or less hovering ever since, but so far I'd managed not to complain. I figured I'd give him through the holiday before I gently, but firmly, told him to get a grip on his overprotective self.

Truthfully, everyone had been kind of "hovery" after hearing the details of my confrontation with Morgan le Fay, including Amity who never "hovered" over anyone.

After the big surprise she'd orchestrated for me at Halloween with the reunion of the WAGWAB women, I'd tried to make sure I paid Amity some extra attention. As a result, our crotchety neighbor had been uncharacteristically pleasant all day to the point that she even told Festus he was looking handsome in his fur.

The werecat almost fainted from shock.

Honestly, the only people in the over-crowded lair who didn't seem to have caught the holiday spirit were Greer, Katherine, and Brenna. I wrote it off to their lack of social experience at big family gatherings and didn't think much about it.

Later I would find out there was more to their reticent behavior than being put off by the eclectic crowd. The two baobhan sith and the sorceress thought we'd gotten off of Avalon, sword in hand, entirely too easily.

Given the steady ache in my shoulder, I wouldn't have taken that assessment well, which is why they didn't say anything. Instead, they allowed events to play out according to the force of the natural order.

Let me pull a Lucas here and go on the record with something. The natural order can be a real pain in the backside.

That Thanksgiving also represented Tori and Gemma's first major holiday since Scrap's death, so they were the recipients of some hovering as well. A few hours earlier I'd found Tori alone in the espresso bar where she shed a few tears for her father on my good shoulder.

Then, wiping her eyes, she'd come downstairs and plunged into the celebration with her usual zest for life, but I knew that a part of her longed for her father and always would.

So that's how we spent the day. Laughing. Talking. Remembering. Playing. Eating too much. Forgetting about all the complications of Fae politics. Even my grandfather, Barnaby, who tends to be well, stuffy, let my Dad teach him to pitch washers.

Looking back, I know those few hours gave me the strength for what came next — a mirror call for Bronwyn from Tír na nÓg that interrupted more than the football game.

The sanctuary was under attack.

By Morgan le Fay and all eight of her sisters.

Sometimes, ancient enchantresses are just like cockroaches. No matter how hard you step on them, they come crawling back.

30

Bronwyn and Katherine went through the portal to Tír na nÓg first, but before I could follow, an energy bolt erupted through the opening. The magic ricocheted off the floor and hit one of the big limbs on the treehouse sending Booger and Marty scrambling for safety. The branch crashed to the ground and burst into flames.

White foam liberally sprinkled with glitter shot out of the ceiling instantly dousing the blaze as I sprinted for the portal. I heard Lucas yell, "Jinx, no!" but his warning came too late.

Or at least that's what I told him later.

Honestly? I ignored him and dove head first through the opening, tucking into a roll when I hit the other side.

The impact sent waves of pain through my shoulder, but I didn't have time to think about that. I came to my feet on soft sand as two more strikes hit the portal. Static webs engulfed the gateway, collapsing it entirely and cutting us off from Briar Hollow.

Before the next incoming volley, Katherine pulled me behind a sheltering boulder at the base of the cliff under the city. "Are you hurt?" the baobhan sith asked.

"No," I said, cautiously peering over the rock. "But from the looks of it, we're outgunned."

Nine black figures floated over the bay with Morgan le Fay in the center. They were all firing on the island. Above our heads, a bolt hit the city's retaining wall sending an avalanche of brick and rock plummeting down the mountain.

"The others will find a way to reach us," Bronwyn said, "but until they arrive, we must hold the city."

That's when I got an idea.

"Katherine," I said, "can you stop time the way Greer can?"

"Yes," she said, "but halting the flow of time won't stop the coven's attack. It will only delay their strikes."

"I know," I said, "but 'delay' is exactly what we're after."

Oblivious to the storm of magic raging around her, Katherine moved to stand against the sheer rock wall. She let her power rise. Her eyes smoldered with lurid, liquid light as a crimson fire began to stream from the ruby signet ring on her index finger.

As she chanted the words of the temporal incantation, the breeze off the water slowed, grew leaden, and died. The coven's inbound magic froze in mid-air, and all sound stopped.

Before I could ask Katherine how long she could hold the weight of time, a hot current of air rolled over us as Greer landed on the beach. Without a word, she joined her mother, calling up the red fire from her own ring and merging the power with Katherine's.

Under their combined strength, the coven's suspended energy bolts shattered and dropped into the bay, sizzling as they hit the salty water.

In the utter stillness that followed, Morgan spoke, her voice carrying easily over the water. "Your pet vampires cannot stop time forever," she said. "When their powers are exhausted, I will kill you and take from this island what is mine."

Behind me, the Briar Hollow portal crackled to life. Sir Reginald and the Rodere came through first astride their fairy mounts with swords drawn. Tori and five mountain lions followed — three with curled ears. The werecats were on the case.

Tori took up a position beside me, with Chase and Festus on either side of us. Merle, Earl, and Furl formed a line in front of Katherine and Greer.

Out of the corner of my eye, I saw Rodney guide his fairy horse to a hovering position just off my left shoulder, while a swarm of GNATS drones took up formation behind us.

Mom, Gemma, Brenna, Lucas, and Rube came through the portal next, completing our first line of defense.

"Sorry we're late to the party," Tori said. "Little portal malfunction."

"How'd you fix it?" I asked, my eyes still on Morgan and the coven.

"You would be surprised what four raccoons with multitools, a Druid princess turned AI, and one reformed Creavit witch can pull off," she said matter-of-factly.

"Works for me," I replied. "Festus, who's running the drones?"

"The Pickle and Beau," the werecat said, "with some help from Adeline. Ironweed and his troops should be here any minute."

Somewhere off to my left, I heard another portal open, and suddenly the air was alive with fairies in combat gear and purple berets. Ironweed fluttered into my peripheral vision.

"Hello, Jinx," he said conversationally. "Understand we've got a coven to take out."

"We do," I replied. "You and your boys go with Sir Reginald and the Rodere. I want the city protected at all costs."

The fairy sighed dramatically. "Great. You do know how the infantry feels about cavalry show-offs, right?"

"You and Reginald can settle that between yourselves," I said, "I'm kinda busy at the moment."

Popping me a smart salute, Ironweed flew away. His men joined up with the Rodere and together they started toward the city, passing a diving flight of dragonlets on the way up. The iridescent creatures banked sharply, kicking up sand as they landed and turned to face the water.

With a series of clacks and chirps thrown over his shoulder, Minreith informed me that he and his companions weren't alone. Hazarding a glance toward the clouds, I saw the skies filled with hovering dragonlets.

Morgan's laughter echoed in the quiet. "You think to stop our immortal Coven with a ragtag army of rats, fairies, and flying lizards? You are even more foolish than I imagined, Witch of the Oak."

My grandfather's voice rang out in response. "Do not be so sure of that, Morgan le Fay," Barnaby said, striding through a portal from The Valley with Moira at his side and Aunt Fiona following behind. "The whole of the Otherworld stands against you this day."

You see, in the first critical seconds after we learned that Tír na nÓg was under attack, and without telling anyone what she was doing, Adeline sent out a clarion call to the realms.

They came from every corner of the known worlds.

Witches. Wizards. Creavit. The Women of the Craobhan. The Ruling Elders. *Nonconformi.* Sentient objects. Ghosts and mythic creatures.

Pouring through portals that opened spontaneously up and down the beach.

The merfolk rose in the waters clutching tridents in their hands, while herds of sharks, whales, and dolphins encircled the island. The shadows of true dragons passed over the land, filling the air with the acrid scent of smoke and brimstone.

There were no races that day. No allegiances to any cause save the preservation of pure magic and the natural order. We stood, shoulder to shoulder, a solid Fae wall united against the would-be corrupters of virtue.

Enraged, Morgan raised her hand only to be answered by drawn wands and raised staffs.

Stepping to the water's edge, I said, "Do it — and the instant you do, I'll tell the baobhan sith to release time. Then you can face us all, Morgan, the united Fae. The races you tried to divide and demean. Do it. If you're big enough."

Beside her, one of the women in black said, "Sister, we are beaten this day. Let us retreat from this place while we still can."

Morgan silenced her with a savage backhand blow. "That will be enough from you, Gliton," she hissed.

"Please, Morgan," another of the women whined. "We cannot fight them all."

At that, the enchantress threw back her head and let out a scream of pure hatred and agonized frustration. Turning blazing eyes back on me, she said, "We are not done with one another, Jinx Hamilton. Mark my words. We are not done."

Then, throwing her arms wide, she engulfed the coven in a cloud of purple smoke. At a sign from me, Katherine and Greer released time. The wind picked up, dispersing the last lavender tendrils to reveal only empty air over the bay as a great cheer rose from a thousand throats.

"That," Tori said, "is what you call dodging a bullet."

~

THAT THANKSGIVING DAY, Morgan le Fay didn't just lose the Battle of Tír na nÓg. She united the realms in common purpose.

As Lucas and I walked among the bonfires along the shore that night, I felt the dawning of a new day for the Fae races. In one group a satyr with a guitar was leading a mix of elves, druids, and werecats in a slightly bawdy drinking song. Nearby, Stan, Fiona's Sasquatch neighbor, was teaching a group of varied *nonconformi* children how to make s'mores.

We'd come down for a walk on the beach after dinner in the city's open-air pavilion with all the people I think of as our extended family. With Rodere and fairy guards on every portal, people were coming and going on Tír na nÓg from all over the Fae world.

When all was said and done, the victory party lasted through the weekend.

Going back to work in The Witch's Brew on Monday morning felt like something of a letdown. I mean seriously. Wednesday, I held Excalibur in my hands. Thursday, I stood at the head of a Fae army. And Monday, I had to unclog the toilet in the store because Darby was off helping Bart with his dusting practice.

Don't get me wrong. We know Morgan is still out there. She still wants Merlin's tools. There are still problems in the Fae world and plenty of business for our special ops team to tackle, but there's also a strong sense of a new beginning.

We all went into the Christmas season feeling lighter. On Christmas Eve, when Lucas and I stood together watching the Brown Mountain guard make their flight to coat the Mother Tree in fairy dust, I couldn't help but think how far we'd all come in just a year.

As for where we'd be in a year? Well, let me just leave you with this tidbit before I go.

The gift Lucas gave me on Christmas Eve?

Think small black box.

But we'll get to that next time.

STAY TUNED...

... for the next chapter
in Jinx's ongoing adventures:
Watch for Book Twelve:
To Love a Witch
Coming Soon

REFERENCE SECTION

(Please note this reference section is a work in progress and will be updated as needed.)

Abe Abernathy - The fishing tournament competitor Howard McAlpin claims murdered him in his office with a brass swordfish.

Adoette - Barnaby Shevington's second wife. A Cherokee witch and the mother of Knasgowa.

Albert (Linda) - Briar Hollow librarian and local historian who has a crush on Beau Longworth.

Alchemy - Historically, alchemy is the medieval precursor of modern chemistry. In a metaphysical context, it is the study of transforming ordinary elements into objects of true merit. This can be expanded to include elements of personal transformation and inquiry.

Ailish - The Elven Gray Loris who is Connor Endicott's pet and companion. A monkey-like creature with enormous eyes who loves "sticky sweet" honey.

Amity Prescott - The owner of the arts and crafts gallery next to The Witch's Brew and a member of the Briar Hollow coven.

Amulet of Caorunn - The amber amulet associated with the Mother Rowan that has the capacity to restore that which has faded. It contains three rowan berries.

Amulet of the Phoenix - The amber amulet associated with the Mother Oak. It encases a feather of the Great Phoenix and contains the powers of protection, rejuvenation, and immortality.

Andrews (Gemma) - Tori Andrews' mother and Kelly Ryan Hamilton's best friend. Trained as an alchemist, but also possesses the powers of witchcraft.

Andrews (Tori) - Daughter of Gemma and Scrap Andrews. Jinx Hamilton's best friend. A descendant of Brenna Sinclair. She studies alchemy and possesses growing powers of witchcraft. Jinx's business partner at The Witch's Brew.

Andrews (Scrap) - Tori Andrews' father who left his wife for a younger woman and was then killed by The Strigoi Sisters.

Anna Koldings - An accused Danish witch and one of the main suspects in the Copenhagen witch trials of 1590. Called the "Mother of the Devil," she was burned at the stake.

Aos si - Pronounced "a-o-she." In both Irish and Scottish mythology the aos si are similar to elves or fairies. They dwell underground in fairy mounds and exist in an invisible world parallel to the human reality. In the Jinx Hamilton books, Myrtle, is known as "the aos si" and is assumed to be among the last of her kind.

Argante - The elf queen of Avalon who took control of the island from Morgan le Fay.

Arthashastra - Written in Sanskrit, the Arthashastra is an ancient Indian text on economics, stagecraft, and military strategy composed during the 2nd and 3rd centuries AD.

Arthur (King) (Pendragon) - The legendary British leader immortalized in medieval romances and histories. Thought to have ruled in the late 5th and early 6th centuries AD. As there are numerous and varied tellings of the story of Arthur, Camelot, and the Knights of the Round Table, our story blends many of these threads.

Assembly of the Realms - The representative assembly of the Fae realms, which meets in Londinium. A co-equal governmental body with the Ruling Elders.

Attu Island - The western most of the Aleutian Islands off the tip of Alaska.

Avalon - The legendary "Isle of Apple Trees," which figures in Arthurian legend. The site of the forging of the sword, Excalibur, and the location of Arthur's exile/recovery after the Battle of Camlann.

Awenasa - Knasgowa's daughter by her first marriage to Degataga, born in 1784 and died in 1853.

Baobhan Sith - Pronounced "baa'van see." In Scottish folklore, a female vampire who seduces her victims before feeding on their blood. Especially fond of young, male travelers. The baobhan sith characters in our books have the power to travel by flight and can stop time. Sometimes referred to as the White Women of the Scottish Highlands.

Bart - A brownie from Shevington who enlists Darby's aid to train for a competitive dusting contest.

Bastet - The famous cat goddess of the Egyptians who was first depicted as a fierce lioness and later changed to the familiar, sleek black form by which she is most commonly pictured today. In Greek culture, she was seen as a moon goddess.

Battle of Camlann - King Arthur's final battle against the traitor, Mordred. The king was either gravely wounded or died. In the versions of the story where Arthur lived, he was taken to Avalon to recover.

Battlestar Galactica - An American science fiction series that first aired in 1978 and was revived in 2004.

Brighid - A goddess popular in the Irish mythology. A member of the race of gods known as the Tuatha Dé Danann and the daughter of the Dagda. Depicted as a goddess in three forms, our books describe three sisters, all named Brighid, with the other two using the names Brig and Bea. The eldest of the three Brighids is the Queen of Summer.

Black Death - A pandemic outbreak of bubonic plague that killed 75-200 million Europeans from 1347 to 1351.

Bouchard (Pierre-François) - The French Army engineer who discovered the Rosetta Stone in 1799, which facilitated the deciphering of Ancient Egyptian writing.

Briar Hollow, North Carolina - A fictional town along the Blue Ridge Parkway in North Carolina that is the setting for the Jinx Hamilton novels.

Brocéliande - A Forest in France associated with Arthurian legend and believed to contain the tomb of Merlin.

Brown Mountain Guard - The fairy troops under the command of Major Aspid "Ironweed" Istra who deflect human attention for portals leading to the Valley of Shevington by staging mysterious light displays over the Brown Mountains of North Carolina.

Brownie - Household spirits common in Scottish and English folklore. Represented in our books primarily by Darby, who has the appearance of a tiny old man and an eternally youthful, innocent heart. He also possesses the power of invisibility.

Cailleach Bheur - Pronounced "kallick-burr." A weather goddess in Celtic folklore used in our books as the Qeen of Winter.

Caledfwlch - Pronounced "catfish-witch." The Welsh name for the sword, Excalibur.

Camelot - The fabled city at the center of King Arthur's realm.

Castañada (Jorge) - An agent with IBIS who assists in creating an artificial intelligence home for the spirit of Barnaby Shevington's first wife, Adeline (Moore) Shevington.

Chesterfield (Irenaeus) - Barnaby Shevington's younger brother. The first Creavit practitioner. In league with Reynold Isherwood.

Claridge's - An historic hotel in London located at the corner of Brook Street and Davies Street in Mayfair.

Conference of the Realms - The meeting of representatives in Londinium that voted to lift The Agreement segregating the *nonconformi* races to the Middle Realm.

Creavit - An individual whose powers have been made (*creavit magicae*) by an act of traitor magic (*veneficus trajectio*.) The Creavit heresy touched off the Fae Reformation.

Cryptids - Any creature popularly considered to be a product of folklore and thought not to exist in the real world.

Dagda - The father of Brighid. A member of the race of gods known as the Tuatha Dé Danann.

Darby - The brownie bound to Knasgowa's grave as a guardian. Set free by Jinx and now a beloved member of The Witch's Brew family.

Daughters of Knasgowa - The line of witches descended from Knasgowa, the daughter of Barnaby Shevington and his second wife, Adoette. Sword in service to the Mother Oak.

de Roquefort (Sir Reginald) - The Commander of the Knights of the Rodere. Father of Robert and grandfather of Rodney.

de Roquefort (Robert) - Son of Sir Reginald de Roquefort. Rodney's father.

de Roquefort (Solange) - Wife of Robert de Roquefort. Rodney's mother.

Dewey - The dwarf who works as Moira's assistant. Darby's best friend.

DGI - The Division for Grid Integrity, the Fae investigatory agency charged with protecting and serving the Mother Trees.

Dirty Claw (The) - Werecat bar in Shevington.

Do dheagh shlàinte - "Your good health" in Gaelic. Approximate pronunication, "ur do ghay slawn-cha."

Dragonlets - *Draco Americanus Minor.* The miniature North American dragon. The size of large dogs, covered with blue and purple iridescent scales. Winged with bird-like heads; faceted, amber eyes; and beaks.

Druid - Historically among ancient Celtic peoples, a high-ranking religious or legal leader serving as a keeper of lore, a practitioner of medicine, or a political advisor.

Duke the Coonhound - The spectral dog with whom Beau played catch in the cemetery, who has now moved into the fairy mound.

Elven Gray Loris - A fae species of Loris. Monkey-like creatures with soft gray fur and enormous, sad eyes.

Elves - One of the Fae races broken into numerous sub-genres ranging from "high" elves of the Old Court to water and wood elves.

Elvish - The language of elves.

Enchantress - Alternative name for a witch or sorceress.

Endicott (Connor) - Jinx Hamilton's brother. Taken to Shevington as an infant and raised by Fiona Ryan's best friend, Endora Endicott.

Endicott (Endora) - Fiona Ryan's best friend, now deceased, who raised Connor Hamilton when he was taken to Shevington for his safety.

Excalibur - The mythical sword associated primarily with King Arthur, but forged by the elves of Avalon under the direction of Merlin.

FaeNet - The Fae equivalent of the Internet.

Fae Reformation - After 1517, during a time of increasing witch hunts in Europe that spilled over into the Fae community due in part to the activities of the Creavit. Barnaby Shevington called for the suppression of the Creavit Heresy, touching off the Fae Reformation. It was a result of these actions that Shevington and his followers split from the European body of magic and came to the New World.

Fairy Mound - The underground magical homes of the aos sí. Each of the Mother Trees on the Grid is associated with a corresponding fairy mound.

Fer Dorich, the Dark Druid - The self-appointed crime lord of the Middle Realm, who has now relocated to Las Vegas.

Ferguson, Malcolm - The rogue werecat hired by Anton Ionescu to murder Fish Pike and harass Jinx and her family.

Folger, Hiram - The star pitcher of the Briar Hollow Spectral Sports League. In life, he pitched one season for the Durham Bulls when they were a Class D minor league team in 1913.

Freak Freeze of '15 - The human name for the intense and sudden cold spell that struck North Carolina when Irenaeus Chesterfield kidnapped the Queen of Summer in league with Cailleach Bheur.

Gareth - The alchemist imprisoned in the Liszt chess set and set free by Connor when they escaped from Irenaeus Chesterfield's hidden cavern.

Glastonbury Tor - A hill near Glastonbury in the English county of Somerset. Topped by St. Michael's Tower. Long associated with the mythical island of Avalon.

GNATS Drones - Drones operating as part of the Group Network Aerial Transmission System under the command of Major Aspid "Ironweed" Istra.

Goddess of the Crows - Alternate name for Morgan le Fay.

Grayson (Lucas) - DGI agent. Currently dating Jinx Hamilton.

Grayson (Morris) - Director of the DGI. Lucas Grayson's uncle.

Great Dispersal - The dispersal of the Mother Trees from Tír na nÓg to points around the globe, thus forming The Grid.

Green (Glory) - A former state archivist miniaturized by Irenaeus Chesterfield and sent into The Witch's Brew as a spy. Taken in by Jinx and her friends, and recently restored to normal size. Dating Chase McGregor.

Grimoire - A witch's working books of spells and notes.

Guinevere - The wife of King Arthur.

Hamilton (Jeff) - Father of Jinx Hamilton. Married to Kelly Ryan Hamilton.

Hamilton (Jinx) - The principal character in the Jinx Hamilton novels. Age 30. A former waitress who inherited her powers and her store from her aunt, Fiona Ryan. The serving Witch of the Oak.

Hamilton (Kelly) - Jinx Hamilton's mother. The Roanoke Witch, in service to both the Mother Oak and the Mother Rowan.

HBH Kids - Three would-be paranormal investigators (Kyle, Mindy, and Nick) who produce a web series called "Haunted Briar Hollow."

Hengroen - King Arthur's stallion, whose descendants are stabled in Shevington.

Henrikkson (Birger) - A lindwyrm enrolled in Shevington University who has aspirations to be elected to the Assembly of the Realms.

IBIS - Acronym for the International Bureau of Indefinite Species headquartered in the British Museum.

In Between - Alternate name for The Middle Realm.

Innis - Barnaby Shevington's brownie housekeeper.

Ionescu (Anton) - The head of the local clan of Strigoi (Romanian vampires). Now deceased.

Ionescu (Cezar) - Anton Ionescu's cousin and the new head of the Strigoi clan in Briar Hollow.

Ionescu (Ioana) - Anton Ionescu's niece. Killed in a car accident in high school. Reanimated as a *strigoi mort blasfematore*.

Ionescu (Seraphina) - Anton Ionescu's daughter. Killed in a car accident in high school. Reanimated as a *strigoi mort blasfematore*.

Island of the Apple Trees - Alternate name for Avalon.

Istra (Major Aspid "Ironweed") - Fairy major in command of the Brown Mountain Guard in Shevington.

Isherwood (Reynold) - Ruling Elder removed from his position for his complicity in the Creavit Heresy and the murder of Adeline Shevington.

Isherwood (Thomasine) - Reynold Isherwood's wife.

JinxBot - The simulacrum (animate copy) of Jinx Hamilton that fills in for her when she is called away from The Witch's Brew for extended periods. Confined to remaining on the premises.

John Johnson (Sheriff) - The Briar Hollow sheriff.

Joseph of Arimathea - According to the Gospels, the man who took responsibility for the burial of Jesus. During the Middle Ages, Joseph came to be associated with a number of myths surrounding the Holy Grail, which he is believed to have brought to England.

Karen the Weaver - An accused Danish witch and one of the main suspects in the Copenhagen witch trials of 1590.

Key Man - Working with Seneca, the raven, in a shop in Black-friars, the Key Man crafts black market magical objects.

Knasgowa - The daughter of Barnaby Shevington and Adoette. The first Witch of the Oak after the murder of Adeline Shevington.

Knights Templar - Historically, The Poor Fellow-Soldiers of Christ and of the Temple of Solomon, known commonly as the Knights Templar. A Catholic military order charged with protector Crusaders to the Holy Land. Founded in 1119. Forcibly disbanded in 1312.

Lair - The basement space below The Witch's Brew and within the fairy mound protected from human detection by a cloaking spell.

Lindwyrm - A dragon or serpent species of *nonconformi*.

Liszt - (Franz), a 19th century Hungarian composer who lived from 1811 to 1886.

Londinium - The Fae city existing in the Otherworld opposite London.

Longworth (Beauregard T.) - Colonel Beauregard T. Longworth of Tennessee served in the Army of Northern Virginia. He died in the hills outside Briar Hollow in 1864 when the Yankees ambushed his cavalry patrol. Beau exists in corporeal form because he is in possession of the Amulet of the Phoenix. Newly appointed curator of the fairy mound archive.

Lucien St. Leger - The seneschal or administrative officer of the Knights of the Rodere.

Lucius Annaeus Seneca - Roman Stoic philosopher, statesman, dramatist who lived from 4 BC – 65 AD 65.

Lundenwic - The *nonconformi* city existing in the Middle Realm opposite London and Londinium.

MacVicar (Greer) - DGI agent and baobhan sith working with Lucas Grayson.

MacVicar (Katherine) - Greer MacVicar's mother. Protector of Tír na nÓg in partnership with Bronwyn Sinclair.

Madam Kaveh - Proprietress of a famous coffee shop in Shevington.

McAlpin (Howard) - Deceased mayor of Briar Hollow currently haunting the courthouse.

McGregor (Chase) - Werecat. Owner of the cobbler shop next to The Witch's Brew. Jinx's former boyfriend. Currently dating Glory Green.

McGregor (Festus) - Werecat. Chase McGregor's father. Has left retirement to serve as the principal protector of the Daughters of Knasgowa.

Memoriae - The spirit inhabiting the Liszt chessboard.

Merfolk - Any number of aquatic Fae species residing in the underwater city of Qynn.

Merlin - The wizard who served as King Arthur's principal advisor.

Middle Realm - Also known as the In Between. The layer of reality existing between the Human Realm and the Otherworld.

Miller (Pete) - Former owner of the Stone Hearth pizzeria. Deceased.

Minreith - The leader of the dragonlet flock in Shevington.

Morgan le Fay - King Arthur's half-sister. Merlin's lover. Head of a coven of witches comprised of her eight sisters located in Scandinavia. Also known as Morgaine.

Mos Eisley - Spaceport town located on the planet Tatooine in the fictional *Star Wars* universe.

Mother Oak - The Mother Tree located in the center of Shevington. The only tree on the Grid ever to re-locate after the Great Dispersal.

Mother Trees - The twelve great trees that make up the Grid.

Munin - One of the ravens in the Tower of Londinium.

Myrtle (aos si) - A member of the Tuatha Dé Danann. Jinx's mentor and friend.

Nonconformi - Various unconventional races confined to the Middle Realm under the terms of The Agreement to prevent their appearance in the Human Realm. Newly freed. Form the bulk of the inaugural class at Shevington University.

Oak Island - A 140-acre island on the south shore of Nova Scotia, Canada, long believed to be the location of buried treasure.

Otherworld - The plane of existence encompassing the Fae world.

Pagecliff (Horatio) - The Shevington bookseller newly appointed as the head librarian of Shevington University.

Pauldrons - The shoulder pieces in medieval armor.

Phoenix pen - The enchanted pen given to Jinx on her 30th birthday by Barnaby and Moira. It will never run out of ink and has the ability to channel Jinx's thoughts, dreams, and visions.

Pike (Fish) - A halfling werecat murdered and left on the doorstep of The Witch's Brew.

Pixie Post - A Fae delivery service run by pixies.

Portals - The trans-dimensional openings that allow travel across the realms.

Psychometry - The ability to touch objects and derive visions from them.

Queen of Winter - The title of Cailleach Bheur.

Quercus de Pythonissam - Latin for "Witch of the Oak."

Qynn - The underwater city of the merfolk located in The Valley.

Ratatoskr - In Norse mythology, the squirrel who carries messages up and down the trunk of Yggdrasil, the World Tree.

Roanoke Island - An island on the Outer Banks of North Carolina named for the Roanoke Carolina Algonquian people who inhabited the area in the 16th century.

Roanoke Pythonissam - Latin for Roanoke Witch.

Roanoke Witch - The title given to Kelly Hamilton when she received the Amulet of Caorunn and entered the service of both the Mother Oak and the Mother Rowan.

Rodney (de Roquefort) - Black and white hyper intelligent rat who lives in The Witch's Brew.

Roquefort-sur-Soulzon - A commune in the south of France.

Rube - Raccoon and consultant to the DGI who runs a "wrecking crew" in charge of scene cleanup for Fae incidents in the human realm.

Ruling Elders - The executive body in Fae governmental structure.

Ryan (Fiona) - Kelly Ryan's oldest sister. The aunt who gifted Jinx with the inheritance of both the store and her magic. Faked her death to move to Shevington.

Samhain - Pronounced "sow-in." Festival celebrated from October 31 to November 1 to celebrate the the beginning of winter

Satyr - A *nonconformi* that is half man half goat.

Seneca - A raven operating a mysterious shop in Blackfriars.

Shevington (city of) - The Otherworld city founded by Barnaby Shevington in 1584 opposite modern day Briar Hollow in the human realm.

Shevington University - The newly founded educational institution located in the city of Shevington to facilitate the re-introduction of the *nonconformi* races in the Fae world.

Shevington (Adeline) - Barnaby Shevington's first wife. A Druid princess who was serving as Witch of the Oak when she was murdered by Irenaeus Chesterfield.

Shevington (Barnaby) - Born Barnaby Chesterfield. The wizard who touched off the Fae Reformation when he protested the Creavit heresy. Founder of the New World Fae city of Shevington. Jinx Hamilton's grandfather (many times removed.)

Shevington (Moira) - The Shevington alchemist and Barnaby Shevington's current wife.

Sídhe - In the Jinx Hamilton books, a High Elf of the Old Court. Known as the "beautiful people," they have become prominent as A-list celebrities in the human realm.

Siegfried - The brownie majordomo of Claridge's hotel.

Sinclair (Brenna) - A former Creavit sorceress who fell through the fires separating the fairy mound and regained her hereditary magic. Tori Andrews grandmother (many times removed.)

Sinclair (Bronwyn) - Brenna Sinclair's mother and the protector of Tír na nÓg with Katherine MacVicar.

Slàinte - Gaelic for "cheers." Pronounced roughly "slawn-cha."

Special Ops Team - An interagency investigatory team comprised of Lucas Grayson, Jinx Hamilton, Greer MacVicar, and Rube.

SpookCon - The annual Halloween and paranormal festival held in Briar Hollow.

Strigoi Sisters - The nickname Tori Andrews gave Seraphina and Ioana Ionescu.

St. Gabriel's Tower - The gateway from Tír na nÓg to Avalon.

St. Michael's Tower - The gateway from Glastonbury Tor to Avalon.

Sword of Merlin - Alternate name for Excalibur.

Sylph - An invisible spirit of the air.

Tarathiel - Elf that serves as a bodyguard to Fer Dorich.

The Agreement - The edict that confined the *nonconformi* races to the Middle Realm.

The Crooked Critter - A bar in Lundenwic frequented by Rube, the raccoon.

The Plague - Alternate name for the bubonic plague or the Black Death.

Tír na nÓg - Pronounced "tur-nah-nŌg." In our books, the Otherworld sanctuary for pure magic existing opposite Oak Island.

Tower of Londinium - The Otherworld prison where Reynold Isherwood is kept. The Fae equivalent of the Tower of London.

Tuatha Dé Danann - In Irish mythology, a supernatural race that lies in the Otherworld but interact heavily with the human world.

Tuath Dé - Translates to "Tribe of the Gods."

Valendorff (Christoffer) - The Danish minister of finance during the Copenhagen witch trials of 1590 who named the home of Karen the Weaver as the site of coven meetings.

Virginia Dare - The first child born in the New World in the Colony of Roanoke. In our books, the white doe.

Viviane - The Lady of the Lake who rules Avalon in partnership with Argante, the Elf Queen.

Volker (Otto) - A cryptozoologist who is the Assistant Director of IBIS.

WAGWAB - An acronym devised by Festus McGregor for the descendants of the Briar Hollow Coven who held a reunion during SpookCon2. It stands for, 'We are the granddaughters of the witches you weren't able to burn," a quote from *The Witches of Blackbrook* by Tish Thawer

Warner (Katrina) - The serving Witch of the Rowan.

Werecat - A shapeshifter with the ability to assume two forms. In their small form they appear to be domestic cats of various species. In their large form, they may be any of the big cat varieties ranging from mountain lions to panthers, lynxes, tigers, lions, etc.

Whiskey vs. Whisky - Single malt Scotch whisky is spelled without an "e" preceding the "y" as would be present with "bourbon whiskey."

Witch of the Oak - The witch in service to the Mother Oak.

Witch's Brew (The) - The coffee shop owned jointly by Jinx Hamilton and Tori Andrews.

Women of the Craobhan - The twelve tree witches in services to the Mother Trees and the covens they head.

Yggdrasil - Pronounced "IG-druh-sill." The World Tree located in Tír na nÓg. The mother of the Great Trees that form The Grid.

ALSO BY JULIETTE

The Jinx Hamilton Series includes:

Witch at Heart

Witch at Odds

Witch at Last

Witch on First

Witch on Second

Witch on Third

The Amulet of Caorunn

To Haunt a Witch

To Test a Witch

To Trick a Witch

Books 1-6 of the Jinx Hamilton Mysteries

are also available in this

specially priced

boxed set.

Juliette Harper is also the author of *The Lockwood Legacy*.

The six full-length books are currently available only in a specially
priced box set.

The Lockwood Legacy

Other works in Juliette Harper's catalog include:

You Can't Get Blood Out of Shag Carpet: The Study Club Mysteries Book 1.

and

Descendants of the Rose:

A Selby Jensen Paranormal Mystery

ABOUT THE AUTHOR

Juliette Harper is the pen name used by the writing team of Patricia Pauletti and Rana K. Williamson. As a writer, Juliette's goal is to create strong female characters facing interesting, challenging, painful, and often comical situations. Refusing to be bound by genre, her primary interest lies in telling good stories.

The Jinx Hamilton Mysteries open with *Witch at Heart*, a lighter paranormal tale featuring a heroine who possesses powers she never dreamed existed. Jinx has been minding her own business working as a waitress at Tom's Cafe and keeping up with her four cats. Then she inherits her Aunt Fiona's store in neighboring Briar Hollow, North Carolina *and* learns that her aunt has willed her special "powers" to Jinx as well.

They say admitting you have a problem is the first step and Jinx has a *major* problem. She's a new witch and no earthly clue what that means — until she's given the opportunity to use her magic to do a good thing.

In Book 2, *Witch at Odds*, Jinx accepts her new life as a witch and is determined to make a success of both that and her business. However, she has a great deal to learn. As the story unfolds, Jinx sets out to both study her craft and to get a real direction for her aunt's haphazard approach to inventory.

Although Jinx can call on Aunt Fiona's ghost for help, the old lady is far too busy living a jet set afterlife to be worried about her niece's learning curve. That sets Jinx up to make a major mistake and to figure out how to set things right again.

By Book 3, *Witch at Last*, a lot has changed for Jinx in just a few months. After the mishaps that befell her in *Witch At Odds*, she wants to enjoy the rest of the summer, but she's not going to be that lucky. As she's poised to tell her friends she's a witch, secrets start popping out all over the place. Between old foes and new locations, Jinx isn't going to get her peaceful summer, but she may get an entirely different world.

Book 4, *Witch on First*, has Jinx walk out the front door of her store on a Sunday morning only to find her werecat neighbor and boyfriend, Chase McGregor, staring at a dead man. Under the best of circumstances, a corpse complicates things, but Jinx has other problems. Is her trusted mentor lying to her? Have dangerous magical artifacts been placed inside the shop? Join Jinx and Tori as they race to catch a killer and find out what's going on literally under their noses.

Book 5, *Witch on Second,* opens a week before Halloween. Jinx and Tori have their hands full helping to organize Briar Hollow's first ever paranormal festival. Beau and the ghosts at the cemetery are eager to help make the event a success, but tensions remain high after the recent killings.

Without a mentor to lean on, Jinx must become a stronger, more independent leader. Is she up to the task in the face of ongoing threats? Still mourning the loss of Myrtle and her breakup with Chase, Jinx finds herself confronting new and unexpected foes.

Book Six, *Witch on Third*, begins where *Witch on Second* left off, the last night of Briar Hollow's first annual paranormal festival. With Chase still stinging from the breakup and Lucas Grayson more than a little interested, Jinx has plenty on her plate without a new evil trio in town. As the team works to counter Chesterfield's newest scheme, something happens in the Valley that changes everything for the Hamilton family.

In Book Seven, *The Amulet of Caorunn*, Creavit wizard

Irenaeus Chesterfield is back, with a bigger, badder plan to go after Jinx and company. In the weeks leading up to Christmas, Jinx starts having dream visions about the mysterious Amulet of Caorunn. Trying to get more details, she and Tori try a dicey double enchantment with shocking results. Join Jinx, Tori, and the gang as they work to recover the Amulet, stop Chesterfield, and enter the mysterious Middle Realm.

In the eighth installment, *To Haunt a Witch*, Jinx, Tori, and the gang have settled down to enjoy some "normal" time after their adventure in the Middle Realm. Then Cezar Ionescu walks through the front door of the Witch's Brew asking for a favor. An abandoned house owned by the local Strigoi clan is attracting the attention of the Haunted Briar Hollow web series. Can Jinx and company relocater the spirit?

As usual, there's more to the abandoned house than anyone imagines. When the group brings home a "helpful" spirit, Jinx finds out things about Fae politics she didn't want to know, and discovers a hidden element of her already complicated family history.

Book 9, *To Test a Witch*, transports readers to Fae Londinium. As the Conference of the Realms convenes, Jinx and the gang settle into adjoining rooms at Claridge's determined to find a way to end The Agreement segregating the In Between.

In the three days before the opening ceremony, Lucas assumes the role of tour guide, taking Jinx to Hampton Court and the British Museum. But it's the sites he doesn't show her that prove to be the most critical after an assassination attempt puts Barnaby's life in danger and leaves Jinx in charge of the Shevington delegation.

From encountering the ghosts of Henry VIII's wives to meeting a troop of gargoyle guards in the Fae Houses of Parliament, Jinx and her friends take the town by storm.

In Book 10, *To Trick a Witch*, Jinx answers the age old question, "What did you do over your summer vacation?" Her story beats everyone else's by a mile.

The Conference of the Realms may be over, but the trouble is just getting started for the crew in the lair. There's an outbreak of cryptids in the human realm, threatening witch hysteria in Briar Hollow, and a covert coven reunion in the works.

Jinx finds herself juggling Fae politics while grappling with new career aspirations and relationship complications — all with SpookCon2 looming in October.

In addition to the Jinx Hamilton series, Juliette's best-selling *Lockwood Legacy* novels are currently available in a specially priced boxed set. The individual titles include: *Langston's Daughters*, *Baxter's Draw*, *Alice's Portrait*, *Mandy's Father*, *Irene's Gift*, and *Jenny's Choice*.

Descendants of the Rose is the first installment of the Selby Jensen Paranormal Mysteries. Selby's business card reads "Private Investigator," but to say the least, that downplays her real occupation where business as usual is anything but normal.

And don't miss the hilariously funny "cozy" *Study Club Mysteries*, a light-hearted spin off of *The Lockwood Legacy*. Set in the 1960s, the first novel, *You Can't Get Blood Out of Shag Carpet*, takes on the often-absurd eccentricities of small town life with good-natured, droll humor.

By Juliette Harper
Copyright 2018, Juliette Harper

Skye House Publishing

License Notes

ISBN: 978-1-943516-65-0

❀ Created with Vellum

Made in the USA
Lexington, KY
15 March 2018